Also by Sterling Watson

BLIND TONGUES

WEEP NO MORE MY BROTHER

THE CALLING

A NOVEL BY STERLING WATSON

DELTA
FICTION

Published by
Dell Publishing
a division of
Bantam Doubleday Dell Publishing Group, Inc.
666 Fifth Avenue
New York, New York 10103

Readers who look for the real geography of North Florida in this book
will not find it. Forms and degrees of the real are here, mixed, as they
always are in fiction, with the exaggerated, the fabricated and the
fantastic. I am not I, he is not he, she is not she and they are not they.
We are all fiction, and therefore real.

ISBN 0-440-55026-2

Reprinted by arrangement with Peachtree Publishers, Ltd.,
Atlanta, Georgia

Printed in the United States of America

Published simultaneously in Canada

February 1989

10 9 8 7 6 5 4 3 2 1

MV

This book is dedicated to Jim Hall.

The intellect of man is forced to choose
Perfection of the life, or of the work,
And if it take the second must refuse
A heavenly mansion, raging in the dark.
When all that story's finished, what's the news?
In luck or out the toil has left its mark:
That old perplexity an empty purse,
Or the day's vanity, the night's remorse.

— W. B. Yeats
"The Choice"

Part I

One

THAT YEAR I LIVED WITH anchorite austerity in a small and still room in a boarding house near the university. It was the year I wrote stories. My dream was a voice, a typewriter, sheaves of creamy paper, and a bottle of bourbon whose age was written in months on its label. To write was all I had wanted since an outfield collision had shattered my left knee and my hopes for an athlete's life. My knee foretold the weather and promised there would be no berth for me on Uncle Sam's orient express. It was 1974. I was a writer and believed in my happiness.

I was happy and the owner of everything I needed, except what I could not construct on the paper that daily curled through my antique Underwood. I needed a teacher, a mentor, a guide in the dream of words. It was Eldon Odom's voice that sang in my head. He had called me to this rented room, this implausible life of typewriter and bottle and think-sweat and masturbatory hope in Bainesborough, Florida. Six years earlier, I had found his first novel, *Naked in Church,* in the library of the Alligood County Consolidated Junior-Senior High School. With paper and paste, the book had been defaced. The censored words were our country voice. They were what we said when things went wrong, or more right than we had a right to expect. They were the idling of tractor engines, the South wind in the live oaks and the moan of animals, the grind of roadhouse guitars, and the sob of riverside salvation — all the collected echoes of my childhood. Eldon Odom spoke the voice of the place I had thought storyless, abandoned. I had never dreamt that homely voice could be found in a book. I tried to envision the hand that had written the words, the hand of Eldon Odom.

Naked, I discovered that warm, dreaming afternoon, was the story of a young man much like me, of North Florida stock who had a yen for new worlds, far places, who left his stern father, taking only his mother's lonesome kiss with him on a journey to Parris Island and Marine Corps basic training. The Corps was this boy's escape from the rural county which was his spirit's prison. I still remember thinking: Even I know better. I ached for the book's innocence. I was one step ahead of its hero and hooked. I read it all the way, finishing just as Alligood County Consolidated closed for the day.

One day, in early June, I went to meet Eldon Odom. It had taken me a year in the rented room to summon the courage to telephone him. The courage had finally come from the bottle with the age written in months on its label. On the fifteenth ring, a grit voice had answered, "Hanh!" It was fully five seconds before I could pluck up to talk. "Mr. Odom, please. This is . . . Blackford Turlow calling." I was ashamed of my name, for even then I knew it was a noise from the pages of a corn pone potboiler. Back home, where improbable names were replaced by jokes, I was called " Toad" Turlow. I was Toad because I was low to the ground and not particularly pleasant to look at, and because, when I was angry, my voice was a croak. Eldon Odom said, "What to hell is a Black-Ford-Tur-Low?" I was shaken, but I summoned restraint, trying not to croak. "You don't know me. But Blackford Turlow would like to meet you. He is a faithful reader and admirer of your work. Also a writer."

There was a pause full of muscular breathing. Finally Odom said, "How old is this Blackford Turlow? Is he a student?"

"Not officially, sir, but in the old sense of the word he is." Another pause.

"Sorry about the ruptured amenities, son." It was the first of many times he called me "son," and though I knew it for a mere manner of Southern speaking, it was as though he had stroked my beaded forehead. I was talking to the father of my art. Moved, I answered "That's all right."

He said, "We been having trouble lately with some shithook calling up and threatening my boy, Presley. Says he's going to do all kinds of nasty things. I call him out ever time, but the yellow dog won't come over here and let me knock his dick off. What do you think of that?"

Clearly, my answer would be judged by the code. I had read *Naked in Church, The Way to the High Ground,* all of his books, and I knew them as well as I could breathe. I quoted him the answer. "Blood is inevitable."

He said, "Come on over, son. It's a few minutes before I got to pick up Missy Sully from her ass-kicking lesson."

I walked the two miles to his house from my rented room. The shorts I had planned for the occasion revealed knees that were shockingly different: one sleek and knit hard as a new baseball; the other as sloppy as a handful of chicken parts and tracked by two long, purple scars. Eldon Odom would see me walk in my slightly lurching way and recognize a fellow cripple.

From my researches, I knew his injuries were mysterious. In

one interview, he had spoken of an auto wreck, a midnight when he had wrestled with the angel and come away with a thighbone's measure of faith in his own prescription of years. In another leaf of the public record, he claimed he'd been stitched by machine gun fire on a Marine night patrol in the Dominican Republic. The interviewer, a university professor, and by genus Odom's enemy, had refuted him on the spot, challenging him to prove it. Odom had only said that proof was in the crucible of art. From the printed page, I heard the dangerous mutter of the voice, its disgust with the professor's interview, with all intrusions upon the privacy of a man who had written six of the best novels the American South had produced.

I had scouted Odom's house. He lived on the edge of the city, at the mouth of the town's single creek, called Hart's Flow, where it emptied into Lake Jenny Jewel. It was choice real estate, giving, as I later heard him say, "the illusion of seclusion." Standing on his cypress deck, you could listen to the serious, secret business of Hart's Flow beneath your feet and never know you were within pissing distance of suburban America. Many nights, when I could neither write nor sleep, I had walked to his property line. There I had stood under the moon hoping to hear the voice from that alcove of oaks, the words that would break the lock.

The house itself was rambling and low and expensive, one of those 1950s sandstone creations with levels split and married to the landscape. As I stood on a little knoll, looking down at it, my impression was of gravity. It seemed to have sunk elegantly into the surrounding hollow. There was no lawn. Love vine and ivy scaled the trunks of the blackjack oaks and loblolly pines, then leapt the driveway to the roof of the house, canopying the dooryard.

As I neared the door, I listened for a sound from the house. There was only the hum of an air conditioner. An iron grill formed a narrow runway along the front of the house and an L at the west corner. On two sides, it caged every window and door. The moment my hand touched the grill, a pair of precise and noiseless jaws slashed at it. Some instinct, asleep in my reverie of what was to come, awakened in time. I jerked back my hand while the ivory fangs of an enormous German Shepherd levered the bars. The dog stood eye to eye with me, only breathing hard, its gums oozing blood which might have been mine. I was drawing back my foot to kick the bars when the door opened and Eldon Odom stepped out.

I saw him superimposed upon his book jacket picture. He was a much diminished man. In the photo, he crouched on a large rock, a promontory somewhere in the rural South. His massive forearms rested indolently across sausage-tight, khaki-trousered thighs. Large, veined hands hung from wrists three inches wide. His face was a landscape of quiet outrage. As scarred and pocked as the far side of the moon, it acknowledged everything and nothing. The eyes, squinting into a setting sun, said, My heart is an open book; you take it up in hazard.

The man who stood behind the dog was thinner, stunned and sleepy-looking, and in the advanced stages of a hangover. I listened carefully while he spoke baby talk to the dog.

"No, Levi. You can't eat this 'un. He just too big. He choke you and you die. And what would ole Daddy do without his fucking big dog?" The dog watched me out of malevolent yellow eyes until Eldon Odom worked his way between us and got the beast up with its paws on his shoulders. The two began to move in slow circles while Odom invented a song for the dog's pleasure. He still had not spoken to me.

When the two had commuted their souls for a good long stretch, and the dog had flecked Odom's shirt with blood, he pushed the beast down and said, "Now, Levi, I'm gone open this gate and when I do, you introduce yourself to this boy. No more of that goddamned violence, you understand me?" The dog stared yellow into the man's eyes. I stepped back from the gate and looked over my shoulder at the steep drive. The hole in the bright summer air at the top of the hollow, a mere wafer of safety, was fifty yards away.

The gate latch clashed and the iron gate swung, but I stood my ground for I was, or so I thought, a ground-stander. The dog padded out and thrust its big, hot snout into the crotch of my tennis shorts and lifted, then jumped up on me eye to eye and looked that piss-yellow malevolence at me. I was damned if I was dancing with a dog, so I looked over the hairy shoulder and said to Eldon Odom, "This dog is quiet."

"That," Odom said, "is Levi's special grace. He don't bark much. He just sit and wait, and when your basic neighborhood intruder stick his hand in that gate, Levi gives him back a bloody stump. His name is Leviathan. I call him that cause he's solitary, poor, nasty, brutish, and short-tempered."

The dog moved behind me, gazing disinterestedly at the summer afternoon. It squatted and kicked itself in the head with a hind foot the size of a flatiron. I wanted to apply a size-nine tennis shoe to its rib cage. Instead, still in the hot clutch of adrenaline, I followed Eldon Odom into the house.

We walked through the living room and through a sliding glass door, onto a cypress deck above the tannic waters of Hart's Flow. If I saw the furniture or the walls of that room, I don't recall it now. What I recall is his walking in front of me — being in his wake — and feeling that I was in place. Eldon Odom gestured me to a sling chair and I sat, remembering myself a bit. In the pit of my stomach, I could feel the fight-or-flight boys throwing down their implements before the swords-into-plowshares people. That dog had scared me. I looked down, trying to think of something to say, and noticed a constellation of dog's blood in my crotch. When I looked up, Eldon Odom was staring at my knee. "Where'd you get them zippers?"

Reflexively, my hand found the two corrugated scars which were now the stuff of a famous novelist's interest. I struggled for a way to say it. There was always a way, a right way, one and no other, and this was the place to use it. The result was a swelling silence. "Well, shit, son, surely you know how you got yourself a second-hand knee."

I found my voice somewhere beneath the constellation of dog's blood and said, "I got the zippers from the university athletic department surgeon. They didn't give me a whole lot but a handshake after that."

"Sorry for yourself, are you?"

I looked into Eldon Odom's face. It was tracked by the caravans of years and the footprints of uninvited visitors, and by the strain of recording it all in deathless prose. Who was I to feel sorry before this monument to the triumph of the human spirit in adversity? (Unfortunately, I was commonly given to such thoughts in those days.) I said, "A little, I guess, but I'm getting over it."

He nodded vigorously and ground his lantern jaws. "Good, get over it and over and over. That's all you can do."

He fixed me with eyes not unlike the dog's, now that I saw them plainly, and waited. I stared and hoped my face communicated understanding. We hung fire for the next minute or so until Eldon Odom looked out at the pines and said, "Jew like a glass of whiskey?"

"Yes, sir."

As I watched him shamble back through the glass doors, his head ducking, his elbows pumping, I tried to recompose him before me. His face had been a Cherokee color, his jowls covered with two days of spotty salt-and-pepper beard. His teeth had been strong and regular and stained by tea or tobacco. His hair was shiny, an extraordinary ruff, deep black and lustrous.

Straight on he looked a little like that famous portrait of Geronimo. And now, this minute, all that was Eldon Odom was off getting *me* a drink of whiskey.

He came back through the door with a fifth of Heaven Hill and two tumblers full of ice. He struggled down into a canvas sling chair and spoke to the label of the bottle. "How do you like your blue-eyed boy, Mr. Death?" He poured two full measures, filling our glasses while I watched in fear and awe and with that strange sense of placement. Noticing the confusion in my face, he said, quietly, "I'm telling you, I took a medium to bad hurt from the bottle last night." He was disappointed. What kind of drinking companion was I turning out to be?

He drank and watched the trees on the opposite bank. It was a moment of transition. It was my invitation to be more than the courteous young man, silent and soft-spoken. It was the benefit of the doubt. I fished in the cloudy waters of my thoughts for a word to say. "Is that something you do on a regular basis?"

Eldon Odom looked at me sharply, and we crossed over. Stiff and definite, he lifted his glass to me; it was more like a punch than a salute. "Good bit more regular than either of us wants to know about." After another pull at the whiskey, he gave me a speculating look. "So, you a writer, are you?"

At this, I tried to get out of my canvas chair. I was sitting on the manuscript of my short story.

Lying in my room with only an oscillating fan to take the edge off my fever, I had dreamt of the moment I would hand Eldon Odom my baseball story, "Chatter." It would be a ceremonious moment. My dream narrative forked in various directions, but the drift was that Odom would cajole the paper from my modest fingers, eager to see what the young man had done. And all of this after the young man's brilliant dilations on the themes in Odom's own work. Now, I struggled to stand, remembering the manuscript in my hip pocket. It was not too badly damaged, only damp and bearing the imprint of the edge of the chair and a trouser button.

"I was hoping to give this to you," I said.

He pincered the damp paper with two fingers and held it up to a squint. "I been given work straight from the heart, the shoulder, and the soul, but never from two inches to one side of an asshole." He laughed and I followed him. My laughter was not half so hearty as his which was a regular fit of self-congratulation.

"Not that I meant any comment on the work itself, you understand."

I assured him that I understood.

What he did next was toss the manuscript to the deck and return to the serious business of consuming the Heaven Hill. I noticed the drink in my hand and got down to business, too. "So, you were a jockstrap, were you?"

I told him I preferred the word *athlete*. He mulled my response in his chaps, along with enough whiskey to sour it to his taste, and said, "Team sports don't interest me. Team sport jocks are not free men." And there, he gave me to suppose, was an end on it. So what now? I watched the manuscript on the boards. It looked as hopeless as I later learned it was.

Eldon Odom nudged the paper with a bare toe, sipped, and said, "It's plenty of mine have come to as much as that one probably will. If you let it bother you, you'll perish of your expectations." I was still parsing his sentence when he rose and pointed to the trees. "Look," he whispered. His body was rigid and so went mine. It was the compelling whisper of childhood friendship, of the boy you follow, the one who sees before you do the object of your desire — the frog to gig, the apple high on the bough, the girl bending to retrieve her pencil. I looked. I saw nothing. "Right there," he said. "Follow my arm." I leaned closer to him, into the powerful masculine odor of his forty-two years, and sighted along his arm toward a high branch where a large, absurd creature polished its bill on a twig. "That's a pileated woodpecker," he said, still in the conspirator's whisper. "I'd change places with that boy in a minute." I thought: You'd be beating your head against a tree. I was a country boy but no bird watcher. I said, "He's strange looking." Odom drew back and let his arm drop. "Is that all you can say to one of nature's very wonders?"

I felt like crawling to my chair. He said, "That bird represents the successful completion of millions of years of genetic honing. On his worst day, that little sucker can hit harder, pounds per square inch, than Marciano on his best. And besides, he's well adorned."

We watched the bird. As near as I could tell, it was hopping up and down and trying to turn its head around backwards. Eldon Odom continued, "I got a neighbor across the hollow sneaks out and shoots his rifle at that bird. I told him if he ever hit his mark, I'd hit mine." He turned to me with another of many challenges: "What you think of that?" His eyes said: Testify to what I say or against it. No middle ground between us. I said, "Go for it," echoing the title of his last and least successful book. He looked at me in a neutral way, then drank and a grin split his big, red-Indian face. And that was the beginning of something.

We sat for another hour on that deck watching the woods and the quality of the light as mid-day became mid-afternoon. The waters beneath us whispered, the birds sang, and the heavens rained light. We finished the bottle of bourbon and got well into another one. The talk seemed to flow between us easily. He seemed interested in me in a tired, quiet way. He asked me many questions. I answered them well in my whiskey-lubricated voice, and embroidered only a little here and there, shading as a writer must, so that a heightened truth might shine. I told him

about the day I had run into an inexperienced freshman right-
fielder as the two of us crossed the warning track. When the
freshman, unheedful of my waving hand and the warning
beneath our cleats, tangled his legs in mine and we crashed into
a brick wall, it was his chance to play center field for the
remainder of a long season.

As I was carried out to the ambulance, the scouts who had
come to watch me play left the grandstand. They knew what I
did not yet know. I learned it when the surgeon entered my room
the morning after entering my knee and bent over my bed to
wake me. I looked up from the black pit of the anesthesia,
nauseous, full of my sodium pentathol nightmare, and saw him
shaking his head from side to side. I spent the morning puking
up the old life, unable to imagine the new one.

"I know what you mean," said Eldon Odom, sipping his
drink, and I knew he did. I gloried in our knowledge of sur-
geons' knives and severed hopes.

A door slammed somewhere in the house, and we started.
"Oh, shit!" Eldon Odom said, and gave a wry, ain't-I-the-one
smile. "I forgot to pick up Missy Sully from her ass-kicking
class." He rose and stretched and began his walk to the pillory
of Missy Sully's disappointment. I could hear the brute panting
of the dog, the click of its nails on the terrazzo, and something
else — an animal noise, a kind of yip.

Missy Sully was a handsome, auburn-haired woman who
wore too much makeup and moved with the manic, bouncing
gait of an overaged cheerleader. She was wearing the white
pajamas and green belt of a medium lethal karatica. She stopped
in front of me, followed by the adoring Leviathan, and as I
struggled up from my chair, she executed a kick that stirred the
air against my forehead. It took me a moment to get all this
aligned. Eldon Odom's wife had just greeted his guest by
practicing her foot attack. As she did it a second time, she

uttered the little yip I had heard. It struck me as a touching thing, that little noise of hers. Both a warning and a protest, a little like the bark of a lap dog but more like a cry from the painful culmination of love.

Eldon Odom followed her onto the deck, locking the dog in. It smeared its moony face against the glass door, snorting and slavering its love. "Sully, this is Blackford Turlow, a student of mine."

I took her hand. It was moist. Behind the stagey makeup and the karate energy I saw a clear, cold intelligence. It was the director of the actress whose violent entrance had ended my idyll with Eldon Odom. She pressed my hand hard before letting go.

"I'm pleased to meet you, ma'am."

"Blackford Turlow." She didn't blink.

My mama didn't raise no fool, as we used to say, and I knew it was time to leave. As I was excusing myself and discovering that I could walk with the load of whiskey in me, I shook Eldon Odom's hand and formally thanked him for agreeing to read my manuscript. The four of us walked through the dark house to the canopied drive. Leviathan exited with me, and as I stood facing the couple at the gate, the dog repeated his best trick. I stood, red-faced, with his moist black muzzle under my testicles. I managed to say, "Thank you again."

Eldon Odom said, "Why don't you come to class. Tuesday night, in the Old Barracks, second floor, south end. Seven o'clock." He turned and was gone.

Missy Sully stood watching me ride the dog. She stared until I knew she had noticed my scars. Finally, she smiled and said, "Levi, save the cheap thrills for me. Come on, boy."

She turned on her heel, and I heard retreating toenails and one little yip.

Two

I DON'T REMEMBER walking home. Perhaps the circuit that held the memory was cauterized by that "drink" of whiskey I had with Eldon Odom. Or perhaps memory has done what it always does against will and logic, stealing what we most treasure and leaving only the detritus of experience. I read somewhere that when we are old, we lose the immediate recall of words but regain that lost world of early life — the first girl, the first terror, the first hero. I look forward.

When I lay again on my army surplus cot in the rented room, I heard voices. Words were the substance of my whiskey reverie. I replayed the tapes of my meeting with Eldon Odom, the better to fix it in memory. In recollection it did not seem one whit less magical than it had as I was living it. I had rent the veil of Eldon Odom's famous secrecy. I had met the man. I fancied he had taken me to the ramparts, shown me wilderness and water. These things were real. His eyes had rested upon them and they had moved him to speak. Any object which could call forth the voice of Eldon Odom was magical. And that included me.

In the sweat of the whiskey and of an exaltation that kept my limbs rigid, my mind began a slow wheeling turn from the afternoon's glories to the coming Tuesday night. I asked myself in seriousness how I could live through the intervening hours until I walked into Eldon Odom's class and . . . What would I do there? Where was my place? Suddenly, I saw myself as the grit I was and, in the exaggeration of fantasy, as a Li'l Abner entering a room full of city sophisticates, all of them with published stories to their names and great expectations. Then I remembered Eldon Odom's words: A man could perish of his expectations.

Somehow I fell asleep. Probably it was the power of simmering, besotted matter over such mind as remains when a twenty-four-year-old consumes half a bottle of whiskey. I awoke to a knock at nine. I knew the knock. It was one of the two I was likely to hear in my present circumstances. One belonged to my neighbor down the hall, a boy named Traymore who usually came to borrow something. Traymore was tall and sinewy and pale, a painter and a writer, whose room was full of botched canvases and bags of roasted soybeans. Absolutely bereft of money, Traymore lived on the soybeans and an herb tea he brewed night and day. His typewriter clacked late into the night, an accompaniment to mine. When it was silent, he was usually swatching acrylics onto canvases liberated from a nearby sail-maker's shop. Traymore was a friend when both of us were capable of society, but he served me a darker purpose. He was the cautionary tale of the writer gone wrong. He was one of my futures. Eldon Odom was the other. Traymore's schizoid politics, his lack of focus, his visionary eye full of nothing lived by me day and night as a reminder of how the dream could die. Some writers needed used car salesmen for this; I needed

Traymore, who was perishing of his expectations.

But that night's knock was decorous, not loud but insistent. It was not Traymore's. It emanated from the divine knuckles of Ardis Baines. I lay in the dark, a little sick and getting worse and thinking I would keep quiet and let the knock go away, but Ardis opened the door. I cursed myself aloud for neglecting the lock. Ardis, in a halo of sticky light from the sixty-watt bulb in the hall said, "Nice talk."

"Give me a break," I moaned.

"I did," she said. "I should have cursed you back."

I sued for peace and Ardis didn't press her advantage, which I suppose meant she was in the peace-giving mood. She closed the door and walked to the only chair in the room. It was dark, but she knew the way. I could hear her stockings frictioning as she crossed her long, pretty legs. Even to someone in my condition, it was pleasant.

Ardis was a frequent, though not always welcome, visitor to my dream. She held the dream in contempt, or at least its props: the rented room, the bottle, the shadows. She wanted to know why I couldn't be a writer without, as she put it, reenacting the life of Byron. I couldn't, was all I told her, and it was all I *could* have told her then. I hadn't told her about Eldon Odom.

We sat in the dark for some time, while she breathed lightly and evenly and emitted the good smell of secret skin. Ardis and I had tangled up in exactly one thousand combinations in my bed. She had told me our first night together that the room smelled like the digs of a pissbum. Her exact words.

"Dog possum?" I had said.

"No, pissbum."

Ardis knew from pissbums, too, for she worked part-time at a free clinic and halfway house for street people, runaways, panhandlers, and rising felons. There were plenty of alcoholics among the spare-change crowd.

From my position atop the warm and ample surface of Ardis Baines, I had asked how she could say such a thing about the altar of art. She had turned to the wall, a maneuver which deposited me on the floor, and said, "You come home with me. I can't stand this place anymore."

Home with Ardis Baines was a trip directly into the heart of the capitalist stronghold. Her daddy was the great-great-grandson of the Baines after whom Bainesborough was named. He was a real estate baron and owned the creosote works whose deadly effluent tainted the waters of Hart's Flow. Hers was a lineage not to be sneezed at in this part of North Florida. Sleeping in the bed of a polluter's daughter did not appeal to me politically, but my writer's eye was wide awake to the possibilities of what it might record at *chez* Baines, and so we went. More about that later.

Ardis sat in the dark breathing evenly, but loudly it seemed to me. My head was beginning to chime. She didn't speak. It was another contest. Finally, I said, "Ardis, what did you come for? I haven't got it, whatever it is. I am barely breathing air. I am, in fact, dying. If you are the ministering angel, you are welcome. Anything else . . ." I left it to her understanding. Her understanding was considerable, try as she sometimes might to mask it with a first-rate impersonation of a junior-leaguer.

She kept on inhaling there in the dark, and I could hear the chair creaking, which meant she was engaged in her nervous habit. Her beautiful legs were crossed at the knee and she was letting one rock on the fulcrum of the other.

"Ardis," I said, "I've told you that's masturbation."

The creaking stopped. She walked toward the door and would have left without turning on the light if I had not called her back.

"Why should I?"

"Because I asked you to. Now, come over here and sit on my nasty old bed and talk to me a little."

"Gross."

"Yes, but come anyway." I heard her feet start in my direction. When she sat down on the bed, her hip against mine, I took her hand. "Let me guess what you're wearing."

"No."

"That blue dress I like, the India print with the drawstring at the neck." Ardis wore dresses. In those days, most girls didn't. Jeans were in. "No," she said, but by tracing the contours of her body in the dark, I could tell it was the blue dress. I said, "My fingers feel blue."

"Your fingers are taking liberties with my tits."

"They have to. Byron in the blood. I can't help it." I undid the drawstring at her neck. "I have to liberate you from the bondage of capitalist contrivance. It's what Byron would do."

"He did underwear?"

She stood up and began to take off her dress while I imagined her doing it. She was a beautiful girl, only twenty, not even legal yet. She couldn't drink in bars, but she had an old head on her shoulders, and a Baptist soul, and a body the 1950s would have admired. But it was 1974, and skinny was in. The girls who were saying yes to the boys who said no were tall and skinny. Ardis was five-four and weighed 130. I suppose she had a little fat on her, but only in the right places. I was only imagining her undressing. I could not see her. I said, "Stop. I can't."

"What do you mean, you can't? You always do." Her voice had the old mocking tone. A you-don't-know-what's-funny tone. Since I usually did know what was funny, and since it was usually not me she was mocking, I liked the voice. I reached up and took her hands, which were holding her dress undone to the waist.

"I'm drunk, Ardis. I can't fuck now."

She reached down and took my hand. "I love it when you talk dirty to me, Toad." The fact was, she did love it to a point. That point was where the Baptist in her lived.

"I'm sorry," I said.

"No, it's all right, Mr. Turlow. I have got better things to do tonight anyway. But I *will* ask you to remember that we had a date."

The memory of the date had gone the whiskey way of all memory. Cauterized, I told her so. She sat down again and let me touch her breasts. The nipples did exactly what I knew they would do and did it very quickly. "Stand right up, don't they?"

"Yes," she said. "Too bad you don't."

"It's not that I don't, Ardis. It's that if I did, my head would bust."

"I see," she said, seizing my hand. "Then don't play with me."

"I thought you liked it."

"I know you do. You got a lot to learn about women, son."

Ardis dressed and left, and I fell asleep, but not before wondering how a girl four years my junior could call herself a woman and me "son" and get away with it. For I had let her get away with it and a lot more besides. She had something that I did not understand, and as long as this was so, she could call me anything she wanted to. I was going to write about Ardis someday and understand the thing she had. She was fair game because I had told her so. The understanding would come. It was only a matter of time, and there was plenty of that.

Three

IN MY SHORT STORY, A crippled center-fielder sat for the last time in the dugout with his teammates. In a gathering twilight, he listened to them call out to one another and their opponents using the game's ritual language, called *chatter*. He did not participate, though he knew all the words. He felt, suddenly and with great sadness, his separation from them, from this lost world of red clay and leather and sweat and Carolina ashwood. He kept silent, his thoughts chewing at the meaning, suddenly revealed to him, of the things they were saying. At the end, he bumped away on his crutches, leaving it all behind, the sound of their chatter ringing in his ears. It was an early Fitzgerald ending. The story was not exactly a work of pure imagination.

As I walked the three blocks through the student ghetto, called Squalor Holler, toward the old ROTC Bachelor Officers' Quarters, called the Old Barracks, I mused upon the fact that I had managed to live, more or less in the usual way, from the time of my visit with Eldon Odom until the evening of his weekly class. The usual way was a comfortable continuum of meals eaten in a greasy spoon called the Gutbomb, afternoons spent at the typewriter spinning skeins of prose, and evenings prowling bookstores, libraries, and bars. I worked in an all-night convenience store, the graveyard shift, eleven to seven.

It wasn't the perfect life, but with stamina, it was bearable. Standing behind the counter in the Lil Colonel Convenience Store, selling beer and wine to such creatures as could still locomote at 4 A.M. in a small, North Florida college town, I earned enough to pay the rent and buy suppplies for my work. I was something of a shade tree mechanic and was trying to coax a '67 Toyota out of retirement. When it didn't run, I walked for my health.

Many times in the hours since Sunday, I had imagined the conference I would have with Eldon Odom. I had pictured us sitting in his university office, a campus vista of sunny splendor unreeling from his window. There were green lawns and brick walks, and along these lesser mortals went in pursuit of unimaginables, such as accounting and engineering. Eldon Odom looked up from the manuscript page he was reading in my mind's eye and told me I was his heir.

Things got pretty vague after that. Sometimes he produced from a convenient nook a whiskey bottle, and we solemnly toasted the future of the lineage. Sometimes Eldon Odom himself was mysteriously missing. I had taken his place. The office was mine. Below my window strode those engineers and accountants, knee-deep in the quotidian.

I'd be lying if I didn't admit that a time or two I had seen it as disaster. Eldon Odom telling me to break the pencil and go back to cutting pulpwood in Alligood County. Such visions came to me but could not survive the systematic attack of my ego.

The Barracks was a split-pea green clapboard building. It had been used to house the veterans who had come to the land grant university after the big war. It had been listed as temporary on university maps for thirty years. It held graduate student offices and a few dusty and settling classrooms. Its peeling paint and sagging floors reminded me of the rented room where the dream lived.

When I stood at the door of the classroom, faces turned to me and turned away. Twenty or so people sat waiting for Eldon Odom and no one said a word. It was a narrow room with Odom's large desk at the head of two long seminar tables. It was Eldon Odom's office and his classroom, but it was like no faculty office I had ever seen. Cigarette butts had been ground out on the bare pine floor. Even the walls were scarred where matches had been struck and butts ground out. Initials and witticisms had been carved in the table tops and along the old tongue-in-groove wainscoting. Odom's desk was disarrayed and covered with dust. None of his few books looked as though they were ever opened. Rows of black footprints marched in the paint above the old radiator behind his desk.

I made my way to the only empty place left, an old armchair at the right hand of Eldon Odom. I sat down and willed myself into obscurity. From obscurity I occupied myself with the task of inventorying the types, for types were all around me. Even I, though I did not know it then, was one.

Directly to my left, knitting, was the blue-haired lady. A pleasant seeming soul whose needles clicked pleasantly and whose knitted product was as indeterminant as I was later to learn her stories were. Across from me sat the body builder, a young man about my age whose face was covered with the angry red scrofula of acne, and whose arms bulged from a skin tight T-shirt, emblazoned SLING IRON. The words were formed by the interlocking bodies of Grecian discus throwers, sprinters, and javelin chuckers. At the head of the second table, situated so that he could stare directly into Eldon Odom's eyes, sat the businessman. His wash-and-wear suit coat was casually thrown over the back of his chair. Rolled sleeves and loosened tie told that he had come straight from work. He had the weight and high color of a jolly man going to seed. Next to the weight lifter sat Virginia Woolf, an attenuated, whippet woman whose wine-dark tresses were elevated in a loose Edwardian bun and whose clothing, in undecipherable layers, resembled an enormous doily.

There were several young long-hairs, known as "hippites" among the wits of Alligood County, and a few smoldering young men in green fatigues. Several wore the Viet Nam Service Medal, and a few the insignia of the newly formed Viet Nam Veterans Against the War. One of them wore a purple heart as well. His eyes were angry; they flashed from face to face challenging the eyes they met. I watched the young man light a cigarette with his wounded hand, a two-fingered claw. He trapped a matchbook against the front of his fatigue jacket, pinning it against the badges he wore, and with his good hand plucked matches from the book. Sweat beaded his forehead. By the time he had lit the cigarette, I was not the only one watching him. After he had dropped the second of the three matches it took, I wanted to help but cancelled the impulse as quickly as it came. When he sat puffing angrily, holding the cigarette in the crotch of the two fingers, I nodded in the accepted fashion, right on brother. The soldier squinted back at me Eldon Odom style, then looked away.

The room was filling with nervous smoke. We were a circle in Dante's pit by the time Eldon Odom strode in. He carried a canvas book bag full of manuscripts and a sixteen-ounce beer. A woman followed him. She was tall and dark, and for a moment I thought she was Missy Sully, the karate queen of the fortress in the woods, but this woman only resembled Missy Sully in some particulars. Her slenderness and the long, dark hair almost to her buttocks were the same, but there, at the stony curve of the buttocks, the resemblance ended. This woman's body, in cut-off jeans and a workshirt, was as hard as mine. She moved with balletic grace and some of the carefully affected airs of male athletes. The stance she took — arms akimbo, hip canted — while Odom claimed his desk and she looked for a chair, was the armament of a stud wide receiver.

And clearly, there was something between her and Odom. She was young enough to be a student, even an undergraduate student, though this was a graduate seminar in fiction writing. She had come *with* him, not merely at the same time. There was between them the conspiratorial air of secret ownership and also its elaborate denial.

I stood to offer my chair, not out of chivalry but thinking she belonged here at the right hand. She curled her lip, slung her backpack into a corner behind the desk, and sat on it. A little laugh made its way around the room, ending at the pale face of the soldier, who gave me the same sneer I had received from the girl.

Odom watched all this with a proprietary grin. He finished the beer in a long, pumping swallow, and wiped his flat, red face with the back of a denim sleeve. "Now then, let's get to the bloodletting."

I had never stayed with a writing class. I had started with a few, so I knew the shape of them. A teacher read manuscripts aloud, and the assembled apprentices did what the sharks did to the Old Man's marlin. The ideal was a Socratic colloquium led by an enlightened but disinterested Master, whose end was the improvement of his student's work. I had not seen the ideal realized. Classes I had attended as an undergraduate had been dominated by one or two carping nit-pickers whose egos soared at the expense of fellow writers, and poorly led by professors who were not themselves seriously engaged in writing. I had submitted work to such a forum only once before. My story had received grudging praise, and the praise had stuck to it for months until I had thrown it away.

Eldon Odom sat down and began shuffling the heap of manuscripts. I guessed from the tension that came among us that no one knew how he would start. Was each hoping to be read, or hoping not to be? I was happy to be out of it. I watched his shuffling hands, and when I saw them holding my sweat-stiffened wad of pages, the air in my lungs turned to ice.

It had not occurred to me that Eldon Odom might read my work. I had not submitted in to be read *aloud*. We had struck an agreement I thought perfectly clear: He would read the story, we would meet at his convenience and talk. I gripped the arms of the chair so hard my knuckles popped. He unstuck my pages, taking his time, I supposed, to heighten the suspense. Even as I tried not to show the others who I was — namely, the author — I asked myself questions. Wasn't I proud of what I had done? Wasn't it, in my own estimation good? The fault in the privacy of my dream began to open before me even before Eldon Odom read a word.

He did not look at me before beginning, nor did he glance in my direction during the reading. It was a good reading, well done, fair. He spoke all of my words clearly, even tried a time or two to accent my characters' voices. There were moments when he enjoyed my story, when a light from it came into his eyes. But somehow the words I had written failed the voice that uttered them. Eldon Odom's voice. They did not fit in his mouth. In the disappointing tones of the last few paragraphs lay buried all the sadness and loss I had reached for and not reached.

When I had read it aloud to Ardis Baines, the first and only time, her reaction had been happy and simple. "It's good. You *are* a writer."

She had spoken with a finality, a certainty only youth confers. I did not press her for more. I liked her dotted I's and crossed T's. Now I hated her as my words fell short. By the time Eldon Odom had finished, the waters of my armpits had met in the middle of my shirt. I had so tortured a cigarette that tobacco shards littered the floor at my feet. I was ashamed.

There was a long silence after the last word, the word that sealed the sorry fate of my crippled center-fielder. He was a sentimental ass to be sure, though no worse a lamebrain than his creator.

Eldon Odom's method was to read the stories anonymously, the better to secure fairness in criticism, but I was certain everyone knew the bad smell was mine. I kept my eyes on the disemboweled cigarette in my hand. It was an interesting cigarette. It smoldered at one end, was bitten like a cigar at the other.

When Eldon Odom said, "Comments?" it was as though lightning had struck us. From the look of my fellow apprentices, it was as difficult to talk as to be talked about. Odom lurched back in his chair, raised a booted foot to the radiator and added new prints to those already marching in the paint. The gesture told he would wait as long as we would. After considerable pause, the weight lifter elevated a slab of flesh. Eldon Odom nodded at it. "It's a sketch," he said. His voice was oddly high, an alto compressed from the bellows of that great chest. I did not know what the comment signified, so I looked at Eldon Odom for some clue. He only nodded a sage head at the muscle man. There was more in the nod than I could see, for the muscles began to swell with gladness.

Virginia Woolf raised her hand; it climbed like a charmer's cobra, wavering and dangerous. "I don't think the character's a fit vessel of consciousness. I mean, who could care about a bunch of baseball players?"

Odom nodded at this, too, but somehow differently. Virginia wrapped both arms around a pigeon breast and let her eyes shift toward the lighthouse. I had read my Henry James and knew where she had got her remark. Silently, I countered with my own Jamesian trope: You can't tell a writer what to write about, only demand that he make as much of his subject as possible.

Odom's eyes pawed the faces in the room, picking locks, stealing what they could, and seeming at the same time to demand silence. At last, the Viet Nam soldier with the mutilated hand said, "No enveloping action. I mean, what's this guy doing playing games when there's a war on? There's no relationship between the action proper and anything universal." The soldier's face and his disgusted voice gave the impression that my story had raised hopes only to drop them like so much garbage. And he looked at me. None of the others had. He knew I had written the story. I had read my Gordon and Tate, too, and knew his comment held a grain of truth.

"Don't have to be the war, but it's got to be something." This came from the body builder, and came without the eliciting gaze of Eldon Odom. The weight lifter offered his comment not to the front of the room but to the soldier, in a sternly sympathetic way. The soldier only stared at me, raising a cigarette to slitted lips. I was beginning to see a little showmanship in the way he used the torn hand. Look, he seemed to be saying. See it. See it. I looked.

The businessman waved his hand, smiling like Elmer Fudd. Odom stared at a square yard of air just above his head. "Yeah, Frank."

"Well, durn it, it seems to me it's pretty good." Frank gestured to Virginia and then back to the group at large, but his eyes were on Odom all the time. "I mean, *I* like baseball. *I'm* interested. I bet a lot of us were." He scanned the room for affirmation. Where were his fellow boosters? All those who are interested, please raise your hands. No one looked at him. It was clear that I had been defended by an armpit sniffer.

The soldier spoke under his breath, as though to the man in the next bunker, "Who cares about a jock's knee?"

The body builder said, "Baseball sucks. No violence."

Odom glanced at the soldier, narrowed his eyes but did not speak. Frank wallowed, stewed, fried, and finally evaporated, leaving a husk of gristle and a dark stain in a summer suit. No one else spoke.

Odom looked at his watch. "Other comments?" We waited while he inventoried all our faces. "Break, then," he said.

The class stood as one man and began shuffling to the door. I looked at my watch and saw that an hour had passed. I could not think how this was possible. I stayed where I was. The hallway was dangerous. The group was congregating there — for what? Coffee? Human blood? I stayed and Odom stayed, too, and so did the girl, there on her backpack. She had taken a Buddha posture, her hands delicately curled into each other, a grim smile on her face. At last Odom pushed himself up and leaned back to stretch the muscles of his back. He did not look at me. I watched him walk out. I wanted to ask him a hundred questions but would have died before uttering one of them. The girl began to rise from the half-lotus, unreeling an incredible geometry of gleaming skin and muscle, all of the stonecutter's art. She said to me, "Don't take it hard. Only the strong survive. Anybody who *can* be discouraged *should* be discouraged."

As I watched her perfect rock-struck calves and buttocks cross the threshold, I knew the words had merely passed through her. I had been given the ground rules for the game as it was played here, and from the source.

Four

I WAS STILL SEATED at the right hand when the class returned from its break. I sat through two more hours, two more stories, two more discussions of shortcomings less grievous than mine. One was a story about a firefight between American Marines and NVA regulars during the Tet Offensive. It was an accurate and compelling account but ended badly. Or so the class said. The other was a story of a lonely old woman whose chief accomplishment and only diversion was her knitting. I did not hear much of either one. I was sunk too deep in my own disappointment. At the end of the three hours, I had recollected and memorized every word spoken about my story, an easy task since very little had been said.

I rose at ten o'clock and, taking my manuscript from the desk top, walked out with the others. At the head of the stairs, Frank, the Rotarian, caught up with me. "We usually go to Moby Dick's after class," he said. "Why don't you come with us?"

"No, thanks," I said. I tried to smile at him. He grinned and we parted on the street outside.

As I walked in the cool night, the manuscript in my hand became an intolerable weight. I dropped it in a trash can in front of the Gutbomb. It was my grand gesture. I would regret it, but it seemed at the moment the only way to get back a measure of control. I walked on, oblivious of the traffic, horse and foot, passing on the town's busiest thoroughfare. I suppose in some part of my mind I knew where I was going, but I did not admit it to myself until I turned at the end of College Avenue and passed through the Spanish stucco portals of Prairie View, where Ardis Baines lived.

Prairie View was a golf course suburb perched on a bluff above Bainesborough's one distinguishing geographic feature, the Savannah. In his *Travels,* William Bartram had called it the Great East Florida Savannah. It was less than great now — most of it had dried up — but on a starry night, what was left was beautiful. It was five square miles of saw grass marsh and cypress hammock, alive with the creatures who had retreated to it ahead of bulldozing progress. It was a treacherous place. The saw grasses were razor-edged. When it rained and the waters rose, long, fat rattlesnakes crawled out onto U.S. 441. A trip across the Savannah on a wet August night could be a mad dash through a gallery of living and dead serpents, reeking like the end of the world. Great horned owls ruled its skies at night. They were big birds whose white faces sometimes flashed unsurprised in your headlights. You could see them carrying prey.

During the day, ospreys, rare so far inland, and red-tailed hawks soared on the summer thermals. There were deer in the Savannah, and ocelots, and bobcats, and some said even the last of the Florida panthers. There were no secondary roads in, only an occasional serpentine canal. Airboats could travel the Savannah but not without hazard. On the far side of this marshy plain, about four miles from the outskirts of Bainesborough, stood a prison farm. The inmates tapped for turpentine in the nearby pine woods and cultivated fields of corn, peanuts, and tobacco. Occasionally there was an escape and a pursuit to the edge of the Savannah. It was local wisdom that correctional officers never went into the Savannah after a running man. They didn't have to.

Ardis Baines lived in the last house on a bluff overlooking the Savannah. It was the last because it had been built first, fifty years before anyone had conceived the idea of a subdivision called Prairie View. Ardis's grandfather had built it, surrounded by twenty acres of the highest, driest, and best ground in North Central Florida. The house was a reprise of an antebellum structure, the original Baines mansion which had stood on the site. It had been the ancestral seat of the Baineses, who had come first in the person of Colonel William, after whom the town was called. It had been destroyed by fire in 1864 by a party of Yankee raiders, a splinter from the Battle of Olustee. Colonel William had fought in the Indian Wars, one of General Jessup's lieutenants, and had stayed on. After he had personally escorted the Seminole chief, Osceola, to St. Augustine to be imprisoned in the Spanish fort, Castilla de San Marco, he acquired the land under a patent signed by a grateful President Jackson.

The long walk was good for me. The moon was high, white-faced, and icy, and it cooled me, flesh and spirit. I could see the lights of the big house ahead and smell the night-blooming jasmine that festooned its stucco walls. The Baineses' old basset hound, Lyndon, belled at the sound of my footsteps. I stood at the bottom of a small rise, staring at the walls that protected this house. Behind me lay the sleeping delights of contemporary architecture. Prairie View had grown up around the Baineses like a medieval village around its castle — for protection and a breath of royal airs.

To secure a measure of independence in her twentieth year, Ardis had moved into a six-room cottage, a miniature of the big house situated a hundred yards to the west. Between it and the mansion lay a swimming pool, two tennis courts, and a gazebo. The cottage had housed the servants until after the big war. Now the black women who served the Baineses commuted from the Negro quarters in Bainesborough. My usual procedure was to walk the long way around the walls to a place just west of Ardis's cottage.

Ardis and I had taken the walk together one afternoon and marked the place where a cedar grew close to the top of the wall. Ardis had pointed it out to me, though I confess I had been a short step ahead of her. "Why don't you use that for a ladder and come see me some night late," she had said. She turned and addressed herself to me, her ample bosom not quite contacting the front of my shirt. I gave her a standard sort of questioning glance, one that said, Are you sure? Is it OK? What if I get caught? Do you really mean it? Aw, come on! She gave me back a stare that was half lover's challenge, half disappointed practicality. Somehow, I got the feeling I had missed a chance to be Ardis's kind of guy.

All this was necessary because Ardis's father, Arnold Baines, creosote magnate and prototypical New South executive, was not fond of me. Ardis had invited me through the front gate a time or two, and he had since made it clear that he did not want me back. We had sat by the pool together, he and I, having the ritual who-are-you-and-why-are-you-trying-to-get-into-my-daughter's-pants conversation, New South style.

Blackford Turlow.

Writer.

Because we have similar views on things political and philosophical (a lie).

I have a great deal of respect for your daughter (true) and because well, (exasperation) . . . look at her.

With that I had slipped. I don't know what made me say it. I usually just thought such things while a smirk tugged at the corners of my mouth. I followed with some lamebrained maunderings intended to ameliorate. Ardis was attractive. I was attracted to her.

The sun was well over the yardarm; it was a perfect May dusk, a rare one when the air was cool and dry. We were drinking martinis. Ardis's father was dressed for golf in pastel slacks of polyester and layers of unneeded sweaters with puffed sleeves. He was aglow with the sweat of a sub-eighty round and a Beefeater martini; aglow, at least, until I made my unfortunate remark. After that he was burnt.

We sat in silence for a time. He did not exactly glare at me, nor did he actually bite the rim of the martini glass, but somehow the damned thing got broken (maybe it came that way) and his lip was bleeding into the gin, and Ardis had to come and lead him into the house. There was a bright red boutonniere of blood on his pink sweater, and his face was pale. As she took him away, she looked back at me, her eyes asking what I had done. I muttered something about the Oedipal struggle. That was the end of me and Arnold Baines. He later told Ardis I was a pseudo-artist shitass and a draft-dodging pinko. People said things like that back then.

I had made the trip up the tree and over the wall without mishap a half dozen times before and was beginning to take the short and well-rewarded leap for granted. It was my practice to squat on the top of the wall, sight as best I could a landing place in the darkness below, and then make the eight-foot drop. That night, I landed on the broad back of Lyndon Baines, the basset. Lyndon was unhurt and began licking my face as though it were a prime cut the minute I was belly up among the sandspurs.

What was prime cut was my knee. It felt like that day on the warning track all over again. I lay in the grass staring at the stars while little things without names, expensive things, began to put themselves painfully back into place beneath my kneecap. After a while, I could tell it wasn't going to be as bad as I had thought. By the time I was ready to get up and limp, Lyndon had given me a very good tongue-lashing and was ready for some real play. "Don't bark," I said. Lyndon nodded his head. I thought, Lyndon, when the urban guerillas come for old man Baines, you are going to do a fine job. I imagined the happy dog leading several ski-masked men to the poolside where Arnold Baines sat, musing into the deeps of a Beefeater martini.

When I got to Ardis's door, I told Lyndon he had to go. "Three's a crowd." Just then, a lizard flashed in the grass and Lyndon was off, humping like a Brahma bull. Ardis opened the door. "Who's out there? Is it you?"

"Yes."

"Oh, it's you." It hadn't occurred to me that there was any *you* but *me*. She was standing in the light from the doorway with a pistol in her hand, to be exact, a Long Colt .38. It made my knee throb to see it. "Put that thing away, Ardis."

"Right," she said.

She went and put the gun in a drawer. I had seen it before. When she moved to the cottage, her father had given her this heirloom to shoot me with. I stood outside the door watching Lyndon eat the lizard. I wasn't going in until I was sure the cannon was safely stored. When Ardis was there in the glow again, wearing a flannel nightgown, I said, "I'm hurt." I wasn't referring to my knee.

"Come in," she said. She looked me up and down, sighting for blood I guess. "Is it your knee?"

I was limping a bit more than was actually necessary. "No, it's not my knee. It's my heart." I told her what had happened,

ending with my grand gesture in front of the Gutbomb. I tried to
be funny about it, because otherwise I would have been wimpy
or mean. Ardis did not take kindly to wimpy. She demanded and
got certain kinds of considerations. I remembered my flash of
anger against her back in Eldon Odom's office. Mean didn't set
well with her either. I felt guilty now on top of everything else. I
wanted to be on top of Ardis. There, at least, I could do
something right.

She took me by the hand and led me into her bedroom. She
had fixed the cottage up nice. It had fallen into a pretty bad state
after the maids had decided it was too Tomish to live in. Ardis
had made it over in her own image — no frills, late-sixties social
consciousness–*moderne*. But I didn't notice any of that as Ardis
led me down the narrow hallway to her sleeping quarters. I
noticed the way her buttocks disturbed the straight lines of the
tent she was walking in. I said, "Ardis, a flannel nightgown in
the summer?"

"I get cold. I'm just cold-natured, I guess."

There was a comfortable looking hollow among the bed-
clothes in the exact shape of Ardis Baines. I reached down to
touch it. It was warm. "Ardis, who was the is-that-you you were
talking to when you weren't talking to me?"

"Oh, don't be silly." Her eyes were on the Ché Guevara
poster over the bed. There were certain considerations I
demanded too.

"Ardis?" She looked straight into my eyes. It was like having
something hot thrown at you. She said, "Let's just do what you
do best and forget about what I said. It doesn't mean anything
anyway."

I stared some heat back at her. We stood that way for some
time, while old Ché exuded revolutionary charm. Finally, Ardis
gave in. "It's just some boy from the halfway house. He says
he's in love with me. Says he knows where I live. He's got an

arrest record. See? It's nothing, like I told you." I remembered her at the door in her granny nightgown with a pistol in her hand, pioneer womanhood. It was funny before, and now I wished we had left it that way.

"Arrest record?"

She seemed tired of it. She sat down on the bed and formed the flannel into the shape of a nest in her lap. I could see the swelling curve of her belly and the little tuft of pubic hair just below. She said, "Minor things mostly. B and E, bar fights, DWI and a little dealing. He did a year in the Bradford County slammer and a couple years in the Nam before that. Nothing to write home about." She could talk tough. She was a veteran of half a year in the halfway house which, as far as I could tell, was halfway between nothing and nowhere. "Ship him back to Bradford County," I said. I watched her belly swell and diminish with her breathing, her hands resting in the nest she had made for them. "I can't. I'm not in shipping. I'm just an intern."

"And your address is in the phone book, and I'm not the only poontanging fool that knows the way over that wall."

I regretted it as soon as I said it. It came from my anger, my fear.

She looked at me, naked and hurt. I sat down. "I'm sorry, but you know what I mean."

"*I'm* sorry, but I don't. Tell me." Tears shone in her eyes. I had never seen her cry. I reached with my thumbs and erased two of them. She made two more immediately. "I'm an asshole, Ardis. You know that."

She nodded, yes, very seriously, yes, unable to speak. I could see now that she had been scared by the sound at her door, more than she was willing to admit. She was not well protected here. Lyndon was no watchdog. I considered Ardis and the Long Colt .38 someone might take away from her and use. It was a mess.

"I'm sorry, Ardis."

She nodded again, and this time took me up against her breast. It was where I'd wanted to be ever since leaving Eldon Odom's class. I let my face rest in the odor of secret skin, against the soft nape of her neck, and tried to purge my mind of all thought. It didn't work but it was sweet trying, and an exercise in humility.

She raised up the corner of her nightgown and wiped her eyes and swallowed away the last of her outrage. When she spoke, it was in the old Ardis Baines way. "I know you are sorry."

I laughed, relieved. "Let's bump bones," I said. She lay back, pulling me onto her, holding me like a wrestler.

"I hoped you'd say that. Only not quite that way."

"Too crude?"

"What we do is not bumping bones, or fucking, except once in a while. Once in a while we *do* fuck, I admit it. We fuck like dogs. But mostly we make love, and I want you to learn to say it."

I thought about telling her it was a good old Anglo-Saxon word, that Chaucer himself had used it, but instead I promised I would learn. And I guess I meant it.

I stayed with Ardis until about two in the morning. She was asleep when I left by the same way I had come.

I was asleep in my monk's cell and was dreaming of Eldon Odom's class when someone knocked at the door. In my dream, I was confounding the weight lifter and the claw-handed veteran by the sheer brilliance of a critical refutation, a theory of fiction invented on the spot and unreeled before their astonished eyes (and by the silent approval of Eldon Odom), even as I took my manuscript from the great man's desk and strode out. I was loath to leave the dream, but finally, the insistence of the knock fetched me up from blissful depths and I stood, scratching myself and wondering who was on the other side. The first thing I saw was a handful of paper coming through my door. The arm and the face that followed it smelled faintly of garbage and belonged to Ardis Baines. "Here," she said, handing me my manuscript.

"Thanks," I said. She was gone before I could offer anything else.

I lay in bed for a while with my mind's eye on Ardis as she prowled the midnight streets, coming finally to the place in front of the Gutbomb where I had discarded my short story. In my mind's eye, she paused, pushed up the sleeve of her long flannel nightgown and plunged her lovely, pioneer's arm down into the swill, retrieving hapless art. I loved that Ardis, the one who moved on now, up the dark street, walking toward the rented room where I slept.

Five

THE MORNING AFTER I visited Ardis and Ardis visited me, I had another visitor. I was sitting at my desk contemplating the manuscript from the garbage can when I heard footsteps in the hall. They were not Traymore's. Traymore, who haunted my doorway with an empty stomach and asking eyes, rarely wore shoes. These heels struck the old heart pine floor like two framing hammers. I dropped the manuscript on the desk and stood up.

I was planning to peek out at the landing and see who was breaking my monkish silence, but before I could ease open the door, those heels were on the other side of it and a fist was rapping. My hand was on the knob, but I did not open immediately. I crept back to the desk, sighed loudly, scraped the chair a few feet and stomped to the door.

It was the lean, hard girl from Odom's class. She wore a dancer's wraparound skirt, and the shoes I had heard were high-heeled black dance pumps. In her tight black leotard, her crushed breasts were like a boy's pectoral muscles. The back-pack was slung negligently over her shoulder. A pair of pink pointe shoes, scuffed and smudged, protruded from it.

Her tanned legs were shaved ice-smooth and accented by the clefts and ridges that body builders call "cuts." Her weight rested on her right leg and I stared at the thigh, at the place where the quadriceps nestled into the knee joint in a neat, hard curve. It was the impossible geometry I had possessed and lost. It was a form of perfection. I knew it was fleeting and, to the extent that it was genetic, also accidental, but in those days, any perfection impressed me. All of this took place in a second or two while she watched me out of eyes as dark and depthless as coffee beans. They reminded me of the eyes of horses — not dumb, but cold in a way that signals an elemental resistance. I might have been angry at her — she was from the world of my humiliation — but I wasn't. Instead, I was suddenly conscious of how shabby my room was.

I hurried to remove a drying pair of socks and a jockstrap from a pool of sunlight on the windowsill. When I had the jockstrap in my hand, I could think of no new place to put it. She walked slowly into the room, took from my hand what the lady gym teacher used to call an "unmentionable," and put it back in the sunlight. "At least let's turn it over and cook the other side." She pulled my chair away from the desk and straddled it in a horsy, dancer's way.

"I remember you," I said.

Something about the way she had invaded me, careless and precise, reminded me of Missy Sully, of that karate kick on Odom's deck. My visitor pushed her short nylon skirt down between her legs and watched me sit on the cot. She gave a heavy breath and said, "I just came by on my way from work-outs to tell you not to worry about what happened in class. It's the treatment they always give a new guy. You could have been Faulkner himself. . . ." She stopped, impatient with her voice. As though her body could tell me better, she stood and tested her calves, rising to tiptoes in those Cyd Charisse shoes. She bobbed for a while with a look of Buddhist concentration on her face, using my chair as a barre. Then she said, "See you in class," and started for the door.

My pride was between my teeth like old leather and bitten through by the time she reached the hallway. "Wait a minute!" My voice rang loudly down the hall toward Traymore's room. She turned with one eye closed.

"Come back here," I said more softly. "I've got some questions." She moved away from the door and distractedly began the tip-toe exercise again. I said, "What do you mean, *treatment?*"

"Just what I said, *treatment.*" She stopped exercising and looked at me straightly. "It's like I told you after class. They don't think anybody who *can* be discouraged *should* stick it. It's too tough. If you stick it, after a while you're OK."

"You keep talking about what *they* think. What do *you* think?"

"Me?" She stared up into the fetid air of my cell, her black bean eyes slitted. "I don't know. It's not like dancing. Dancing is different, probably better. Not so much ego. Anyway, Daddy liked your story."

I said, "Who's Daddy?" knowing the answer.

"Daddy Odom." She stood flat-footed. She was altered as soon as she spoke his name.

"He liked it?" I couldn't keep the note of hope from my voice.

She smiled and maybe a little tenderness for my hope came into her face. She said, "Yeah, he liked it. He told me so."

"Why didn't he tell *me?*"

It was the question I had been turning over in my head since Ardis had left at four in the morning.

She answered without hesitation, as though reading from a book of codes. "Because no one told *him* when he was your age." She stared at me, his strange messenger.

I could not respond. Eldon Odom knew what I wanted. There was a room full of us, all yearning to be cut and shaped by him. If I entered the contract, the choices were mostly his. If the cutting hurt, so be it. But there was something I hated in it. Something that reminded me of that collision on the warning track.

I was on the second floor overlooking the street, and after she left — "See you in class" — I watched her walk off proud and stiff. Occasionally, one of those hammer heels would hit the pavement dead solid with a report that sounded like my father's Smith and Wesson .32. The traffic of the student ghetto parted before her, and people turned after she passed.

I watched her out of sight but not out of mind. I did not know Traymore had invaded my dream until the odor of burnt soybeans and herb tea brought me around. "Was that Lindy Briggs?" he asked from the doorway.

He was tall and rangy and had the pale, starved look of long-distance runners. His long hair was tied in a ponytail. He wore a greasy suede vest and no shirt. His cut-off jeans were fringed at the thighs, and fist-sized slices of his buttocks could be seen moving around, pale and hairy, through the holes in them.

I left the window and lay on my cot, staring up at the ceiling, thinking about Odom liking my story and how he had chosen to show it. I said, "I don't know who she is. She didn't tell me."

He waited. Finally, he said, "That *was* Lindy Briggs!"

Unable to resist, I asked, "Who's Lindy Briggs?"

"Her old man's the Rotcy commander. He's a badass. Eats hippies and fag writers first thing in the morning."

Colonel Briggs was a campus character, a professional soldier who once had publicly called Eugene McCarthy a communist and had advocated the use of tactical nuclear weapons in Viet Nam. During the campus demonstrations after Kent State, he had led a group of cadet officers to the ROTC armory to keep an all-night vigil between the freak legions and the two thousand M-1's moldering in racks inside.

"Where do you know her from?" I asked Traymore.

He scratched his butt by sticking two fingers through a hole in his jeans. It made a sandpapery sound. "Oh, I had her in class once. She's no dummy. I guess you know she hangs around with your idol."

"As of last night, I know it." Traymore walked to my desk, picked up my manuscript and sniffed it, apparently assessing its food value.

"What happened?"

I didn't know whether he meant to the egg-stained manuscript or to me. In either case, the answer was the same. I said, "Nothing much." A grin was festering under his mustache. I said, "How about, none of your goddamned business?"

He parked his infectious ass exactly in the place where Lindy Briggs had sat. "I went to that class once."

I was supposed to ask him what had happened, but I refused to play the game. He shook his head and stared with me at the ceiling. "They just couldn't see it."

"It" was his vision. When I looked at the ceiling, I saw peeling paint, or if fancy was at work, a lunar landscape of flyspeck and woodgrain mountain ranges. Traymore saw his Vision. It was the concoction of rock lyrics, William Blake, and puréed *Bhagavad-Gita* he had been trying for years to congeal on paper and canvas. The writing class obviously had not seen his Vision.

I said, "Well, I guess that makes us even."

"Yeah," he sighed happily. "Even."

It was Traymore's particular gift to sink us to common ground. I was always astonished to find myself there with him.

Six

I WILL NOT SAY that when the next Tuesday night turned up, I was oblivious of its malign intent. I conducted my affairs as though the day were no different from any other, but inwardly I seethed with indecision. I had sought something special from Eldon Odom, and in a way, his way, I had received it. Now, I was called back to the class. He liked my story. Lindy Briggs had said so.

All that Tuesday I worked on the story, but only in fits and starts. By mid-afternoon, I had invented a way of guaranteeing my absence from Odom's class. I called Ardis and invited her to the Beau Geste, our local art film emporium, to see *Jules et Jim,* our favorite foreign film. She would complete her shift at the halfway house at six and then drop by to pick me up. In her father's Mercedes convertible, with the eyes of Squalor Holler upon us, we would drive the three blocks to the Beau Geste. The whole thing was a *geste* of some kind, though Ardis didn't know it. She thought it was a regular date.

I was ready early and pacing the heart pine floor in front of my window, watching for the flash of powder blue that was Ardis in the Mercedes. Instead, what I saw coming through the oak treetops was a shaggy head and a shoulder bearing an Army surplus backpack.

She was not wearing the heels, so I did not hear her on the stairs. It seemed like forever before she knocked, quietly this time. I was thinking of what I would say in the note I would leave for Ardis, of Ardis's anger, of what she would think, all this before the hard little fist rapped on the door. I considered hiding. No one could possibly know I was behind the door. Finally I acknowledged what I had always known: I would go, had wanted all week long to find a way.

My part was to open the door and feign surprise. I said, "Lindy Briggs!" and stepped back into the room. She stood in the hallway. "Come on, we got to hurry."

"Just a minute," I said, forgetting surprise. I wrote the note to Ardis. In it, I told most of the truth. *I decided to go to class. I guess I knew I would all along. I'm sorry I didn't get this to you sooner. See you after? XXX, Toad.*

Triple-X Toad Turlow and Lindy Briggs walked down the middle of Squalor Holler. Lindy was striding along like there was no tomorrow, and Toad was hoping to heaven that a powder blue Mercedes did not turn the corner. In the event that it did, there was no tomorrow.

After a few blocks, when I could breathe again, I said, "Slow down. It's not that big of a hurry."

"Daddy don't like late." She kept walking fast. I suppressed the impulse to drop back a few steps and stare at the back of her. I wanted information from her. That room was a hostile place.

"Does Daddy ever talk, in class, I mean?" Since that first

night, I had wondered why Odom kept silent. She looked over at me, annoyed. From the moment she had opened my door, she had done her best to show me this was business. We were supposed to hurry along in hushed anticipation.

"Does he?"

She stopped short and stood with her hands on her boyish hips, a look of patience on her face. "The group says what needs to be said. If it don't, you'll hear from him, believe me."

She ignored me the rest of the way.

Lindy Briggs separated herself from me before we entered the classroom. Muttering something about toilets, she left me to climb the stairs alone. She came in late, following Eldon Odom, and again she perched behind him in the corner, on her backpack. I took the old armchair again. Before long I sensed a difference in the way I was regarded by the group. The sneers were still in place but directed now at the doorway, where the next newcomer might appear. Or perhaps they were aimed at emptiness, the difficult problem we all faced. The one-handed soldier stared at me long and hard and then nodded. I nodded back. The body builder said, "Hey, bud." I nodded again. My reserve knew no limits.

I was waiting to see how Eldon Odom would register my presence. I should have known better. He came this time drinking whiskey from a paper bag, carrying the batch of manuscripts. Tall and gaunt and wearing a work shirt, denim trousers, and hiking boots, he sat down heavily, took a pull from the paper bag, and began by reciting the title of the first story. He spoke the title twice and then started reading in that red clay voice of his. We all settled in to listen.

It was a night much like the first one, three stories and three eviscerations led by the wounded soldier, the weight lifter and Virginia Woolf. Once, Frank the Rotarian attempted a meager defense but was stopped by the silence that grew around it. He didn't sulk, only smiled, wallowing in shallow optimism. There were miscellaneous voices, too, but it was clear that the class had its power elite. Since I was not much interested in the stories themselves and did not dare speak, I gave myself the task of discovering the source of the power. It wasn't long before I located it in the world of Odom's work. In his stories, a character achieved significance in direct proportion to the severity and cosmic perversity of his suffering. I had written a paper on the topic in school. Suffering was often self-inflicted in Odom's books. The opinions that mattered in this room were, by the look of things, those of the self-created fictions.

A body builder made himself every day, and by pain. The one who sat across from me, glistening in the florescent light, could not cure his own acne. Steel defying gravity could not tear from his throat the silly squeak of his voice and replace it with a muscular one. But what he could build, he had built, and it had hurt.

Some kind of flying steel had taken the soldier's hand, too. But the soldier was more difficult to parse. He had enlisted again, this time in a class of outsiders whose war was with words. Perhaps he wanted to punish the world that had not gone to war with the voice of one who had.

And Virginia, whose name was Sarah Fesco, conformed to the pattern. One of the stories that night was hers. Its principal character was a lonely, waifish girl, an office worker who had conceived a passionate attachment to another woman. This beloved was the gum-chewing blonde queen of file cabinets and copying machines and the apple of the boss's eye. The story ended when, deep in the revels of an office party, the young waif discovered her blonde Juno riding the hips of the boss in the janitor's closet. Along with love died the chance for a new world. So said the story's closing line.

It was obvious. They had escaped from the pages of Odom's books. They were his fictions. He did not speak; they spoke for him. They had made themselves writers in the image of his characters, his obsessions, and were creating a new generation of self-transmogrifying souls in the pages of the manuscripts they brought him.

By the time the class had adjourned, I was hooked. If not on Odom's method, or the medicinal powers of the class for my own work, at least on the personalities in this room, on their brand of group sickness. It was like a baseball team's common obsession. I knew I was going the distance with them. The distance, for the time being, was to Moby Dick's.

Moby's was one of several university bars, the other option in Bainesborough being country and western dives. It was also a seafood restaurant with a big smiling neon whale out front and a keep-it-dark-if-you-can't-keep-it-clean attitude. The lights were low for deep-sea atmosphere, the interior was styrofoam fo'csle and belaying pin. There were spots where you could step into the swampy carpet and disappear. Plenty of drunks had done it. Moby's clientele, I had learned, was mostly graduate students, professors, and the writing and art crowds. But these three groups kept well apart in the large dark interior of Moby's. Odom's class usually occupied the back room by the toilets. The owner, an admirer of Odom, made it available every Tuesday night.

This time I took the ride Frank offered in his big salesman's Buick. On the way, I questioned him about who he was and deflected questions about my own identity. He was Frank Lagano, novelties salesman. Novelties were sexual devices. He sold dildoes, vibrators, and various phony fluids, and had just put in a new line of something he called "butt plugs." "It's an interesting life, you know. I been writing it going on ten years."

"How's it going? The writing, I mean."

"It's tough, but I keep plugging."

So did I. "What keeps you going to class?"

"It's Odom, I guess." He stared up at the Buick's plush headliner. He seem embarrassed.

"What about Odom?"

I had my own need of a piece of Eldon Odom, but when it came to admitting it to another soul, I was reluctant. Frank was willing to talk about it.

"I don't know," he said. "You feel. The class makes me feel. . . ." He looked over at me and grinned like a dog that wants a petting. I nodded and smiled. He turned back to his driving. "It makes me feel like I used to feel, that's all." He clamped his jaw as though he'd said it right and wouldn't revise.

As best I could, I tried to remember how I used to feel. It wasn't all that good, how I used to feel. But I could see how it might have been different for him. I watched the night come streaming up the hood of that shiny Buick, filling our little cockpit with neon come-ons, cut-rates, hotcakes and the general brainwash and soul-kill of the strip. I figured Frank had logged close to a million miles of four-lane shock treatment. No wonder he needed to feel like he used to feel.

I said, "Frank, you're all right." To me, it meant something that I thought Frank was all right. It seemed to mean something to Frank, too.

The group was mostly assembled when Frank and I walked in, and placements around the big table were like those in the classroom. One vacant chair was close to Odom. I didn't want it and didn't want to be seen avoiding it. I stepped back and took Frank's arm just above the wrist. My gesture was deference to his seniority. But his arm stiffened in my grip and he turned to me with panic in his face. He couldn't go close to Odom. We stood urging each other forward like two comedians, while the eyes of the group settled on us. Finally, I stepped past him to the closer seat. Odom did not look at me; he watched Frank take a place on the furthest edge, and with an interest I could not read.

Odom sprawled in a captain's chair drinking bourbon warm and neat from a water glass, scratching and flexing while the group spoke for him. Sometimes he flagged a big, Indian-skinned hand to indicate the worthlessness of someone's word, or called "Huzzah! Huzzah!" to designate a winner. All the vectors of ego and hope and all the sightlines converged at his brooding face. He was the great, lolling, indolent vortex of the evening. The talk went from book to book, branching now and then into that world of fools that walked outside the door. After a while, I could see that each of the principals here had a voice. Whether half-formed or glib, purple or prudent, each voice was an instrument in the recital. Only Odom, who sat and watched, had earned the luxury of silence.

I had grown used to silence when suddenly it was broken. The talk had come to *The Ballad of the Sad Cafe,* to Cousin Lymon, Marvin Macy, and Miss Amelia, the monstrous battle that ends McCullers's story. Frank, who hadn't spoken all evening, ventured praise in his jolly way. Odom pushed forward in his chair, his Geronimo face two shades darker, his neck swelling with outraged arteries. "You bleeve that, Frank? You bleeve that?"

Frank pressed his fingers to his throat in a manner almost feminine; he seemed to prod his larynx, kneading for words. His voice was seized. The smile, his business grin, sickened on his face. Odom watched, crouching forward like a sprinter. Finally he shoved back and picked up his bourbon. He circled the whiskey in the glass, then sighted through it at the candle that burned between himself and Frank. "Frank, what *do* you bleeve? Is it what you *sell* you bleeve? What is it? It ain't in your work, Frank."

Odom's words were tired, slow, discreet, emphatic, and as blunt as bullets. "Go on, Frank," Odom said. "Go on out and find it. Go on."

Frank's fingers still hung at his throat where the words were sticking. He seemed to be pointing at himself. Me?

"Go on, Frank. Go find it. It ain't here. *I* don't have it. Go find it and bring it back and show it to us."

Frank slunk out.

After a long and, it seemed that night, a fitting silence, the body builder ventured the first word. Odom looked at him sharp, then opened a smile and the talk began again.

Somewhere in all of this, I noticed Lindy Briggs. I had watched her while Frank struggled with the hand at his throat. (She had told me I would hear Odom speak when he wanted me to.) She had sat through the bloodletting with her shoulder pressed tightly to Odom's forearm, moving with him when he moved. She was still flushed, nerved from that contact. She swallowed hard and her small, boyish bosom moved. She was like Steinbeck's Elisa, the woman scorned who asks her husband, "Will there be blood?" She had that blood lover's high color in her cheeks. I remembered the holiday hog-killing at home, how the hogs that waited sometimes licked up the blood of those that had gone before them to the hammer.

When the evening was winded, its discussions and dissents blown out, the fringes of the group began to unravel. Sitting by the heart, I was becoming conspicuous. To get myself out gracefully, I decided on nature's call and announced to the group that I had to go point Percy at the pavement. Because I believed that such locutions were colorful, I used them whenever I could. Odom turned to me with a bent grin on his face. "You gone go shake hands with Lindy's best friend?"

I smiled, then frowned. I looked at Lindy, who gave me back a surprised but good imitation of Odom's grin.

"Something like that," I said.

In the men's room, I wondered what Odom had meant. Surely I was shaking hands with Ardis's best friend. As far as I knew, anyway. Since our meeting on his cypress deck, Odom had spoken only this once to me, to mention Lindy's best friend. It was a phrase I carried in my own quiver. I pondered it as I walked home, enjoying the night and the sobering effects of exercise. I kept coming to the same conclusion: Odom was telling the others there was something between Lindy Briggs and me. This could mean only one thing: There was something between Lindy Briggs and him.

Part II

Seven

ABOUT TEN MILES south of Bainesborough, across the
Savannah, there is a sinkhole called Bell's Bottom. Those who
know this part of North Florida will tell you that the word
sinkhole means many things. A sinkhole may appear in the
middle of your front lawn one droughtful August day and end by
swallowing half of your town. Not long ago a hole near Ocala ate
an elementary school — buildings, playgrounds, parking lots
and all. When it finally stopped devouring, an entire block of
new houses was perched on the crater's edge. No one knows
where the elementary school has gone. Geologists speculate
that it rests at the bottom of an underground river. They say it
may someday surface.

Most sinkholes are dry, or at least only damp at the bottom —
small earth cones good for climbing and fossil hunting. A third
kind, however, is springfed, and these give the finest swimming
in the inland parts of the Sunshine State. The water in them is

clear with a turquoise tint, very cold and deep. It is known that most of the water which once covered the huge area of the Savannah was drained away in a day or two at the most. Natural historians believe a logjam at the apex of an enormous sinkhole somewhere in the Savannah suddenly unraveled, and all the water fell away into the earth. The Indians of the area recorded this event as *min-ea-tooh-lloola*. The day of the drinking earth.

The night before, I had drunk all but a drop of the goodwill which Ardis Baines bore me. I decided to call her and accuse myself. Then, Wednesday being her day off, I would ask her to accompany me on a swimming and sunning expedition to Bell's Bottom.

"Hello, sweet. It's me."

"You, who?" It was her pooh-on-you tone. I had heard it before.

"Me, Toad. Ardis, don't be that way. You know about my work."

"I know about your work and I know about that class."

"They're close."

"That ain't what you said the night you came whining around my doorstep looking for, as you put it, 'a snow-white breast to spill bitter tears on.' "

"Jesus, did I say that?"

"That and a lot more I could quote you verbatim." Ardis had a good memory for the foolish things I said.

"I was *in extremis.*"

"You were in heat is what you were in."

"Same thing. Anyway, let me come and get you and take you out to the sinkhole, and we'll swim some and drink a very few medicinal beers and turn a shade darker in the Florida sunshine."

"Join the chamber of commerce."

"Ardis, don't be like that." I let my voice go a little milky.

"Toad, I won't be stood up by you. That's the second time."

This puzzled me and there was silence on the line while I dredged up the whiskey-damaged recollection of that afternoon when I had visited Eldon Odom and come home too drunk to remember my date with Ardis. I said, "Oh, yeah."

"Oh, yeah," was all she said.

I drew myself up to the lofty height where dwelt the benefit of the doubt I would have extended to Ardis had our situations been reversed.

"If it was me, I'd sure-god give you a chance to make it good. I'd give you that, at least."

She considered this for a space, and finally I heard a sigh of resignation. The sweet sigh that meant I was once again lifted from the spit of her disapproval. I almost said thanks before she spoke.

"Toad, I'm giving you another chance. Just this one."

"You won't regret it, Ardis." I saw us lying on a quilt under the cypress boughs by the edge of the sinkhole. We were sipping the purest essence of the waving grain and occasionally exchanging sweet kisses. Then came an X-rated sequence, which I cancelled in favor of a properly contrite vision of a family-style afternoon.

"I'll pick you up in about a half hour," she said.

Driving across the Savannah with Ardis was one of the chief pleasures of life. It was a fine, sunny mid-morning in May, and a warm wind flooded the Mercedes convertible. We were riding along in the comfortable aftermath of strife and reconciliation. I kept sneaking looks at her. Her thighs, bare from her yellow two-piece bathing suit, were splayed on the tan leather seat, and the delicate skein of capillaries under the tanned skin was nature's art.

Ardis was the heavy but brutally desirable woman of the Reubens paintings I had seen in the Ringling Gallery in Sarasota. As I have said, her type was not fashionable in those early seventies, but for me she held magic. Her hair whipped about her face in the sunlight, and it seemed to have caught dark fire, and occasionally she raised an indolent hand to pat it into place. The hand was an afterthought, the briefest concession to propriety from her woman's stupor of heat and speed. I reached over and touched her shoulder and could not let go. The heat, the tautness, the youth of her flesh held my fingers. I was hurting her and she was looking at me in pain and delight before I realized what I was doing. I was having a premonition of loss, of old age and death, and something nearer, too. I let go her shoulder and smiled at her, and my lips made the word, "Beautiful." She smiled at me and mouthed back across the distance and rushing wind, "I love you."

To be loved by Ardis Baines in that moment, in that speeding and wealthy automobile on that weird wonder, the Savannah, in the rich odor of serpent and vegetable madness, was as fine a thing as life held, and I had the good sense to savor it.

By the time we got to the sinkhole and began unloading the car, I pretty well understood some things. Ardis was good and worthy and not to be trifled with. Whatever good there was in me responded to hers, and my paltry evasions and silly vanity were nothing against that goodness. I wanted to say what I was thinking but couldn't, so I took her to me there under the trees. I held her, and suddenly near us again was that sense of loss and the admonition that came with it. The admonishment was to do something, be someone of consequence, because time was passing. I just held her, knowing nothing else to do, silently promising myself I would know more later.

The approach to the sinkhole was a one-lane track that wound into a pasture and ended under a stand of water oaks. A few whited pine logs had been arranged to border a parking lot. A narrow sand path led down to the lip of the sinkhole. A state of Florida sign read No Alcoholic Beverages on These Premises. Someone had discharged a load of buckshot into its white face.

Bell's Bottom was at the crest of a hill. After climbing up to it, you did not expect what you found. It was good to stand at its edge and feel the cool air rise from the cavey depths and to know that feeling of vertigo that comes from suddenly being on the edge of a precipice where none was anticipated. The trail zigzagged down some two hundred feet to the water, a shining blue bowl surrounded by white limestone shelves. It was a difficult trek down. Briars and saw-edged ferns grew across the path, and there were slippery spots and washouts and places where huge roots came spiraling out of the earth to block the way. I had to help Ardis across the rough spots. She accepted my help and resented it in some deep female way. That pioneer woman who had stood at the cabin door holding a Long Colt .38 didn't want any help. A couple of times we slipped and fell. I hooked my arm on a briar and Ardis sucked the wound for me. She was a big believer in the healing powers of suction.

We were alone at the sinkhole, an uncommon piece of luck. Even on weekdays, there was usually someone. The place was close enough to the city to be an uneasy intersection. Freaks from the university came to swim and smoke dope and go naked, indulging in the Rousseauean ideal lately revealed to them in Humanities 101. The locals, who had been coming to the sinkhole for generations, resented long hair and dope and all nakedness exept their own. The locals rarely swam. Most couldn't. They drove to the sinkhole in powerful, four-wheel–

drive trucks with winches and gun racks and stickers that read
Honk If You Love Jesus. They stood around hustling their
trousers and drinking from paper bags. Occasionally they'd
walk to the lip of the hole and remark darkly on the goings-on
below.

Alcohol, drugs, nudity, tribal differences, and the Viet Nam
war had not made a very congenial mix. Once a couple of the
good ole boys, well oiled by Jack Daniels from a paper bag and
Merle Haggard from a tape deck, had retrieved a deer rifle from
the cab of a truck and sent ten rounds of thirty-ought-six among
the gaggle of sunbathing hippites. The papers said only the hand
of providence had kept those copper jackets from going home to
human flesh. I knew it was a lifetime of disciplined aim and a
last shred of redneck restraint. But who was to say what would
happen the next time? I kept my hair short and my pants on.

Ardis and I spread our quilt on the limestone shelf and pegged
down the corners with books and bottles. Someone had climbed
a gum tree near the water's edge and tied a rope at the top. The
looped end of the rope hung about six feet out over the water.
The trick was to get it swinging back and forth so that you could
grab it and carry it up the bank to the place where a ladder of
two-by-four chunks had been spiked to the tree trunk. I looked
around, since the tools were usually nearby. Finally I saw a
blanched pine bough about the length of a cane fishing pole
lying among the ferns, and I used it to start the rope swinging.
Occasionally I'd look over my shoulder at the quilt where Ardis
lay, generous and golden in her skimpy yellow suit, and reading
Deviant Behavior in the Adolescent Male.

"Are you watching?"

"Yes, Toad," she'd say without looking up.

The purpose of all these goings-on was to show off for Ardis,
more or less. She was never an easy audience. Climbing to the
makeshift diving platform, I swung out over the blue bowl of the

sink, gave a hoot at the cold water, let go and plunged, legs running.

I struggled up the shelf near Ardis's feet and said, "Just starting out with the simple stuff. Nothing too difficult to begin with. Got to get it all warmed up."

"Mmmmm," Ardis said, furrowing her brow at something truly deviant. She had not even looked up.

After a while, my joints were limber and used to the shock of the cold water and ready to begin the advanced phase of the show. From the platform, I called down to the brown creature with the two yellow stripes. "This one is a little specialty I invented. It's been in the developmental stages. I'm unveiling it now, just for you. Watch."

Ardis turned a page and adjusted her glasses. After a space, she let go the corner of the book and scratched her thigh. I noticed that the yellow strip of cloth disappeared into a furrow of flesh near the intersection of thigh and belly. I swallowed. "Ardis?"

"Mmm?"

"Watch."

"Mmm." She underlined something with a yellow marker.

I swung out over the sink and, at the farthest point of my outward arc, jackknifed my toes at the sky and flung my hands down behind me in a perfect, prayerful plunge. I saw myself reflected, blue and terrified before I cut in without a splash. I let myself glide down and down into the blue depths and filled my mouth with clean spring water, swallowed, and surfaced with a modified whoop of triumph.

When I climbed out next to Ardis, I asked her how she liked it. "It was fine, Toad."

I stood there dripping. The cold was a local anesthetic in my knee joint. I sat down on the corner of the quilt and picked up a towel. "You're just used to this wonder. You'd miss it if I took it on the road. All this dash and accomplishment gone from your life, all this death-defying legerdemain."

A shadow passed over her face. She said, "Gone?" still reading.

"Gone," I said. I would have done just about anything to beat that book. It didn't occur to me that Ardis had been finishing second behind the book in my life for some time.

A little furrow was working its way into her forehead. Finally she surfaced. "What are you talking about?"

I turned and gazed out over the blue hole. "Mmmm?" I said.

"Toad?"

"Yes, ma'am?"

"Quit messing with me."

"Put the book down."

She did, and I covered her with my wet, cold self, and she adapted pretty well. We were doing what was popularly known as eating face when we heard the sound of a big engine up above. It echoed down into the bowl of the sink and told us to get ready for company.

Eight

THERE IS SOMETHING DISQUIETING about being approached by strangers in the woods. Looking up at the top of the sinkhole, I could just see faces, a wisp of auburn hair and blue denim through the trees. I took the jackknife I had brought to cut fruit and put it under the corner of the quilt near me and sat watching the lip of the sink. I did not let Ardis see me do this. I felt silly for my paltry arsenal but nonetheless a little better prepared. I did not try to imagine myself using a knife. Thought should not go that far.

When we could see them well, I knew there was nothing to worry about. They were a family, parents and a small boy. I gave Ardis's hand a squeeze, and she went back to her book. I sat watching them come down, enjoying their moments of awkwardness, the woman's cries, "Ho, now, son!" not to her son, but to the hillside as she slipped and slid down it. I watched the boy's billy goat sure-footedness and touched my knee and remembered when I could rimrock like that.

When he saw us, the father stood on a little outcropping of limestone and shaded his eyes with a flat palm. In the other hand, he carried a small wooden box. I waved up at him and called, "How y'all?" pleased that my Isle Hammock, general purpose, long-distance greeting still sounded right.

He fished in his front flap pocket for an object I knew would be a bag of Red Man chewing tobacco. He balled a shred of tobacco, inserted it into his cheek, and called out, "Awite. You?"

"Good," I said. If he'd been closer, I'd have said, "Can't complain." If he'd been dressed slightly differently and closer, I'd have said, "As good as I can in an imperfect world." A lot depends on the opening moments of an encounter in the woods.

When the family was down among us, we were like a bunch of cousins at a wedding — embarrassed but good-natured and ready for some society. Ardis sat up and put on a peasant blouse. I put the jackknife back in the pocket of my jeans and stood and repeated, "Hi y'all doing?"

The woman smiled at the man, who chewed. The little boy looked at my wet hair and then at the water with envy. The man reflected a bit. "Might do better if it'd rain."

He looked up at the sky, a blue circle bordered by green trees. He wore a Moorman's Feed baseball cap, a khaki shirt and trousers, and high-cut work boots. He limped like I would in a few years but from different causes. I said, "Too dry for the corn?" It had been good weather for sunbathers but hard for farmers.

"The peanuts ain't famous either."

His wife stepped toward us a bit and changed the subject. "I see you two are pic-nicing." She was a big woman in horse clothes — high-heeled western boots and a pearl-buttoned shirt. She was buck-toothed and had what Ardis called the Dixie

County mouth. I had told her if that mouth was good enough for Loretta Lynn, it was good enough for Dixie County. What could she say to that? Half the women north of Ocala would have given their daughters' eyes to look like Loretta Lynn.

Ardis said, "Yes'm, we brought along a little something. Can we offer you a cold drink?"

This embarrassed the family. The woman said, "That's nicet of you, but we brought our own. Just didn't want to truck it all down here."

"Too much work," the man said, looking at the empty sky. He stepped closer to the water and stared in as though wishing he could transport what was at his feet upward and get it to fall on his corn. He held the box he was carrying at his side and gazed across the sinkhole. It was a fine, polished box of walnut or some other hardwood, and I knew what was in it.

"We was planning to do some target shooting," he said, still looking across the sink. "But I know that'd bother you folks."

I looked at Ardis, who looked at me, puzzled. We both looked at the back of the man who watched the other side of the blue hole. His wife smiled and said, "Delbert don't get to shoot his pistol that much. They're dusting the corn at home, else he'd be working. We don't like to breathe that stuff." She sat down on a stump, and the little boy placed himself between her legs and buried his head in her shoulder.

I said, "Go ahead and shoot. We don't mind."

We did, but Delbert had climbed all the way down here on his bad leg.

"Well . . . ?" said Delbert, which meant that I had not sounded certain enough. I walked down beside him and said, "I'd like to see you sink that beer can over there."

The sinkhole was about fifteen yards across. Ferns grew in dark marl to the water's edge. By the far bank, a beer can floated halfway under. Delbert looked at me quick and sharp. In his grin was the old I'll-bet-you-would, and I knew the beer can was as good as gone. I had Delbert figured, so I stood there wondering at myself. I was conditioned to do what I was doing now, to be polite, to relinquish this place, to polish Delbert's pride. They were a couple of my parents' generation and had come up in the same world expecting the same things. They would have relinquished this place to us, but only by thinking less of us and of the world we shared. Carefully, lovingly, Delbert removed from the purple velvet inside the box the stainless steel Smith and Wesson .38 with a 4½-inch barrel.

Next he took a treated cloth from the walnut case and a plastic box of evil-looking bullets. Carefully, and without speaking or looking up, he wiped the already immaculate handgun, then loaded it, wiped it again, and hefted it in his right hand. When he was ready, I stood behind him, knowing that most of the noise would come from the front of the chamber. It would be outrageously loud here in this natural bowl. I motioned to Ardis to cover her ears. I saw a rigid anticipation in her limbs, and in her eyes, genuine interest. I remembered the night she had walked away from her door, holding that pistol of hers like a dirty shirt between two fingers.

Delbert was a shooter from the old school. He did not squat and hold the pistol with both hands like the cops on TV. He stood erect, side on to his target like a duelist, and shot the beer can out of the water. It was there, then gone. Even expecting it, the noise shocked me. I looked at the little boy. He was proud of his dad and scared. His eyes said one was enough.

Delbert lowered the pistol to a place above his damaged right knee and watched the gouged water slowly become placid again.

I said, "I guess you meant that one."

"Mean 'em all," he said, grinning. He reached down left-handed and took the pistol by the barrel and handed it to me, butt-first, aiming it for a moment at his own heart. The gesture was formal and primitive, and his vulnerability was there and gone in an instant as I took the pistol from him. I looked into his eyes. He said, "Go ahead, have a try."

I stepped to the spot, holding the pistol by my right thigh. I said, "What?" I was conscious of all of them watching me and of the fact that I was no good with a handgun. I had been raised around firearms, the kind we thought of as useful — shotguns that could bring home supper on a fall day when the doves were flying or when the quail could be pointed by a good liver-and-white dog. This short, cold thing was alien in my hand. I wanted to hand it back to him. He said, "That cypress knee there, right next to where the beer can used to be." He drew a line under "used to be" with his toney country voice. Before I addressed my target, I glanced over my shoulder at Ardis and tried to grin. Her eyes surprised me. They said, *Toad, hit the target.*

I raised the pistol, standing as I had seen Delbert stand. I fitted the upright into the V, then swung them both to the middle of the cypress knee twenty yards away. I drew half a deep breath, held it, and closed my hand. The pistol was in the air above my head. There was a red, star-shaped gash in the clay a foot to the side of the cypress knee. I had heard nothing. A little smoke rose from the round, red hole in the middle of the star.

I handed the gun back to Delbert the same way he had given it to me, conscious of that moment when the muzzle projected a lethal dot on my heart. I laughed and said, "Flying with his heart shot out." It was an old bird hunter's lament, to be used when you had stood before a clean covey rise and missed a bird quartering to your right against a background of dark green pines. Delbert knew what I meant. He also knew that I was uneasy. He laid the pistol in the walnut box, but did not close it. It was time to go. I turned to Ardis, thinking to signal as much and saw her coming toward us.

"May I?"

Delbert stared at her, eyebrows arched.

"Course you can, missy." He glanced at his wife.

Behind us, she said, "Lordy, Lord," in a comic, prayerful voice. Her interest was up too.

The little boy said, "Mama, can I?"

"Ask your daddy, hon."

Ardis took the pistol from where it lay in the box and stepped forward to the shooting place. She didn't hit the cypress knee, but she came closer by six inches than I did. She raised the pistol and fired it without hesitation, without a backward glance at me. Apparently without aiming. When she had finished, she watched the smoking hole in the earth for a moment, then laid the pistol in the box. If the target had been a man, she'd have lunged him at fifteen yards. Delbert said, "You might have a gift for that pistol, darlin."

Ardis smiled at him, then looked at me with the smile hardening, then was suddenly flushed and embarrassed. She said, "Thanks for letting me."

He said, "It was a sight to see." The family all laughed, even the little boy, one of those country kids who learns early when to laugh at women. Delbert turned to his wife, "Mama, you gone shoot?"

"Naw," she said. She meant, not this time. She had done it before and would again, but she was not much interested in it. When Delbert picked up his pistol and got that gleam in his eye, she had two little boys on her hands.

We said good-bye to them. Delbert wouldn't shoot again until we had made the climb out of the sinkhole. He was that kind of careful. As we climbed, we stopped and looked down from time to time and there they were, watching the placid surface of the spring, the gun still lying in the open box.

When we reached the top and loaded the car, it looked like

Delbert might get the rain he wanted, and so we put the top up. As we were driving out to the hard road, I turned to Ardis and said, "What you think about a little visit?"

It was about two o'clock, and for what I had planned, we had plenty of time. There was something about meeting Delbert and Mama and their boy that put me in mind of going home, just to say hello, an extravagant gesture, and maybe to walk around the place with Daddy and look at things, and kick some clods and show Ardis how it all was done in the county time forgot.

Nine

I CAME FROM the back of beyond, a little pig and pulpwood community called Isle Hammock situated on the banks of the Suwannee River which marks the Alligood County line for more than two hundred miles. Isle Hammock is the spot where the Suwannee turns north and becomes one of the American rivers that defies gravity. A lot of things in Alligood County seem to defy natural law.

For one thing, most kids grow down, not up. They put down roots, not altogether a bad thing. Like many well-tended growing things, they become immobile and incapable of conceiving any other condition of life. While most of my friends were growing down in Alligood County, I was growing up in it. And contrary to natural law, I took flight and left it altogether. And a large part of this growing up, as I have already explained, was reading Eldon Odom's books. They were, in a way, maps of the sky.

People get old before their time in Alligood County. This is not so much a defiance of natural law as it is the inevitable defeat of one of nature's prescriptions, the body's allotment of time on this earth; by another, the hard life on the land. Whenever I am near a conversation in which the participants rhapsodize about the good life on the land, I move out of earshot or make vulgar lip flutters. Though the life on the land is good in certain ways — nobody mugs you on a farm, although somebody or some thing may beat the living shit out of you if you are not very careful — it is hard in most ways. If you do not believe me, line up twenty city men, aged fifty, alongside twenty of their country counterparts. There in the hard-bitten, sloe-eyed faces of the country men will be written the story of the good life. My father, Mr. Talbot Turlow, is one of those country men.

He looks at me now across the years, and I am shocked at the damage weather and worry and toil, and not a few fists, have worked in the face he willed to me, not pretty to begin with. I am his son but also like those city men, and so, for the time being, I must put myself in the other line.

Long about the time I was entering high school, already quite proficient with the baseball bat, my family made one of its bi-monthly, forty-mile journeys to Bainesborough, the county seat, not so much for supplies and provisions as to get another look at civilization and its discontents. Also, its contents. Things like chain stores and the shopping malls that were beginning to house them contented my mother very much. She was not herself when standing in the middle of a boutique with a name like Serendipity or Nonesuch, staring at the plenitude of finery. She was somebody else, and it was worth the trip to get that way. My father, standing behind her and slightly to the side, looked wilted and expectant in his Lee western shirt with pearl buttons and a pinching pair of Sunday oxfords. If she isn't herself, his face seemed to ask, who am I?

What contented *him* in Bainesborough was to walk through
the hardware departments of Sears Roebuck or Montgomery
Ward and remark that, even though the prices were lower here,
the product was the same as in Murchison's Hardware in Isle
Hammock. He'd just as soon take his trade to Harry Murchison,
the same Harry he'd known since Tige was a pup. Harry stood
behind what he sold. Walking along with my parents in a stupor
of boredom, I would listen, envisioning Harry Murchison,
noble son of commerce, gaunt and freckled and soon to die of
Hodgkin's disease, standing behind a twenty-five-cent handful
of fishhooks, or maybe a John B. Stetson hat.

On this particular trip, I was let loose for a while with my
sister, Patricia "Trish" Turlow, while our parents attended a
meeting of the county chapter of the Peanut Growers' Association. It was a free feed, provided by representatives of the Field
Tested Fertilizer Company, Limited. They'd get fried mullet,
hush puppies, cole slaw, and some talk about having the good
sense to fertilize floor-runner peanut vines with Field Tested
V-119. Neither of them would expect or want an alcoholic
beverage.

My seventeen-year-old sister Trish, on the other hand, was
already something of a lush. She had been blessed with the good
looks that came from my mother's side of the family, the
Blackfords. In the genetic raffle, she had also drawn a nose,
knee, and ankle from our paternal grandmother, Delia Turlow,
née Talbot. (My father and I were both cursed with Christian
names derived from the families of the maidens despoiled in our
making. Such things are common as dirt in Alligood County.)
Blessed with beauty, Trish was popular in Isle Hammock and
surrounding environs, and many were the nights she came home
late enough to make my mother threaten to cut a switch. One
night in particular, I recall hearing Trish come in and get the
usual tongue-lashing, and then walk to her room with a circling

gait. My mother's suspicions did not carry her as far as mine took me — to demon rum. I got up and padded down to Trish's room to see the spectacle.

"Trish," I said, "don't get next to an open flame."

"Jump up my ass, Toad."

I took a speculative look at her ass. In a pair of Levi's, it was wrapped as tight as summer sausage. You could read the date on the dime, her mad money, in the hip pocket. "Naw, thanks," I said.

"Well, then?" She turned to me where I stood in the doorway, scratching myself and about to render a service I was ill-suited for, that of the protective brother. No reasonable son of the South wants the burden of a round-heeled sister. I said, "Which of the Price twins was it?"

She smiled, a memory rolling in the alcoholic waters of her cortex. "Sonny. God, is he tough." "Tough" in those days meant handsome. We spoke in code. A "tough hide" was a pretty girl.

"He's a bad dog, too," I said. "You better stay away from him when he's drinking." I figured the proper tack was to suggest only guilt by association. Sonny Price's response to a skinful of Jack Daniels was the same as his twin brother Donny's. They went to the nearest roadhouse, usually Larup's up on the river, to kick ass and take names. You could purchase trouble cheap at Larup's six days a week and half day on Sunday.

Trish looked at me as though to say, Aren't you getting a little big for your Presbyterian pants? What she said was, "I can take care of Sonny Price, thank you very much." Visions of Trish taking care of Sonny Price tried to get into my brainpan, but I didn't allow them. I turned to go. "At least take off your boots before you go to bed." She was already sprawled with one eye shut.

"You do it, Toad."

I walked over and she put one foot and then the other one on my behind, and I pulled while she pushed. She said, "Now that you had your ass massaged Japanese style, you can go to bed happy." I considered asking her how happy Sonny Price was, lying in his bed tonight, but padded down the hall instead. Trish had "broke bad," as the town liked to say, and there was not much I could do about it but hope.

Anyway, on this particular trip to Bainesborough, Trish was supposed to be keeping her younger brother Toad out of trouble. What she was doing instead was looking for it as hard as she could. We had wandered a good distance away from our rendezvous point with the homefolks. We were in a part of the city I did not know very well. There were bars, which was fine with Trish, and there were antique shops, which interested me. I had noticed that common things were enshrined in them just because they were old. Half of what was for sale in these stores was discarded as useless in Isle Hammock. I could have made a small fortune just carting in the town's trash. It was an early inkling that the life I was living in Isle Hammock might be exportable to foreign parts.

As luck would have it, Trish and I finally found Eighth Street, where an antique store shared a wall with an establishment called the Black Cat. There was an estate sale sign in one window and a winking neon cat's eye in the other. On the sunny sidewalk, my seventeen-year-old sister looked at her own reflection in the mirror windows of the Black Cat and said, "You go on in there and look around if you want, Toad. Take your time. I'll just stand here and get some rays."

Yeah, I thought, you'll have some Bobs and Bills and Dons and Eddies, too, by the time you're through. I peeked into the dark hole that was the Black Cat. All I could see were a couple of somnolent Saturday afternoon drinkers. How much trouble could Trish get into in ten minutes, anyway? They'd probably card her at the door and put her back on the sidewalk. I said, "OK, but behave yourself," and went into the antique store. When I peeked out at her a few seconds later, she was as good as her word, basking in the Saturday sun, a bright smile on her face.

Inside the antique shop, I was strangely moved. All manner of old things had been polished back to life. What impressed me most were the letters, journals, tax records, and account books, some of them from the mid-1800s. I had once helped my mother clean out our attic. She was shuffling old records and letters. Her hands slowed down as they lifted and examined some of her great-grandmother's letters. She hesitated, but finally Presbyterian cleanliness defeated history, and she dumped them, parchment crackling, in a heap of sweepings. From the top of the heap, great-grandmother's spidery script begged for the attention of yet another eye. I reached down and rescued the words. Now, in this store, I saw such things respected.

An old woman approached me from a corner where she had been quietly reading. "Can I help you?" Her face was the sepia color of the parchment I held in my hand.

"I'm just looking." I must have flushed red. I had given her the answer I would have used in a boutique. "Go ahead," she said. "Only take care. These things are fragile." Her voice was small and soft, as though she spoke in the presence of someone asleep. I had been under the spell of the papers for some time before I remembered Trish. I looked at my watch. How long had she been alone? *Was* she alone? I had the strong feeling I was needed, yet the papers held me. Finally an image of Trish laughing in a slightly giddy way came between me and the hundred-year-old journal I was holding. I paid the women ten hard-earned tobacco cropping dollars for an old ledger book, half-filled with the scrawl of someone's household accounts. The dates were spring 1891 to fall 1892. I wanted the book not because it was half-full but because it was half-empty.

Trish was standing in the dark at the back of the bar, her hip shot as far into no man's land as she could get it without standing beside herself. She was trying to be casual while two drugstore cowboys contemplated white slavery. The smile I had envisioned in the antique store was there, all right, as brittle as lead crystal. As I walked toward the three of them, my eyes growing accustomed to the dark, the look on Trish's face changed. It was two things at once — Glad to see you, Toad, and What is my little brother about to do now? I had no idea what I was about to do. I had never been in a bar before.

One of the cowboys was tall and lean and wore a Duane Allman belt buckle and high-heeled, snakeskin boots. He was leaning into Trish's face and whispering something I couldn't hear. It made her eyes freeze solid and turned the crystal smile into a mouthful of gritted teeth. The other one was about my size and well built. He was just grinning and listening to the tall one, who seemed to be their voice. I walked up and stood too close. I was obviously no stranger. Out of the corner of my eye, I could see the bartender moving over to get a better look at me.

Trish said, "Hey, Toad! This is my little brother, Toad." I could barely see her for all the western apparel.

I said, "Hey, Trish," quietly.

The tall cowboy said, "Your *brother?*" He didn't believe it, or was pretending not to. The other one just grinned. His belt buckle said he was proud to be an Okie from Muskogee.

I said, "Trish, it's time to go." I almost said Mom and Dad would be waiting for us down at the convention hall, but then I heard the sound of myself standing in a bar for the first time and talking about Mom and Dad.

I watched Trish's face. I didn't look at the other two for fear of giving them an excuse for what they wanted to do. From years of watching her operate, I knew that Trish was considering a little fun. With my eyes, I tried to tell her this was not the time and certainly not the place. She was not with Donny and Sonny Price, who were mean as two yard dogs and had their way wherever they went in Alligood County. This was Bainesborough, and her two escorts were not interested in courtship and marriage. Before I could think what to say, Trish slipped from behind the two loud shirts and said, "Toad, this is Tommy and Frank."

For the moment, she had us in the amenities. They shrugged and reached for my hand. Each in his turn tried to give me a handful of broken phalanges, but I had been digging post holes for more years than they had been cowboys. I shook hands with Tommy, the tall one, and watched an artery leap to the surface under his left eye while he gave me his best and I gave him back a medium-to-heavy Toad Turlow crunch. Then I did Frank, and the only difference was the way it took him; he broke out in a sweat.

Trish watched, not knowing what to think. She had her mysteries and I had mine. Tommy and Frank had theirs, too. Tommy said, "How come they call you 'Toad,' Toad?"

"It's just something that . . . happened."

"Ain't because you look like a toad frog?"

"It might be. You know how it is." My voice was beginning to croak.

Frank found his voice. "Sounds like 'turd' to me, *turd.*"

And that was when it started to come apart.

Trish decided that things weren't working out and stepped between us, trying to grab my arm. I took a step forward, too, but I was perfectly willing to be dragged out of there. I knew the subtleties of honor well enough to know that only Trish could make the compromise. But Tommy and Frank would have none of it. They worked in tandem. Tommy reached out and gently removed Trish from between us. It was that gentleness that did it.

Even as I went for Tommy, the tall one, and Frank went for me, I knew it was the Price twins I was going for, and all of them who had gently put their hands on my sister Trish. And it was all those nights when she had come home not knowing me or the farm and not caring; all those things I was after getting out of my system.

With my right hand, the stronger of the two post hole—digging implements, I went for Tommy's neck. With the other hand, which still held the antique ledger, I swung at his head. Trish was calling, "Toad, Toad!" I remember thinking my name sounded funny as a three-syllable word.

When I woke up on the sidewalk, looking up into the blue air, my head was in Trish's lap and so was a lot of blood. "Toad," she was calling. "Toad!"

"I'm here," I said.

Inside the bar, someone put a dime in the jukebox and punched in "Your Cheatin' Heart." The old lady watched us from the window of the antique store. The ledger book lay bruised at my side. The old lady shook her head and drew the blinds. Trish was telling me the story. ". . . and then the little one put his head down and shoved you over to the bar, and that's when the bartender hit you with about half of a Louisville Slugger like you use in your games at school, and they had to pry your hand off that other one's neck, and even when they stomped you, you never did let go of that silly book of yours until I got you out here and you went to sleep. We better get back to the convention, or Mama and Daddy gonna have the law after us. Can you walk, Toad, can you? I don't think I can carry you."

After I had puked into the gutter for a while, we started off toward the hall. I had a bad headache but found that I could navigate, with Trish's help, if I kept my eye on the blue canyon up between the trees. It sounds strange, but holding my head back and watching the blue stream of the heavens there in the trees got me all the way back to the hall and into the car before I had to do the big spit again.

With a stripe of vomit drying along the door outside the car (Daddy said, "Son, if you got to whoop up, at least stick you head out the winder"), we drove back to Isle Hammock. Trish had made up a pretty good story, and on the way back to the car she made me promise to stand by it. I had been attacked by some boys on the Bainesborough baseball team. They were angry because we had beat them last time out. We had been walking innocently down the street when they had jumped me. I had fought a good fight, but the four of them — or was it five, Toad? — had been too much for me, even with Trish getting in an occasional lick.

So said Trish, making it all sound plausible. Our parents knew Trish's potential as a storyteller and were suspicious, but I had bled to validate this tale, and so they didn't let their suspicions take shape in words. Trish and I had a few words, though, in a manner of speaking.

Two days later, after I had the back of my head stitched in the county clinic and had got over a thirty-hour headache and was sure I could think straight, I went to her bedroom late at night to invite her to go for a walk with me. I had plans to take her out behind the hog pens where there is a lot of squealing anyway and give her ass the spanking it had been needing since she was old enough to wedge it into a pair of Levi's. She had been unusually quiet for two days and hadn't been out with the Price boys. I had even heard her tell Sonny on the phone she couldn't go to the rodeo in Kissimmee.

I knocked on her door and entered. She was sitting at her vanity, naked. I turned away immediately and waited for her to dress. But she didn't move. I said, "Get dressed. We'll take a walk." I don't know why I turned back around. She was still sitting at the vanity, staring into the mirror. I could see my face in it next to hers. I don't know which was the saddest. I was the Turlow, she was the Blackford. I was the one with the black eye. She looked pale and small and hard-used for a high school girl. And she looked as pretty as she ever would look to me.

Finally, she got up and faced me, and I turned away again to wait for her to get dressed. I had glimpsed the front of her, though, and it was as pretty and more as the back had been, and I thought again of that hand in the bar reaching gently and confidently toward her. A brother has to lose his sister. He knows it. But he doesn't have to lose her to that hand.

Her hand was on my shoulder, turning me, and she was pressing herself to me, the whole long length of her and clutching at me and crying. I tried to push her away at first, embarrassed and something else, too, at the touch of her like that, undressed, but finally I realized she needed me. I held her as long as she wanted me to. She cried on my neck and pressed herself to me, and we said things that are lost in my memory. Finally, she stepped back and looked at me hard, as though to say, that's over. We won't speak of it. I looked a question at her, but she looked back a very firm no.

We never did have that talk. I never gave her that spanking. I knew we were far beyond both. I know I must have told her I loved her while we were standing there, and that I didn't want that hand on her anymore. I know she must have answered in words, but all I can recall now are her warm limbs against me and the little bit of her in my hands, and her crying not for her troubles or my bent head, but for the whole life of loveless love she was living and did not understand.

Late at night I think of her. She comes to me, all these years later, just as she came that night, bare and broken to my face, and purified of all but the terror and glory of her body. It took me years to learn it, what she tried to show me that night: Toad, this is all I have. I don't have the farm like you do. I don't have those hands that dig and grip, not that voice that croaks. I am Daddy's daughter and this boy's sister. It's why I let them touch me. If you belong to one, or two, then you belong to all of them, and then who are you? Late at night she comes to me, and now I know what she would have said, had she known the words, had I known the way to listen.

It wasn't far from that night in Trish's bedroom to the day I started writing in the half-empty ledger I had used as a weapon. The first words I wrote were about the feel of a man's throat in my hands, and later, about the feel of my sister. I had been more frightened of what my hands might do than of what two pairs of cowboy boots and half a Louisville Slugger had done to me.

Ten

MY FATHER'S HEART, which was reborn Sundays twice monthly at the Friendship Freewill Presbyterian Church, would have stopped if someone had suggested he go down to the sinkhole of a mid-week afternoon. His constant sorrow was that he could not get caught up. Getting caught up, as near as I could tell, was having no more work to do. When I was old enough to discuss things with him on a more or less equal footing, I had protested our bondage. "Daddy, we can't get caught up. There will always be something."

"Maybe so, but you got to operate like you can. It's the only way."

I can't remember exactly when we had this talk; I know it must have been on a day when I wanted to ease up and have some fun, and he didn't or couldn't. Corn blight, peanut mold, drought, rain — he feared every fingerprint of the Almighty hand. So if we were not working daylight to black dark cropping tobacco in the August heat, or picking corn by headlight on the kidney-killing Alice Chalmers Four-Row Gleaner, we were mending fence, or building pens, or castrating hogs this week that could not, for fear of some lurking calamity, be mended or built or castrated next week. If you worked until your ass was dragging out your tracks, as some of my friends used to say, then you could use what little energy was left for fun. I had not been having fun very long in the local cut-and-shoot dives like Larup's before I realized that country life was a long secondary road with a tobacco allotment at one end of it and a bottle of whiskey at the other.

I knew my daddy would not be around the house when Ardis and I arrived. He would be out somewhere getting caught up. Mama, I knew, would be in the parlor. She could not get caught up either, but it bothered her less, so she rested occasionally. At three in the afternoon, she would have cleaned up from dinner, fed the yard dogs and cats, made dough for supper biscuits, and would be sitting down to her one indulgence, "The Search for Tomorrow." In recent years, she had shown a growing tendency to fall asleep in the middle of "The Search." There was a big bleached bone of contention between her and Daddy over this. On the few occasions when he had been near enough the house to drop in during "The Search" and had caught her sleeping, he had awakened her and lamented to her face the loss of every good thing in their common life. Like the little Dutch boy, he was a hole plugger. If he, and the few other good folks who stood likewise at the dike, failed in their task, then the rest of us louts and ne'er-do-wells would all be "drownt." For all I knew, he was right. Mama knew he was wrong and told him so. She was not going to give up "The Search." And she never once admitted to falling asleep. "I was just thinking," she would say.

It was strange driving Ardis's fancy car into the shade of those tall pines by the dooryard of that house, the third and best house my parents had built on the six hundred and fifty acres they owned, the only house I had lived in. A powder blue Mercedes convertible was an unlikely presence hard by those pens and sheds and silos. Before turning off the engine, I looked back to see if we had drug Bainesborough and all of its complications with us into this world. I didn't see a thing, and I was proud of myself for showing up in style, even if the style belonged to the daughter of the New South executive, Arnold Baines. Mama saw us from the kitchen window, and by the time our wheels had stopped turning, she was standing on the grass wiping her hands on an apron.

Ardis had not asked about our destination. She was nothing if not stubborn. As I got out and she slid out beside me, still in the peasant blouse and the yellow bathing suit and sporting those ample golden thighs, I wondered what she thought of our visit. I went to Mama. "Hug my neck, Blackford," she said to me. In our family, you had to be commanded to give affection. I squeezed her a good hard one and she giggled a little. "I always forget how big you are," she said, the old glint in her eye.

"I always forget how little you are and how good looking," I said.

She punched me a medium-to-hard shot in the middle of the chest, loving it. I danced around in front of her for a minute, feigning hurt and begging her not to make me cut a switch. Ardis, I could see out of the corner of my eye, was watching with genuine interest.

"Mama," I said, letting my face grow a little solemn, "this is Ardis Baines. She and I have been keeping some company."

Ardis stepped forward to meet my mother, letting her fingers trail along the hot car hood as though seeking a last association with her own world. Before they spoke, their hands joined. My mother owned two handshakes. The first was her after-church, thanks-for-the-good-word, Reverend Ethridge, shake. It was crisp and sisterly but warm. The other, the better of the two, which Ardis was getting, was a lingering grip with a good squeeze at the end and a slow withdrawal. Women got it, the ones she liked. Family got their necks hugged.

"I'm pleased to make your acquaintance, Mrs. Turlow." Ardis's smile was pleasant.

My mother matched it. She said, "Any friend of Blackford's is welcome here." It was getting a little ponderous for my taste, so I said, "Hey, Mommer, what's for supper?"

My mother grinned at me. I was her same old greedy guts, same old hollow leg. "Nothing but red beans and rice."

Red beans and rice was my favorite. What its title doesn't tell you is that it is liberally reinforced by homemade pork sausage. There had been years when the Turlows ate beans and rice without the sausage, because the Turlows were not caught up enough to have time to make sausage and could not have afforded it in any case. But now there had been seven fat years, and the sausage would be good, and I was pleased to have come on this day.

"You gone like Mommer's red beans and rice," I said to Ardis, laying on the accent a little thick just for the fun of it. You can't stand under those pines and not talk that way. The voice I served, that I believed, that I had read in Eldon Odom's books, was whistling up in those trees, coming from the engine of Daddy's tractor in the field. It was all around me and catching from my mama.

We went inside and indeed the TV was on, and they were searching for tomorrow. Doctors were doctoring and committing adultery, nurses were nursing, and doing it, too, housewives were wifing and committing it. Even kids and dogs and cats had the glint in their eyes. It was a sacrifice when my mother walked over and switched off that steady beam of lust. I pictured her sitting in church on Sunday with a little less of the blush on her face as Reverend Ethridge decried modern times.

Things got pretty stiff when we sat down. We talked about the dry spell, and Mama repeated for the hundredth time what her father, Mr. Blackford, used to say: "Dry weather will scare you to death, but wet weather will starve you to death." I have never known what he meant. We talked about the neighbors and what the weather had done to their crops, and finally we talked about Carole Sue Portis. Carole Sue had dropped by the other day with her latest, a perfectly adorable little towhead, and had asked about me. Now, isn't that a coincident? Yes, Mother, it is a coincident.

Carole Sue and I had gone at it pretty hot and heavy there for a while. My mother made no secret of the fact that she had hoped I would stay in the county and make little towheads with Carole Sue Portis. Her hope got mistranslated one night during an electrical storm. Supercharged in the back seat of a '54 Chevy, Carole Sue and I had come very close to making a little towhead. Carole Sue had got back into her stride, though. She had the kind of instincts that had skipped a generation or two — backward. In Bainesborough, when I saw friends of mine from the county on their twice-monthly binges, I sometimes asked about her. Year by year, the answer was the same: "Carole Sue? She's bigged again."

"How many is that, Mommer?"

My mother didn't think this the most tasteful of questions, mostly because it caused her to have to count on her fingers and contemplate the removal of one shoe. Finally, she said, "Seven . . . I think."

We talked about the new addition they were planning, a Florida room with a big fireplace and the corners Daddy needed for his gun cabinet and arrowhead collection. When things trailed off a bit, I asked her if she would show us around. I knew she would tell me that it was Daddy's to do that, but I also knew she could be persuaded and that her tours had a fine feminine charm. She made no secret of her good-natured belief that she could farm better than most men. She just didn't care to.

As we were walking out the door, my mother turned to Ardis. "I got some trousers that will fit you. You'd best put them on. It can be snatchy out there, with the briars and all." My mother was not going to be seen walking around the hog pens with a half-naked city girl in tow.

With a good breeze blowing, we set off in the direction of the pens and feed bins. Those long brown needles came boating down from the pines, silent and mysterious, each one a message. It was a fine summer afternoon.

I knew my mother would take us first to the pig parlor Daddy and I had built my last winter at home. It was the symbol of my maturity and of my leave-taking. It had been a hard, cold, knuckle-busting time in the January wind, the kind of job farmers do only in the stillest month of winter. We had formed a concrete slab, plumbed it to a five-degree slant, and ringed it with troughs so that the runoff would flow to a septic tank. We had installed a methane storage unit above the septic tank, and now Daddy used the effluvium of hog manure as fuel to grind feed corn for hogs. Dust to dollars, ashes to progress.

The roof was tin on pressure-treated two-by-four rafters, and I remembered us up there, our cold blue fingers fitting those corrugated sheets of tin together and troweling on Black Jack roofing cement as thick as pine gum.

I liked working with my father. He had taught me to work without talking, except in grunts and with hand gestures. Our silence was the sign of our competence, our foreknowledge of each other's needs. That winter of my maturity, we had been perfectly silent in our work. The pig parlor was a good job. The county agent had come to see it, and we had stood around acting like it was nothing. He kept calling it progressive, downright progressive. I suppose it was. I made my father a lacquered shingle to commemorate our work that January. It read: The Close Enough Construction Company, E. T. Turlow and Son, Proprietors. We had been close working on that roof in the bitter wind. Perhaps even close enough.

Now a bed of brown pine needles lay on the tin roof and little circles of rust had formed around some of the galvanized nails. Ardis admired my handiwork and said, "Toad, I didn't know you were good with tools." She turned to me and whispered, "What hath Toad wrought?"

I looked off in the direction of the far fence, the fire tower at the Bronson crossroads. "I was just gophering for Daddy."

Mama looked off that way, too. I wondered if parallel eye-beams met in infinity. She said, "I thought the two of them were going to freeze solid up there. I kept coming out to see if I'd have to burn it down to thaw them out."

Ardis said, "Well, it looks good." She might have been talking about somebody's new shirt.

We watched the hogs, and I told her about them. They might *look* good, but they didn't act it. I had bought a joblot of mongrel hogs from a man who owned a sawmill up near Lake City. They were what the local men called termites, or piney woods rooters. I had got them cheap and had topped them out at ninety pounds or so and sold them dear. I had wagered with Daddy I could turn a profit, and I had done it. He believed in lineage, but the environment we had built won the bet for me. A few of the heirs and assigns of my batch of termites were faunching around the pen in front of us. You could tell them by their bent yellow tushes, casty yellow eyes, and generally wormy aspect. They were the living mark of my hand on this place, and I was proud of them. I told Ardis about how the little shoats would eat your shoelaces and bite the valve stems off the tractor tires. Nothing but little mouths and maws, I said. "But cute?" she asked. The notion of the cute little pig is deeply important to all city girls.

We walked on out to the pens where the sows were put back with the boars after farrowing. Things could get a little X-rated out that way, so we didn't linger. The big boar, the boss of the bunch, hooked a sow or two out of his way and sauntered over to the fence to ask for a handful of feed corn. He stuck his snout between two cypress slats and gouged out a chunk of rotten wood. Mama reached down and tumped him a good one on the jaws. He looked a careful eye at her.

"That's Fisher," she told us. "He's the father of it all."

Ardis stepped up to the fence and said "Hi, big fella."

Fisher looked at her carefully. I wondered what sort of electrical storm was going on in the brainpan under that mat of wire hair.

We wound our way back past the feed bins and the shed where the peanuts are dried by the big gas blowers. Mama explained it all as we went, and I had the feeling that she, not I, should have been the writer. She had the gift of simple, clear explanation. It wasn't long before the two women were walking along side by side, and I was an extremity. I was pleased to see it. And it gave me time to look around, to seek out the places, sunlight and shadow, where I had stood, or bent or ached, or dripped my blood. All the hours and blood and discomfort were my investment, and the sadness was that I had left it without even looking back. Nor had I missed it much. Yet now, here with Ardis, I felt a longing for the simplicity of mind that was my father's, that kept him toiling and improving and trying to get caught up, and would always keep his eye in a squint and his hand to the task. Always until he had the heart attack this life had been promising him for half a century. I tried to stop my thoughts but couldn't, and I saw the place going to what it would inevitably become, a goddamned subdivision, somebody's Green Acres or Lonesome Pines. I ducked into the welding shed by the first of the big, aluminum tobacco barns and kicked over a can of welding rods.

My mother knew my moods. Her voice came winding into the shadows. "What's the matter with you, Blackford?"

"Nary a thing, Mommer." I ran to catch up.

About five, Daddy came in from the field. It was early for him, and I knew he had come because he had seen Ardis's car. His curiosity had got the better of him. In the eternal ledger, he was two hours in debt. He drove up in the battered International pickup, and we all walked out to meet him. He had lost more hair since I had seen him last, and when he removed his John B. Stetson, he touched the crown of his head self-consciously. His boot laces and trouser cuffs were matted with chaff and burrs, and dried salt made white whorls on his gray work shirt. As he walked toward us, a slow smile grew on his lined and reddened face. When he stood before me, shaking my hand and already turning to Ardis with a Scotsman's courting glint in his eye, I watched his face, noting the changes. There were more of the exploded capillaries. The patches of incipient skin cancer were larger. Age caricatures everyone, and he was a cruel exaggeration of the man in the photograph I kept in my desk drawer in the rented room in Bainesborough. Time had violated that picture. The essential unfairness of this always astonished me. As he shook Ardis's hand and, unable to help himself, began to try to charm her out of those work pants my mother had given her, I wondered how many years, how many more of these visits before someone, a stranger from the highway, came knocking at my mother's door to ask if she knew the man lying out in the field by the machine that was still running.

Already, my father was calling Ardis "little bit" and asking what she thought of the place and poking fun at her ignorance of all that lay around and getting her to tell him about her family and interrupting her with corny jokes about idle city men. Through it all, my mother indulged him. He was a natural flirt. I knew it must have caused them some trouble once upon a time. I also knew my father would have held his hand in flame sooner than break faith with my mother. If he had not flirted with Ardis, I would have known he did not care for her.

When Ardis told him she thought the pigs were cute, he threw back his head and laughed in a way that shook years from him, and I saw again briefly that fiery, funny man who had taught me how to live and work. He told her he agreed with her but was no longer keeping them in the house. His wife didn't like their table manners, though she did prefer them to her son's. For an instant she believed him, and this made him laugh again, and again this small circle of our ground was delivered from the hand of time.

Ardis reached over and took my hand. She would not have touched me had she not loved my father a little. We went in to help Mama prepare supper. Ardis would help by shelling field peas. Daddy and I would stand around the kitchen and get in the way. The kitchen would smell of twenty years of fried pork and fresh tomatoes and of Daddy. He was pretty strong after a day's labor, but it was what three of us were used to, and none of us wanted it any different. I was proud of my parents for not changing, except in matters of heightened politeness, around strangers. They were what they were and did not give a tinker's damn who knew it.

After two glasses of sweet iced tea, Daddy said, "Toad, let's you and me see if we can find some pinders to boil."

Daddy had three eighties in peanuts that year, but it was early. I think he just wanted to go for a ride with me.

We walked out to the old International. In the kitchen window, I could see Ardis beside my mother. They were leaning over the sink, both their mouths going at once. I waved but she didn't look up.

Daddy and I drove to the field. I noticed again the way he drove, leaning back in the seat and very slowly, the dashboard so covered with spare parts and half-empty boxes of shotgun shells that he could hardly see over it. He didn't hurry. He worked long and hard, but by his farmer's standard, hurrying, except in emergencies, bespoke disorganization.

We passed some of our stock, grazing in a field where last year's corn had grown. The animals were gleaning the ears the machines had missed. Their own ears were tagged with numbered white disks. They watched us pass, bolted, then stopped to look back. For years now, high feed prices had made beef cattle nothing but an expensive hobby. Soon Daddy would be getting out of the cattle business. Ours were mostly Santa Gertrudis, big and bronze and competent for hot weather, low moisture grazing. My father had been the first farmer in the county to bring in Santa Gertrudis stock, and like most things he did, it had paid off. At least for a while.

When we came to the peanut field. I got out and opened the gate for the truck, then closed it after. We drove with the green rows fanning past us, looking for the lushest, greenest vines. We were in no hurry.

"What you think?" Daddy asked me.

I looked ahead, knowing anyplace was fine, and yet knowing he wanted me to make a decision with him even if it was a small one.

"Right up there," I said as we rolled. "Right here."

He braked the old International. We got out and walked up the rows of peanuts, and Daddy began to pull vines from the earth with that rough energy, a definiteness I had never achieved except on a baseball diamond. I walked behind him, gathering them in bunches and spreading them on the tailgate of the truck. I beat the dirt from the gray legumes the world knows as peanuts. They emerged white and hard from their coats of soil, too young for boiling. We stood together looking down at them.

"What do you think?" My father asked me again, the old question, always a test and a lesson.

"Not quite yet."

He threw up the tailgate, shoving the peanuts into the truck-bed, and we walked to the cab. Inside, I watched his hands, but he did not reach for the ignition key. He gripped the steering wheel, his two fists like tools, heavy and whealed and abused. Those hands had never struck a Turlow. Mama had done the punishing in our family. "Go cut yourself a switch," she would say. Daddy's hands were too strong and somehow too delicate also. I watched the knuckles grow white on the steering wheel and listened to the ticking of the cooling engine in front of us and the sounds of the afternoon softening into evening. Daddy stared through the windshield. "She's a pretty one, that Ardis."

The way he said it was solemn, reflective, careful. I had never brought a woman home before. I did not know how to tell him this visit had not been planned, that it had come from a chance meeting with a family of country people at Bell's Bottom, from a feeling that certain connections of mine were growing thin. We were in the midst of something, and I had to go carefully, too. For a moment, I wished I had planned this day, that I was as serious about Ardis as my father knew I must be. I said, "Yes, she's . . . pretty. Ardis is."

He said, "And nicet too, seems to be."

"Yes, sir, that too. At least *I* think so."

He waited for me to say more. The air swarmed around us, warm and conductive in the cab of the truck. It was mine to say the next thing, but I couldn't for there was none.

Finally my father said, "That her car?"

"Yes," I said. "Her daddy gave it to her."

"Hmm," he said and started the engine. We drove in silence

back to the pasture. I got out and threw the peanut vines to the grinding jaws of his Santa Gertrudis cattle. We drove back to the dooryard and dinner.

My father's prayer of blessing has changed only once — the day after my sister, Trish, died. This night, we sat by the table and I watched Ardis as she bowed her head, her neck coloring a little from the heat of the kitchen and maybe the intimacy that family prayer brought among us. She was pretty, so pretty, and nice, too. She *was* those things. I closed my eyes to my father's quiet, tired voice. "Lord, bless this food to our bodily needs and us to Thy service as we grow in grace." He paused and drew breath. "We ask You to intercede for the soul of our beloved departed." It was his homely, not entirely Protestant way of asking the good God to look after his daughter who had sat by this table with us until the night of her nineteenth birthday, the summer after her graduation from high school.

We raised our heads and the bowls of acre peas, creamed corn, and of red beans and rice began to go round. We were still in the quiet spell of the prayer. I saw Trish sitting where Ardis now sat and wondered if it pained my parents to look at that place and see a young woman in summer bloom, with lights in her auburn hair, and a fresh, honest humility. A good, grateful guest. Somebody's daughter.

That night seven years before, we had sat at this table, and my father had said, "Damn it." He was damning his daughter's lateness from an afternoon with the Price twins at the river. He was angry. Later he must have regretted his anger and much else besides. My mother had soothed him, but they were both tired of Trish's break-bad ways, her drinking, which was finally out in the open, and her late hours with the Price twins, neither of whom had proved to be any good. My father, who valued friendship and loved the land, who had invested a lifetime in it so that he could rise in the morning knowing who rose nearby to begin the same day's work, never forgot that it was a stranger who told him his daughter had been killed with the Price boys in the Taylor County roadhouse fire.

For a long while, it was the good God he did not forgive. When at last he did forgive, the prayer of blessing began again with the change I mentioned, and always with a pause before the words, "beloved departed."

A deputy sheriff, a Negro named Reston, had come to the door. We all stopped eating at the knock, the sound of quietly scuffing soles. When my father opened the door to the troubled black face, the sad smile, the spangled, immaculate uniform, I was standing by his side. My mother sat behind us. In my mind's eye, I saw her still at the table, a spoon in her hand, her face pale. The deputy was not good at this. We knew it was bad by the way he swallowed, as though trying to take back the sad smile. Still, I hoped it was a steer on the road, even a fire in one of our tobacco barns. I took a step closer to my father, wanting his strength. We stood that way, not speaking, waiting for the messenger to collect his wits. Finally, he said, "Sheriff Mumford sent me. Said he known you. Said you's to follow me, please, sir." He was in hell by the time he was finished. We were in the yard, hatless, coatless, my mother running behind us, before the idiocy of driving God knew how far in an agony of doubt occurred to us. My father's rough hand took the man's shoulder and swung him around. The eyes that looked at us were big and scared. Daddy said, "Tell me."

The deputy drew himself up then as best he could. "You got a daughter named Patricia Blackford Turlow?" My mother was crying without sound, wiping her eyes on the hem of her apron as she watched the black man's face.

There wasn't much more to ask. The deputy seemed to have

caught up enough to begin to explain, but none of us could listen. My father pushed me gently in the direction of my mother and then drew the black man, who was beginning to talk about a fire, smoke, the county rescue squad, and too late, away under the pines. They talked while I stood by my mother who would not let me hold her, who seemed to want to hold me but couldn't, who cried more quietly and with a fiercer passion than I had ever thought possible. As I watched my father, I saw him grow smaller. He was a small, thin, middle-aged man when the deputy finished his story. My father let the deputy drive off alone, knowing by heart the way we had to go. He asked my mother to stay but she would not, and so I, who would have stayed with her, got into the truck with my parents and drove to the Starlight Lounge hard by the Santa Fe River. It was a wet, misty ruin, smelling of burnt heart pine and seared paint and something else I did not recognize at once. We stood in the headlights of a sheriff's car before a row of wet corpses shrouded in blackened and yellowed sheets to identify the remains of my sister Patricia.

She wore a heart-shaped locket. That was how we knew her. The engraving on the locket, which my father will carry with him until the day of his own death, is: *Blessed is the virtuous woman, for her price is far above rubies.* His own mother had worn it.

I did not want to look at her, but I did. A human being who has died by fire is stiffened and bloated and continues for hours after death to exude the yellow fluids which the body hopes will appease the consuming heat. I looked at her. I wanted to be as strong as my father was, and if he was not strong this once, I would be for him. To see her, or to know that locket, for nothing else was knowable, made me weak in a way I will always be weak. We have strength for such things, but it is measured. I have no more of it.

We sat around the table in a mood of goodwill, and save for the pause in my father's prayer during which I had seen Trish's face where now Ardis's bright, interested expression was, we did not have sadness. We had good food and good fellowship, and our common memory of what was lost had been beaten back beyond the circle of the light. Ardis could be thanked in part for that.

We left them at eight o'clock. Ardis and I had our ministries. I would hurry back to stand my midnight vigil at the counter of the convenience store. I would purvey Mad Dog 20-20 at a buck-twenty a bottle, and she'd dispense methadone all the next day to our faithful interchangeables.

My parents stood side by side. My father's arm was firm about my mother's waist. They waved to us as we drove away. "Drive safely," my mother called. "Keep the rubber side down," my father said, laughing. When we had made the county hard road, the artery that led back to the twentieth century, the way from which the bad news always came, I looked back at them. They were standing there under the tall pines, a promise which was forever. My father bent to kiss my mother's face.

Eleven

IN THE CONVENIENCE STORE, where only the winos are higher than the prices, human frailty eddies and collects in the small hours. After serving as ringmaster to all that metaphysics, I was usually exhausted and often too wired to sleep. On my way home, it was my practice to drop by the Gutbomb for the Early Bird Special — two eggs, grits, toast, and juice: ninety-nine cents. From the Gutbomb, I went home to sleep, if I could, until noon. I spent my afternoons writing. I was thinking of starting a new story. It would be about a young man who worked in a convenience store, about the people he met there and the long thoughts he juggled late at night in that carnival of crotch magazines and other discardable delights.

That morning, perhaps because of my country visit with Ardis, I was more than normally sick of the florescent light, the hermetic air and stale odors of my job. I decided to violate the morning routine.

It was seven-thirty when I reached Butterbutt Landing, a little park and boat ramp on Lake Jenny Jewel about a mile from the mouth of Hart's Flow where Eldon Odom lived. I hoped to have the place to myself for an hour or so. I wanted to see the sun take possession of the lake and watch the ospreys, whose driftwood nests clotted the trees near Odom's house, make their first morning passes over the lake. I was just spreading my towel and opening a copy of Bartram's *Travels in Florida and Georgia* when I saw two swimmers churning hard for a landfall fifty yards up the lakeshore from me. By the shock of black hair and the churning red arms of the leader, and the graceful, effortless stroking of the woman in second place, I knew them instantly. As they neared the shore, Lindy Briggs gave a burst of speed and outdistanced Eldon Odom.

Like an otter, she pulled herself up the grassy slope of the landing. She seemed to slip up the bank without benefit of legs. She lay like an offering to Odom's predatory rising form. Water poured from him as he knelt over her, then flung himself across her heavily, and I heard her laughter burst across the lake startling the awakening world, and then the answering cry of an anhinga. Then I heard the low murmurs of Odom's ardor. I was about to roll my towel and go softly when Odom turned his head sharply toward me.

It was an animal movement, quick and frightened. He raised himself from Lindy's body, and we confronted each other across fifty yards of dewy grass. I could feel the hot blood of embarrassment rising in my neck. I don't know what was in my face. Anyway, what could he see at that distance? Limply, I waved my book at him. A double gesture, it said, Hello, and I'm just here reading. Then it came to me; inadvertently, I was a spy.

We both turned to stare across the lake toward Hart's Flow. There in the creek mouth, in glimmering miniature, were the stalks of Odom's cypress deck. The slate roof of the house was just now catching the glow of the sun. I imagined Missy Sully awake, maybe brewing coffee to drink on the deck. When I turned back, Lindy had seen me. She said something to Odom and raised herself quickly to an elbow.

When Odom motioned to me, I could do nothing but get up and start walking. As I drew close, he said, "Join us, big'un. Move that spectacular ass of yours over and let Coach Turlow sit down, Missy Briggs." I watched closely as Lindy Briggs, in a black string bikini, slid herself across two feet of beach towel to make room for me. I heaved myself down, shirtless and white-skinned and feeling pale from my night of florescent light. And there we were, the distance between us lessened by the exposure of our flesh, a tight, naked circle on the small towel. Odom said, "What you doing out and about so early?" A spy, I searched for suspicion in his voice.

I said, "I just got off the shit shift down at the Lil Colonel."

Odom's eyebows climbed: So you haven't been spying. His face was heavy from a night's gravity. Lindy Briggs was as weightless as Zeno's Paradox. Gravity wasn't getting to her. I felt only a kinship with gravity. I said, "I thought I'd come out here and breathe some un-air-conditioned air."

"I know what you mean," Odom said, but he looked across the lake where the cypress deck was resolving itself out of the mist. Even after his swim in the lake, I could smell the musk of human cohabitation rising from him. Lindy Briggs leaned back on her elbows. Her stomach was ribbed and tanned and as smooth as the surface of Ardis's Mercedes. "If it's shit," she said to me, "why do you work there?"

"Usually for the money," I said. "You know, body and soul?"

She brushed a piece of grass from her right kneecap and glanced across the lake.

Eldon Odom said, "Right, sir!" as though answering a roll

call. "I know it well."

I guessed he meant the convenience store trade.

"I had me some jobs in my time, I can tell you," he said, "and the payback was bigger than the paycheck."

"It always is," said Lindy Briggs. The words rolled up from her stainless throat and spilled from a mouth that was Solomon's rose. She was ridiculous and perfect. Scarless beauty is a target, and I wondered if that was what Odom loved and if Lindy loved his scars. He was the bard of experience, of the broken place which, after it heals, is supposed to be stronger but never is.

Maybe Odom was thinking along similar lines. He leaned toward me and used the voice of experience. "Coach Turlow, what do you think of this beast here? Do you think we can use it?"

I looked at Lindy Briggs, thought of using her, then turned back to Coach Odom. I said, "Look to me like she can throw the pee-hole block. Let's try her at tight end."

Odom threw back his head and laughed. Lindy Briggs just kept staring. "I-god, coach," Odom said, "I bleeve you right. We put her in there at tight end, and if we get in a tight, we might use her to go both ways, maybe at corner back."

"She built for speed, too," I said dispassionately, in the dialect called "grit." "Got them good wheels and that ass-kicker look in her eye."

We could have gone on like that indefinitely, or nearly, and I suppose we did for a good long time. Lindy Briggs sat through it all staring defiant love at Eldon Odom. Then she rose, sleek in black cloth and tanned skin, and slipped into the lake. Odom let her go, grinning and watching me.

I said, "Looks like she done quit the team."

"She ain't earned her way with me yet, not by a long one. Back to the taxi squad." But he watched her striking out strongly in a direct line between his eye and the mouth of

Hart's Flow.

I nodded. "She'll have to knock some people down before we look at her again."

Odom turned back to me. "You writing?"

He said it distractedly, but still the question warmed me. It was the one I had wanted him to ask. I thought about my troubles with words and knew he did not want to hear them. I considered asking him a question about technique, but none came to me. I looked at his big red-Indian face and said, "Sure."

"Good."

"You?"

He drew himself up and arched his brows. The wrinkles in his face realigned themselves, all outrage.

"Always!" he said. "Never stop. Can't."

"Time's winged chariot?" I asked.

He looked at me, wary. "Something like that. You know it?"

"Yes." I was thinking of Trish.

"Not like I do."

"No, not like that."

A new seriousness was in his face. "Do you think we pissed her off good and completely?"

"Who?" I asked.

"Missy Briggs!" he said, exasperated.

"Oh, I don't know her well enough to say . . . coach."

He frowned. "Next time you see her, you tell her you're sorry. She'll like that." He winked at me.

I could not locate us. Was I being chided for taking the smaller part in our recent crime against sisterhood and solidarity? I had only followed his lead. I stared back at him, letting my puzzlement show.

"Do it," he urged. He rose and stretched his long, muscular frame, cupping his hand to slap an expanse of red belly. He watched Lindy, who was swimming strongly. "How far do you think she'll go?"

I told him I didn't know how far.

"Keep your helmet on and stay in a crouch," he said, heaving himself up.

I nodded and watched him wade in and breast the water strongly, leaving behind him that musky odor. Lindy was far ahead, but they were both swimming in the direction of that ravine where the vine-shrouded house lay in morning mist and the green-belt wife waited, and so did the big dog whose special grace was silence.

Twelve

ELDON ODOM'S GROUP were not students in the usual sense. The multilated soldier, the body builder, Sarah, Frank the salesman — they were not seeking degrees. They needed Eldon Odom, and so they came, had been coming for years. Watching them, I reasoned that one way to learn Odom was to learn the lives of those who stood closest to him. If pain was his research, they were his laboratory subjects.

The body builder, Tory Hubbel, and the one-handed veteran, Mike Shine, were roommates in a house by the borders of the Savannah. Hubbel and Shine were a marriage, a symbiosis. The house they shared stood on the lowland rim of the Savannah, miles from the fashionable heights occupied by the Arnold Baines family and other expensive Bainesborough folk. It was a bachelor's rebellion against cleanliness and order, a body builder's gym and a Viet veteran's parody of brothel and barracks, a place where ambush was always imminent.

Once a month, Shine and Hubbel threw a party for the writing crowd and its satellites and for the occasional researching visitor. The first time I went, with Ardis, I was such a visitor. I had heard the parties discussed often enough to know they were bizarre, violent, and considered successful only when the unforeseen occurred. They were the laboratory.

Ardis and I arrived a little early so that we could witness things before they got out of hand and, if need be, retreat in good order. But this does not say it all. I was anxious to see what went on at the Thrash Palace, as Hubbel and Shine called the old house. "Thrash" was their word for the act of love — it was a neat trope, combining sex and pain, the staples of their lives.

The Palace was an old cracker house, a large two-story frame structure surrounded by gardens which had once been elegant. The long beds of day lilies and arbors of rambling rose were now in wild riot. An old boxwood hedge followed a fluted course from the house to the drive and then off into the night. We parked by a swimming pool, empty but for two feet of black ooze. It reeked of the Savannah whose rim was only a hundred yards away. In the last light, we stood by the car watching bullbats hunt the insects rising from those grassy fields. A lone red-tailed hawk, a high delta against the orange light, wheeled toward its roost. From the house we could hear the rumble of the Rolling Stones, "Under My Thumb." Every room was lit, and the odor of marijuana drifted on the night breeze down toward the swamp. We followed it uphill, carrying a bottle of bourbon in a paper bag.

In a kitchen full of bright light and music, I put the bottle on a counter-top. A few strangers, all of them young hippites or athletes, turned from the stereo as we entered. None of them spoke. They drank and smoked in an elaborately casual way and watched the loud record spin.

I poured two bourbons and considered asking the whereabouts of Shine or Hubbel. I was on speaking terms with the
two, though I wouldn't have called us friendly. They were using
their wait-and-see attitude on me, and I knew it would not be
long before I was tested again, though I had no idea how it
would happen.

Ardis and I moved out of killing range of the music into the
largest downstairs room, the place where a family of farmers
had once rested after supper. It was a chaos of weight benches,
racks of weights, and piles of metal saucers with embossed
numbers on them. One wall was painted blue, another red. Fists
had punched holes in the plaster. One half of the floor was
covered by a wrestling mat. A wooden box was nailed to the
wall beneath a dispenser for the hand-drying chalk gymnasts
use. Two mirrored walls doubled us as we walked. Over it all
hung the ammonia smell of sour sweat.

"It's different," Ardis said, sipping bourbon.

"It's that," I said, as we smiled our secret smile.

We walked through the front of the house, to a parlor and a
screened verandah. Vines and creepers scaled the windows and
pierced the tattered screening. Paintings and posters were hung
on the walls, their frames thick with dust. We heard voices
coming from the screened porch, and from upstairs the sounds
of running water and padding feet. Before crossing the threshold, we looked at each other; the expressions on our faces asked,
Should we?

Three adolescent girls sat on a fetid old chaise smoking the
marijuana which had wafted out to us by the car. They watched
us. One of them said, "What it is?" and they all giggled.

We nodded. I said, "How y'all doing?" They were dressed
alike, in loose-fitting gauzy shifts from the Goodwill Industries
counters. Perhaps they had learned their clothing from Sarah

Fesco. One of them extended the joint to me, but I held up my bourbon. Ardis examined the night through a hole in the rusted screening.

From the kitchen, the Stones were belting out "Factory Girl," and the three swayed together on the chaise in a sexy mime of a rock group. The one who had offered me the jay stopped swaying and said, "You know Tory Hubbel?"

I nodded. Ardis took my arm. I could feel her there wondering who Tory Hubbel was and how I knew him. The girl who had spoken, a waifish flapper with big dark eyes and a headband of costume pearls, turned to the other two and helped them burst into giggles. Tory Hubbel was their joke, or I was. I asked, "Do you?"

The three arched their eyebrows and giggled harder. Ardis and I saluted them with our drinks and walked back into the parlor. I tried to make out some of the signatures on the paintings, all violent upheavals of color and form, while Ardis leaned against me, bemused, giving herself to the experience for the time being.

"Ah-HAH!"

Tory Hubbel stood on the landing above us. He wore red Swedish clogs and a white towel. His hard, hairless chest glistened with beaded water. "Come to see how the beast lives, did you?"

I waved to him, "What you say, big'un," and whispered to Ardis, "That's Hubbel." She shaded her eyes and looked up, though the light of the chandelier was not really bright. I think she wanted that hand in position in case she had to cover her eyes. Hubbel stood there posing for us, a wide grin on his pocked and livid face. For an instant, I thought he might drop the towel and expand like a man on a dais. Finally he shut the grin and said, "I be down in a minute." We watched him stride through the nearest doorway. There was laughter and a loud whoop and then the low note of another voice, Mike Shine's. It was the sound of one of their conspiracies, of something to be played on us later.

Back in the dining room, the record had changed and the voices were louder, more raucous. Arrivals were marked by shouts of "All right!" the fraternity boy's all-purpose exclamation, or "Far out!" the clan cry of freakdom. Ardis and I plunged back into the fray. We were standing by the kitchen sink when Shine and Hubbel burst through the doorway. Both were shirtless and glistening, though Hubbel was by far the more glandular. Shine had clamped three joints between his lips and held two more in his hands. His eyes were slits from the smoke. He passed them away as he walked. He wore camouflage fatigue trousers, a webbed belt, and heavy jump boots. Hubbel was throttling a quart of Jack Daniels, and as he strutted through the pressing, cheering crowd, he bent his knees and wobbled, raising the bottle and letting the big bubbles slip up its neck.

They were the signal. The party took off and flew high and fast. Ardis and I stood by the sink while it eddied around us. People raided the bar, clamored for ice, demanded matches, and cadged liquor. Mike Shine stood across the room, arms folded, master of all he surveyed. Girls and women surrounded him, pressing close. I waited for him to come for an introduction, but he kept his distance, a joint pinched in his fish lips. Finally, with a quick cant of his head, he summoned us. We obeyed. "Who is it?" he demanded, his face cold and stern.

It took me a second to realize he meant Ardis.

I said, "Ardis Baines, Mike Shine."

He looked at her, his head cocked back, smoke veiling his eyes. "Baines?" He thrust his mangled hand at her. She took it without flinching, looking him in the eye. She was used to having her name recognized, and usually it pleased her to be the daughter of all that history.

"Shit," he said. "Baines. Bay-nuh-uhs! Your daddy the Creosote King from down by the flow?"

She nodded, hardening a little.

"Mr. Pollution. Puts more shit in the water than a Shriner's convention at the Hilton."

"Shine?" Ardis threw her own head back in mimicry.

"Yeah?" he asked, a little wary.

"Shi-i-inuh!" she mimicked. "Let me see now. Your big brother is Bobby Shine. Buicks and real estate and the Shine Corporation that does the environmental impact statements for my daddy's plant. If it wasn't for the Shine family and its way with government regulations, my daddy wouldn't put half as much shit in the water as he does. I'm pleased to meet you. We got a lot in common."

You could have knocked Mike Shine over with a puff of smoke. He turned and said, "She's a goot one, big'un. Keep her," and walked away.

"You've just been crowned queen of the hop," I said to Ardis.

"Creosote queen is more like it."

"Come on," I said, "let's finish the introductions."

We found Hubbel on the screened porch, on that grimy chaise under a pile of giggles. We stood sipping and watching. It was good clean fun. Hubbel's false protests, "Off, jailbait," were breathless and sweet in the half-darkness, like the secret noises of children heard through a nursery door. When he noticed us, he picked them off and set them upright like giggling bowling pins. It was easy. "Now, stay. Goddamnit, stay!" he commanded. They stayed, giggling. He was breathing hard.

"I walked out here and they jumped me. Bubble gum vampires. Gawd, I *love* it!"

I said, "Tory Hubbel, this is Ardis Baines, my date."

"Date?"

We nodded, Ardis was smiling, waiting for what was next.

Hubbel considered for a moment, then smiled that shark's smile of his. Even his teeth had muscles. "This is an *oasis* party. EVERYBODY EAT YOUR DATE!" Nearby, someone began to scream, "EAT YOUR DATE! EAT YOUR DATE!" They were echoing it out in the kitchen. The girls attacked from three sides, rebuilding their pile of bones and soft places with Tory Hubbel at the bottom.

As we wandered back through the living room toward the heart of the party, we met Traymore. He was carrying a beer as though he didn't know what it was for. He kept holding it away from him and examining the label. He was sad and sulky. I guessed there wasn't enough millennial seriousness in the air. I said, "What's wrong, Traymore?"

"Aw, these guys are phonies," he said. "They don't know what art is. Look at all these people."

I was beginning to feel the bourbon and didn't want to hear his rap about the great mandala. "This is the world, Traymore." It seemed true at that moment. We were standing at *axis mundi*, 1974.

He looked hurt. "It's a fraternity party is all it is. Listen at those jocks."

A series of tremors shook the house. Forearm shivers had reduced the refrigerator to cubist sculpture and had started on the plaster walls.

Ardis said, "Don't worry," and put her hand on Traymore's shoulder. He headed for the screened porch and Hubbel's pile of giggles. I did not try to imagine his reaction to Humbert Hubbel.

The party aged, faded, then rallied. It got mean but was cajoled back to smashed conviviality. A young man I didn't know invited another out into the vegetable garden beyond the screened porch and pounded him into submission. The fight didn't draw much of a crowd. No one seemed to know what it was about, and soon we saw victor and victim together in the kitchen, treating their wounds with bourbon.

At about midnight, I lost Ardis for a moment, then found her with one of the two fighters. He was much too close to her, leaning with a predatory leer and whispering something that was making her neck turn red. I stuck my face in between them and said something gallant and stupid and pulled her away before the young man with the blood on his shirt could grind her into the wall. She said, "I thought he'd break my back," and we laughed and headed back into the stream, which was coming to a final froth. Then I felt a sharp pressure and looked down at our clasped hands. Ardis was gripping my fingers so tightly that a pain was starting up my arm.

A young man had just passed by the kitchen doorway. Tall and dark and well-built, he walked with an athlete's insouciant grace and had mastered the Eldon Odom grin. I inclined my head to Ardis, waiting for a word, but she only stared at him and squeezed my hand all the harder.

The young man pressed into the crowd, and the drunks made way for him as though they still possessed working radar. He walked straight to Mike Shine, who occupied a corner, speaking passionately to a group whose military dress, like Shine's, suggested politics. The newcomer parted the circle, pushed close, and whispered something to Shine. They shook, hook to hand in the thumbs-up fashion, and walked off together.

I said, "What's wrong, baby?"

Ardis said, "Come outside with me."

In the night air, away from the pounding music, Ardis stood in front of me, her hands cold in mine. "That's him."

"Him who?" I asked. There was something about our words that I remembered.

"Him that said he was coming to see me that night. Him from the halfway house, the boy I told you about." There was a rising note of exasperation in her voice.

"How does he know Shine?" I was thinking about the membership of the group.

"How the hell should I know how he knows Shine?" She let go my hands and stood there holding herself, shivering.

"Well," I said, groping, "don't worry about it. You're with me." I suppose I was remembering the bloody boy at the sink and how I had rescued Ardis from that warrior's ardor. It had been easy. But she didn't seem much consoled.

"Let's go," she said. "I want to go."

Immediately I said, "Eldon Odom hasn't even come yet."

It was necessary for Odom to see me here. To be seen was the next step, my reason. Ardis waited for me to say more, but already she was stirring in her purse for her keys. I could only watch. She looked up, giving me another second. "To hell with Eldon Odom and you, too."

I just stared at her.

"He isn't your work," she said, cold anger in her voice now. "He isn't even his own work."

Suddenly I was cold, too. This was the week of my last chance with Ardis, who had just told me to go to hell, to go there with Eldon Odom who held the keys to the doorway of words. I thought, *I will.*

I let her drive away while she hoped I wouldn't. I stood there in a false nonchalance that was obvious to both of us. After the blue Mercedes was out of sight, I thought about my promise that no harm would come to her. And later, as I was weaving up that sandy track toward the lights of Bainesborough in a dim and whiskey-misted dawn, I replayed what had passed between us. A week before, under the tall pines, we had seen my parents' kiss of faith. Somehow then, and earlier with my father in the peanut field, I had known Ardis and I would come to nothing. I had broken the faith when I left the farm to follow the voice, and it was somehow the same faith I could not keep well enough to keep Ardis Baines.

Thirteen

WHEN I RETURNED to the party, the hard-core celebrants were still at it, but the pile of giggles had laid permanent claim to the sofa and whistled its child's breath sweetly at the night beyond the screens. Traymore had long since wandered off into that night, but not before lining his pockets with plastic baggies stuffed with food. Hubbel and Shine, the two iron men, showed no signs of slowing down.

At about one o'clock in the morning, Eldon Odom arrived with Missy Sully. A short time later, Lindy Briggs came, too. Without acknowledging one another, the three invaded us like the story whose minor characters we were.

As Eldon Odom swaggered past me, dressed as usual in khaki and denim, I watched Missy Sully. (I later learned she was Rebecca Sullivan Odom, of the Sullivans who owned the Ocala horse farms.) She was a slender, dark-haired, green-eyed Irish-woman with pale, translucent skin that set her apart in this South of suntans. She was very handsome, though just on the far side of her best years. I asked myself how a man with a wife like this could be back-dooring with Lindy Briggs. It was a stupid question. It reminded me of Ardis's untethered hair flying behind her in the moonlight as she dug that Mercedes into the sand, leaving me in my dream.

Missy Sully walked to the kitchen with the bottle she had brought. Hubbel and Shine went to Odom, just as, earlier, everyone else had gone to them. They stood before him, two young lieutenants. He put his hands on their shoulders. "I-god, I bleeve you two boys have been misbehaving yourselves again. Look at this place."

They stared in mock wonderment at the wreckage. So did we all. It had happened over a span of hours, but now, taken all in all, it was a stupendous mess. The refrigerator was a new thing, a thing to be admired. Discarded articles of clothing lay among bottles and cans, empty and half-empty on every surface. It was as though Cossacks had raided us. Someone had vomited in a corner of the wrestling mat. Someone else had stepped in it. Someone had knocked over a weight bench with a two hundred and fifty–pound barbell on it; as a consequence, there was a hole in the heart pine floor big enough to put a head through. Someone had put someone's head through the hole, and it had taken a fire axe to make the hole large enough to get the head out. The fight that had ensued had smashed a picture frame and smeared blood along the mirrored wall and across the base-board. The winner had been restrained from running out into the Savannah to celebrate under the moon.

Yes, nodded Hubbel and Shine, grinning: We have been misbehaving ourselves. They laughed and Odom took the bottle of Jack Daniels that was always in Hubbel's hand. Then Odom turned and spit a stream of whiskey above the crowd, and people danced in this amber baptism and the party continued, rolling toward light.

I circled close to Odom and stood in his glow, but he did not speak to me, only rambled to his public in the way I had come to know was the public man. I found myself remembering that first day we had talked on his deck and how forthcoming he had been with me and how silent since. I told myself this silence was part of my apprenticeship, but the idea was hollow. The whole thing, my waiting for him tonight, to be seen by him here, suddenly seemed an initiation into nothing. I shook my whiskey head and backed away from the glow of Odom, out of the circle, stumbling through the debris, looking for a place to rest.

They were starting a weight-lifting contest when I left the room, using a comatose young girl for their weight. She was blonde and unremarkable except for the depth of her sleep. The expression of rest on her face did not change as she was passed from hand to hand, lifted high and let down.

I found Missy Sully alone with the three sleeping teen-agers, the giggle factory, on the screened porch. She was not the rest I wanted, and I was turning to slip away quietly when I heard, "Wait."

It was a command. I stepped close, and she patted a place beside her on the edge of the chaise. She was sipping bourbon, straight without ice, and leaning back against the warm bodies of the three kittens.

We sat in silence. I held my tenth bourbon but did not drink.

"First time here?" she asked me. She tilted her head and drank, then quietly gagged, and I noticed the fretwork of wrinkles at her throat. I remembered the karate kick, the flash of white foot under my nose there on the deck and that strange animal cry of hers. "Yes," I said. My voice was slurred, and I resolved to speak precisely. After a space, she turned to me. "You're a nice boy, aren't you?"

I had lived long enough to know that women did not like nice boys. They liked bad boys who were nice to dogs and small children and their sainted mothers and who were otherwise ass-kickers. I squirmed, but finally the unvarnished truth came rising out of the whiskey. "I *am* a nice boy."

She patted my knee and said, "Good. That's good. Why don't you go home now." Her voice was weary, and in the weariness was a warning.

"I'm not *that* good." Her hand was still on my knee. I could feel the heat of it start. She said, "I remember now. You've got those terrible scars."

"On the other one," I said. The other knee was not within her reach.

She drank again and shuddered. "I hate it when a young person like you is hurt. Why don't you go home?"

I stood and her hand fell from my knee into her lap. She stared through the screening. "Sometimes," she said in a weary voice, "enough of this" — she showed me her empty glass — "and I can see in the dark. The things out there." She gestured at the night outside. "Why don't you get me another bourbon?" I took her glass but did not plan to come back.

In the kitchen, things had changed. The crowd had thinned by half. A group of silent drinkers — all men — stood by the back door. The women had separated themselves to the other side of the kitchen. They were tense, detached somehow by more than physical distance. The two groups wouldn't look at each other.

As I turned the corner, I looked up at the landing and saw Odom and Shine and Hubbel and the new boy, the one Ardis had been afraid of, carrying the young blonde girl through the doorway. They were still laughing and holding her like dead weight, the equipment from their contest, but there was something more. I watched the silent, expectant women, thinking of films I had seen of deer drinking water on the veldt; it was that same skittish expectancy. I stood with Missy Sully's glass in my hand and listened to the ceiling. Finally, unable to make any sense of it, I turned to a young man near me, one of the football players who had been breaking down on the refrigerator. "What's doin'?" I asked. I heard myself say, "Whath doin'?"

He smiled vaguely and held a finger up to cancel his lips. He lifted a thumb to the ceiling. "Yeah," I said, "I know, but what?"

He said, "A train. They pullin' a train on some ole girl up there." He pressed a thick fist to the middle of his face and giggled.

I was confused. "A train? What's a train?" As I asked it, the ridiculousness of the question came home to me. The Orange Blossom Special, that midnight train to Georgia. A train was a train.

"You know, a *train*," he said, urging his loins toward me and grinning obscenely. Suddenly I knew what he meant. It was an apt image. They were raping "some ole girl" up there. The sodden heap they had carried upstairs was still in use.

It was time for me to get off the bus. I put Missy Sully's glass down, grabbed the bottle I had brought, and walked outside. I was standing unsteadily by the back door when I heard a noise, something wild. At first I thought it was from the Savannah, but it was too close for that. I made my way around the corner of the house.

There was a lighted window above, and I heard muted voices. But the noise was someone climbing an ivy-covered trellis, making steady progress just above me, weeping into the cackling ivy. In the moonlight, I knew the glistening definition of those bare legs. It was Lindy Briggs.

She did not see me. I called out, in a whisper, but she didn't hear.

I started climbing, too. I did not know whether the trellis would bear us. I was finding my holds in the ivy, avoiding the wood which was rotten and noisy. When I was just beneath her and looking up at those working buttocks, that moon-silvered silk of skin, she heard me and turned, startled, and by reflex kicked at my face. The blow took me on the cheek, and I smelled the rubber soles of her hiking boots. I said, "Wait a minute! Don't do that!"

"Go back," she whined. Did she know it was me? "Get down," came the whine. "Can't you see . . .?"

Couldn't I see she was hurt, humiliated, was weeping? My curiosity and a new feeling of closeness to her were too strong. I could not find the decency to go down. I kept climbing and would have fended off the next kick with force. But she did not kick again, only clung until I was close beside her, the two of us out of breath, aching, perched in the moonlight with the lighted window, the voices just above us. Carefully, flank to flank, we pulled our eyes above the sill.

The walls were painted black. A bare bulb hung by a braided wire from the ceiling. The floor was covered with a dirty thickness of foam rubber. Hubbel and Shine and the boy I did not know stood passing an almost empty bottle of whiskey while Odom worked at the girl on the floor. They had pulled her clothes halfway off and piled them beside her head. She was lithe and tanned; the design of a brief bikini was sunburnt on her. Her T-shirt had been pulled up and twisted at the top to make a bag for her head. Odom rode her in a sitting position. His face, not ten feet from us, was a mask of concentrated anger. Her legs twitched at each stroke like the extremities of a body in seizure, and once, just as he finished, gritting his teeth, arching his neck and releasing a low dog's moan, the girl raised a limp hand to pull the T-shirt away from her face.

She was pretty, anonymous, the kind you see at busy intersections in the city waving bouquets at passing cars. She was the high-school dropout who would walk to your car window and exchange pleasantries with you before handing you a bunch of carnations. She'd count change for you, but not without moving her lips, pulling money from the pockets of her cutoff jeans.

With the T-shirt down, I could see that she was breathing heavily from Odom's weight. She did not open her eyes. Odom stood up, his softening penis aimed at us, dripping seed. With his right hand, he shook it, smiling. A constellation of semen fell on the girl's mat of pubic hair, and Lindy Briggs beside me moaned a reprise of that dog who was Odom at his pleasure.

Odom raised his eyes to the window and squinted, and I froze, knowing Lindy didn't care if we were caught. After a space, Odom turned away, still holding himself. He took the bottle from Hubbel, drained it, and tossed it in a corner. We watched as the new boy stripped himself, revealing strong white limbs, and knelt to the spread legs, the mat of hair and the lax, breathing mouth. He lifted the T-shirt and pushed it back over the girl's face. Her limbs twitched as he entered her, and Lindy Briggs sobbed beside me.

I pulled her down. She tried to stay, but it was descend or fall, so insistent was my grip on her shoulder. I took her with me out past the cars to the swimming pool that stank of the Savannah. I offered her the last of my whiskey. She drank, sobbed, and drank again, clutching at her chest.

I said, "I know. . . ."

"Shut up!" she cried, "You don't know. You're just like them." She shoved the bottle into my hands. "No, you're *not* like them. You think you are, but you're not." She had calculated what she thought would hurt me. She pressed both hands to my chest and shoved me toward the house. "You're a *writer?* What are you doing with *me?*"

I didn't answer, only leaned against the hands that pressed my chest. She closed her eyes and said, "Did you hear him . . . did you?" I looked back up at the window where the light was just now going out and thought of the girl waking up in that room, maybe just at dawn when the house was still asleep but the Savannah was awake outside the window. I saw her rise from the rubber pallet, holding her forehead and belly in her two hands, saw her go to the window and look out, and there, looking in, were our two faces, Lindy's and mine.

Lindy lifted her hands from me. "Leave me alone."

I said, "Promise you won't go back there."

I had no idea what would happen if she went back. I suppose I had some notion that if I kept her with me, then neither of us had ever been at that window. She balled her fist and hit my chest using all the strength she meant for Eldon Odom. It hurt. "Get out of my goddamned movie, will you? You don't know shit!"

I left her sitting by the pool and walked toward the road, exhausted. The eastern sky was paling, and the white moon was a speculating face above the sill of the Savannah. I had made half a mile up the dirt road when I heard the music stop, and then Lindy raced past me in an old Ford with an ROTC sticker on the bumper. She didn't look at me. In her wake, I thought I heard the moan — "Did you hear him?" — that same dog's moan, but it must have been the Savannah behind me, full of predatory sound. I turned and tried to see it in the dark.

Fourteen

MY HEAD WAS SO badly bent the next day that I could not go to work. I called Billy Soomers, the old alkie who coordinated what he called his "team" of Lil Colonel Convenience Store clerks. He said, "OK, but you owe me one," meaning a night shift in one of the ghetto stores, the ones usually operated by large black gentlemen who sold trouble cheap.

After trying to sleep most of the morning, I called Ardis at work. She was "not available at the moment. Can we take a message?" In my state, it required every human restraint not to give a message that would violate state and federal codes. "No," I said.

Coming back from the phone downstairs, I met Traymore, who had left the party early. He smiled when he saw me. "Your hands are shakin', big guy. You want some herbal tea?"

I asked him to lower his voice. He protested that he was speaking in a normal tone.

"I was afraid of that."

He smiled a somatic smile and walked on, immaculate. I went upstairs again and tried to see the pages of my new story through the metallic sheen of my headache. No luck. I lay down and stared at the ceiling and concentrated on keeping rivers and hills separated, gave names like "Tranquility" to a few of the craters in the plaster and generally occupied myself with the cartography of a long-haul hangover.

I had almost found the valley where I could lie down beside still waters and sleep when someone knocked at my door. For a space, I held to sleep, but the knocking persisted. When I had both feet on it, the floor tilted thirty degrees to starboard and then rolled back sixty to port. I called, "Can you come in? I can't. . . ."

Lindy Briggs opened the door. She wore the leotard and wraparound skirt and soft dancers' pumps and carried the backpack. She had the fevered look of those bereft lovers in nineteenth-century novels.

She said, "Will you fuck me?"

I was trying to steady the floor and to convince myself I had not heard what I had heard. I considered just lying down to pretend she was not there. Then I had a moment of intense clarity. I pressed both palms to my hot face, dragged my fingers downward to straighten my vision, and said, "Fuck you to spite Eldon Odom, who would like nothing better than to get shut of you? No, thanks."

She came toward me, a few steps into the room, and stood with pleading eyes. I said, "Go home and sleep by yourself, and I'll try to do the same. What do you say?"

Suffering heightened her. The sallowness of a night's boozing and grief gave her skin a more believable texture. She was no longer Lindy the ice maiden, Lindy the movie. She was Lindy strung-out on Eldon Odom so bad she wanted into my bed.

She stood in the middle of the dusty pine floor for a moment watching me. Then she dropped the backpack and hooked her thumbs in the straps of the leotard and was bare to the waist before I could stop her. She shivered as she stood there pulling at the knot that held the wraparound skirt in place. I was on my feet and struggling with her, trying to keep her hands from what they were doing, and all the time fighting nausea and wondering if I was crazy.

Finally I had both her hands. We stood very close together, her hands trapped in mine, angry and awkward. I wrapped her arms around me and pulled her close, naked against my naked chest. "Please," I said. She was rigid in my arms, still wanting to fight, so I said, "Don't," and pulled her to the bed. We were sitting down and the floor was steadying beneath us. I put my Salvation Army blanket around her shoulders. We sat that way for a long time, and when I looked at her again, a tenderness was in her eyes. She reached out to my face. "Did I do that?"

"What?"

She gently touched the bruise below my right eye, and the little stab of pain brought back the scent of the rubber sole of her hiking boot and all of the night before, all of it. I said, "I guess so. It don't hurt. Don't worry." My face was the least of our worries.

"I shouldn't have done it. It wasn't you I wanted to hurt."

I looked at her and said, "And it's not me you want to . . . make love to either, is it?"

She looked at me for a long time, then gave me the first real, unsullied smile I had seen from her. "I don't know," she said. We sat for a space, looking at each other. There was nothing she could have said to scare me more.

I said, "Believe me, you don't." Then I said, "Let me help you," knowing she wouldn't. She turned away and pulled up the straps of the leotard.

She walked to the doorway, then came back for the backpack. "You know he pushes us together, don't you?"

I nodded yes. I remember the first night at Moby's. Eldon Odom's crude comment about Lindy's best friend, and later, that morning at Lake Jenny Jewel.

"Do you know why?"

I did, but I shook my head no.

"He wants me at the back door. He wants to keep up appearances, the bushwah bastard. But I won't. . . ." She was about to cry again, and I held up my hand as though to ward off a blow. She mastered herself and laughed at my upraised hand. She stepped forward and took the hand and stroked it. "You're a good guy." It was the second time in two days my virtue had been praised by a beautiful woman.

I gave her hard, perfect hand a little pressure and said, "I try to be a bad guy, but it just don't work out. Raised wrong, I guess." I almost told her that it was mostly because of my sister, the way I had seen her abused when she was drunk and sorry. But I heard those words coming out of me into this room, into the ears of this stranger with whom I had shared two of the strangest moments of my life, and I knew they were better left buried in my bent head.

"My father would like you," she said. "But not if he knew you been staring at my tits."

We both laughed. I said, "Listen, you got great tits." And then, "Was I staring?" It was bad and delicious to talk to her like that.

"Thanks," she said. "From you, it means something."

I sat there feeling like a boy scout, and the second thoughts came crowding in. My mind's eye watched us thrashing on that camp bed. I said, "Are we going to let him push us together?"

She said, "No." Said it firmly, but with the sadness that told me she could think of worse things.

I said, "OK," but not very convincingly. She came forward and touched my bruised cheek again.

Finally, wanting a clean ending, I said, "I like you, Lindy. Let's be friends."

She said yes and picked up the backpack, and the next thing I heard was her dancing the stairs two at a time. When I lay back and stared at the ceiling and tried to locate once again that green valley, those still waters, I saw Lindy Briggs walking naked on grassy banks, and the words, *in the presence of mine enemies*, came to me. It was hours before I could fall asleep.

Part III

Fifteen

I TRIED ARDIS at work during the rest of that week and finally at the big house. The maid told me "young Missy Baines" was on vacation.

"Where? With whom?"

"Fambly. Whole fambly done gone."

Then I remembered a reunion with the northern branch, the Baineses of Richmond and Chapel Hill. We had talked about her going. It had seemed a long way off, nothing to worry about. Now it seemed everything to worry about. She had gone without a word to me.

Or so I thought until her letter arrived, and I sat in the light of my desk lamp with the voice of Ardis Baines:

> Dear Mr. Turlow,
>
> As you know, I have to leave town to visit connections in Virginia and North Carolina. It's a family

obligation, and while I cannot say that I will much
enjoy spending three weeks listening to my daddy
brag up our branch of the family, I can say that I have
not much enjoyed recent hours spent with you. I have
always respected your art but do not see the connection you seem to see between art and the life and
times of Eldon Odom. He and his bunch strike me as
degraded. I hope we can talk about this when I am
back. I know a brief separation will do us both good.

She signed herself *A. Baines* and provided a return address in
Richmond. Her clear intent was that I should respond, and soon.

I knew what I should say. I knew what I should promise, and
knowing this, knew I could not write just then. I don't know why
I couldn't promise. Perhaps it was the need to keep two worlds
separate, the knowledge that with Ardis fortuitously gone I had
an opportunity to experiment with my life. Perhaps I was
learning to see in the dark.

The writing I did was my own. I worked and waited, and the
days passed. Sometimes, as I lay on my cot in anxious half-
sleep, I saw the bewildered face of the flower girl. She came
holding her troubled head just as I had imagined her that night at
the Thrash Palace, and sometimes she brought her sister, that
white-faced speculating moon who had presided over my stumbling departure. And yet, I had not departed. I was still with
Odom.

Finally I set aside an afternoon to reread the passages from
his books I loved the most, to wonder whether the voice still
sang simple and sweet from the pines and cypress hammocks of
the uplands north of the city. I read them and it did. It thrummed
on in those pages unchanged. How could Odom rape his life and
woo his work? How could he be the man in the room and the
voice in the work, that dog's moan and this singing, both at

once? I could not understand it. I put aside his work and looked at my own. It was the naked revelation of myself; in it there was no difference between private and printed man. And it was getting better. Page by page, sentence by sentence, I held the tone and pitch more firmly. And the change, I knew, came somehow from these new circumstances of my life.

One day Eldon Odom asked me, "Toad, when are you bringing that story back in?" Anger rushed in me. I stopped my tongue, for it would have said, "Never." I remembered my humiliation.

I said, "What I hoped was that we could have a talk about it, you and me." I recall what it took for me to say that. I looked at my shoes when I was through.

He looked me straight in the eye and grinned, "I never do it, Toad. It's the group you need to hear. The lonely voice is fallible. The group knows what I know. If the group fucks up, maybe sometimes I know it, but the group is the world and the world will kick your ass every chancet it gets."

I wanted to ask him how a man whose entire life had been disaffiliation from everything organized, everything *inside,* how such a man could believe in the group. I wanted to ask what was the group when it went upstairs to that room. What was it then? But I didn't ask. I had said all I could find to say. I only nodded, resolving never again to bring a story before the group.

I began to see Lindy Briggs, who had seen me in one moment of strength and would not forgive it. We met at the Gutbomb or went for walks in the city or along the rim of the Savannah. I even took her to Bell's Bottom. I did my flying rope tricks for her while she lay below, immaculate and impossibly beautiful in a narrow black two-piece. When I was finished, she duplicated what I had done, added a few capers of her own, and suggested I imitate them. I resigned from the circus. What I could do by main strength, she did by dancing.

She was the daughter of Colonel Briggs, who had commanded a division in the early days of Viet Nam. After her mother's death and some blunder of his own, he had been abruptly rotated stateside. Since childhood, Lindy had lived with his rage at being dead-ended in ROTC, or since, as she put it, "they stuck the turd in Daddy's file." No one knew what the Colonel's mistake had been. Lindy loved and feared her father, and I supposed she loved Eldon Odom for being everything her father was not. I did not ask her why she loved Eldon Odom. I was afraid she would ask me the same question.

I told her stories about my family, about the father who had raised me, who was strong and gentle and enduring, and who rarely spoke of anything but corn and rain and the hope of catching up. My stories made her sad, and so mostly I listened. As she talked, she became real to me, and this, in a sense, was a loss.

Her extraordinary body was the result of years of self-denial and pain and education, all to make her what her father respected most — a warrior. She had made herself as hard as he was but could not become the last thing, a man. At times she hated herself so intensely that she wished to die. One day she told me this: The night we had clung together on the trellis, part of her had wanted to enter that room and take part in the male rite.

"But what about the other part?" I asked her.

She looked at me, her face bent in pain. "It's the girl on the floor."

We went to class together, which seemed to please Eldon Odom. We walked in, side by side, as close and as distant as brother and sister. I began to participate in the criticism, using my opinions as I saw fit. I spoke my own, not the group's voice, and offered help because help was what I needed. I ignored most of what others said. When Eldon Odom spoke, I was rapt, wanting the untranslated truth. Occasionally he turned to me with questions. He favored my answers, showing the others I was his boy, hoping they would think Lindy was my girl.

By stages, I became accepted, and I began to learn more about my fellow students. The group was a living thing whose heart was Eldon Odom. Shine and Hubbel and Sarah were our vitals, too, and now there was MacEvoy.

The Tuesday night after Ardis left town, the boy who had frightened her at the party came to class. Mike Shine brought him in. His name was Tommy MacEvoy. They had served together in the First Air Cavalry. MacEvoy was from the outskirts of Bainesborough, a little hamlet called Dillingham. Whereas Shine's family was Old Bainesborough, MacEvoy was from grits, the son of a diesel mechanic who worked for Fleet Trucking. Their bond was strong. It was MacEvoy who had stood close to Shine when a sniper's bullet had torn his right hand.

That night at Moby's, the test I had expected came for me. Our bunch was in its usual back room by the evil-smelling urinals. We had been especially loud and foul this night. There had been raucous arguments, arm wrestling, and once Shine and Hubbel had hoisted Sarah Fesco and handed her back and forth across the table to give her, they said, a little humility. When they put her down, she was livid and rumpled, and it took Eldon Odom to stroke her feathers back into place. "Aw, Sarah, stay with us. Help me keep these goddamned animals in their chains." Sarah stared at him, and he grinned his hooked grin and his eyes pleaded and she belonged to him, and to us.

When the conversation grew thin and it was time to leave, I

said so, and my announcement met with no protest. Lindy rose with me, her eyes on Odom, and said, "Wait for me, Toad."

Just then a tall, fat man, an English graduate student who frequented the bar, lurched into her. In his embarrassment, he held her close and danced with her a few steps before passing on to the men's room. It was the innocent grope of a surprised drunk, but one of his hands had pressed her buttocks. Mike Shine said, "You gone let the Feds get away with that, Toad?"

Shine and Hubbel held Odom's contempt for the "Feds," their word for Ph.D.'s. The Feds were parasites on the body of art.

I looked at them. My face must have asked, Me?

"You gone let a footnoter do that?" asked Hubbel.

Shine rose and stood by Lindy and me in the narrow passage. Tory Hubbel joined us. I watched Eldon Odom's face. There was a mock righteousness in it and something else — simple meanness. I could not believe what was happening.

When the fat man emerged, still zipping himself up, I saw that he was soft and scholarly and wore the wire-rimmed spectacles that hippites favored. He was one of the legion of Trotskys that lurked the hallways of the English department. I knew what they were about to do, and I felt sorry for him.

I turned to Shine and said, "Come on, let's get out of the way." I tried to say it right, not belligerently but with the small authority I owned. While Shine smiled at me, Hubbel pushed Lindy against me and her elbow caught me in the cheek, just where her boot had hurt me already. My impulse was to turn on Hubbel. The flash of pain, the ridiculousness of it, the sudden shouts from our table of "Go for it!" and "Kick ass and take names!" all inflamed me. I was cocking my fist when the fat man grabbed me from behind, locked me to his chest and tried to use my body to push his way through.

Tory Hubbel's bulk was against my chest. The fat man panicked. I heard his ragged breathing against my ear. He was lifting me, and little things were beginning to stretch in my neck. In pain and rage, I reached back and hooked a thumb in his eye socket and gouged until I hit something neurological. When he let me go, screaming, I turned on him using all the anger meant for Hubbel and Shine, and it took Lindy Briggs and Eldon Odom to pull me back. My fists were bloody and so was my shirt, and the fat man's glasses were somewhere beneath our feet in blood and beer. He was moaning, "Oh, Jesus," and Lindy was pulling at me, crying, "Stop it, Toad, you asshole."

A crowd of drunks rushed in from the bar, but our group bowed up on them. Then I heard Frank whisper, "The cops," and we all rushed the back exit.

In the silence outside, I spun and spun and somehow did not make it into any of the cars which burnt rubber out of the parking lot. The last thing I saw was Eldon Odom handing Lindy into his car. I scaled a fence and landed on unsteady legs in the sand of a junkyard just as the sirens and rolling blue lights converged on Moby's. I ran with a bouncing neon carnival in my eyes until, wobbling and exhausted, I fell among cardboard boxes in an alley and lay staring at the heavens while my breath came back to me.

Shame lay with me like an infected lover on my cardboard bed. I had used my hands in a way I had sworn I never would again. Standing between two louts and an intellectual with a beautiful woman at my side, I had failed at compromise. My neck throbbed and my zippered knee was howling in outrage at my long, stumbling escape. I could still hear Moby's, the shouts and the scratchy voice of the dispatcher on the police radio. I lay trying to purge my mind of thought while my bloody knuckles congealed, but I kept seeing Lindy Briggs driving off with Odom.

Finally I got up and walked out to the street and looked at

myself in a store window. I had to be careful. There was blood on the front of my shirt and on my face, and my hands looked like the weapons they were. I looked up and down the street for police cars. This block of bars and restaurants was heavily patrolled at night.

I was starting the walk home with my hands hidden in my pockets and my face averted when an engine idled up beside me. I kept walking, knowing I was under arrest.

"Hey, Turlow!"

Frank swung a car door out to me. I peered up and down the street and then slid in beside him. It felt good in the air-conditioned interior where he lived.

He looked at my hands and face. "Good thing I happened along."

"Yeah," I said. I opened the glove box and removed the pint he kept there. After I had taken two healthy swallows, he said, "Help yourself," without a trace of irony.

We drove along in silence while I let the whiskey percolate down to the hurts and the guilt and start to make them warm. I was about to tell him where to turn when he said, "You really cold-dicked that guy. Man alive!"

I looked over at him, at his unending capacity for idiot wonder. He waited, watching traffic.

"Look, Frank," I said, "Hubbel and Shine cold-dicked the guy. They used me. All I did was lose my temper like a kid in the schoolyard. I'm not proud of it."

We drove along in the hermetic hum of Frank's air-conditioner and the high, cold whine of his tires and the green glow of his dash lights. I took another drink and offered him one.

"No, thanks, I got to drive."

He said the word "drive" as though it meant something, a special talent.

He glanced over at me. "We talked about you when you left,

after the cops got through with everybody."

"I thought everybody ran."

"Naw, hell, Hubbel and Shine and me, we just moseyed on out to the bar and sat down like we knew what we was doing. They went right past us. Didn't get to us till later. By then, we was innocent. Know what I mean?"

I nodded and saluted his moral ingenuity with the bottle in my hand. "So, you talked about me?" I was curious.

"Oh, yeah," he said. Frank was pure salesman.

Finally I gave him the satisfaction. "When you talked about me . . ."

"Yeah?"

"When you talked about me, Frank, what did you say? I mean, what did you say *about me?*"

"Oh, yeah," he said. He turned a corner and, as near as I could tell, drove aimlessly.

"Well, actually, it was me an Hubbel an Shine an that new guy, MacEvoy."

He looked over at me and smiled his excitement. I said, "Yes?"

"Oh, well, Hubbel just said he thought you hooked the guy pretty good, considering, and Shine, he said, yeah, said you had a pretty good left, all things considered, you know and . . ."

"And?" I tried to drink whiskey through gritted teeth.

"And . . . ah, well it went on like that, you know. We was just skating the bull about what happened, the fight and all."

"Frank," I said. "What were all these things considered?"

"These things . . .?" He looked at me, mystified.

"You said 'all things considered.' Twice you said it."

"Oh yeah, well, they didn't say. They didn't. . . ."

He drove for a while. Then his face brightened with a real sales item. "That MacEvoy's really something. He's the goods, you know what I mean?"

"The goods?"

"Yeah, you know. . . . He takes out this little kit he's got and the four of us, we go back in the head, and right there, you know, in Moby's . . ." Frank put a thick forefinger to the side of his nose and tapped twice, then gave a couple of stagey sniffles.

"Yeah?"

"You bet," he said. "Right there in the head. Shine, you know, he does a lot of drugs — speed, coke, and downers. And Hubbel, he does that glandular shit to make himself big. Near as I can tell, MacEvoy gets it for them. He's their, what you call it, connection. You know?"

I knew. I asked him where MacEvoy got the drugs. He didn't know. I asked him what it was like. He smiled. He didn't know. Then he turned to me and whispered, "Well, I do know a little."

"Coke?" I asked him, whispering, too. "How does it make you feel?"

"Oh, I don't know."

"Does it make you feel like you used to feel?"

He smiled. He was pleased I had remembered his words. He said, "No, better. Better than that."

Sixteen

I DID NOT KNOW the date of Ardis's return, but after a time I knew she was back and that her period of internship in the halfway house would end with the end of summer. She would return to school in the fall. Having failed to write the letter, I convinced myself that I could not call, that nothing less than a visit would do. Twice I walked to that ivied wall on the bluff above the Savannah, but I could not climb and jump. The wall had grown too high. As the silence lengthened between us, impossible to cross, I lay on my bed nights wondering how I, or we together, had made something into nothing. It had happened so quickly.

Then one day I saw a flash of shining powder blue metal and a fan of auburn hair, and my heart moved. I hurried along the hot sidewalk. I was close enough to see her face, those brown eyes. I saw them clearly, and they saw me, and clearly, as she turned the corner.

I attended class faithfully as summer became that queer, subtle North Florida fall, and fall became winter, chill and miserable because Florida is not built for cold. I went with the group to Moby's after class and made a place for myself there as a drinker, a ground-stander, and an arm-wrestler of more grip than strength. I learned the don't-fuck-with-me look and walk that Shine and Hubbel had mastered years before. I went to parties at the Thrash Palace, and I made a place for myself there, too, and wondered whether it was one I wanted. My life was a round of writing and work and class and riotous cruel celebration. I celebrated existence which I knew was cruel and riotous and learned what I could of my craft, and in exactly this way the slow wheel of the seasons made one revolution. Spring came again, cool and sappy, and the dogwoods bloomed virgin white, and I knew Ardis would be home again soon, and I hardened my heart to that homecoming.

She had written me during the year. Hers were the letters of a college girl having a good time, meeting interesting people, becoming more sophisticated. They were studies in cool nonchalance. Naturally, I hated them. I lived in a small, dirty, rented room, and a pile of manuscript pages were my only becoming. When I wrote to her, my letters were riotous and cruel, and after a while I did not hear from her anymore. In the spring, when she was expected, I kept a winter heart within me.

Through all this I saw Lindy Briggs. She confided in me and, after a while, I confided in her. We were strongly attracted to each other, but neither of us would break that contract we had made the day she stood bare-breasted in my room. My half of it was the restraint that did not allow her to love me as a surrogate. Hers was the respect she held for that restraint.

Meanwhile, a war was being waged between Lindy Briggs and Missy Sully for the possession of Eldon Odom. I was a soldier in that war. My fascination, my curiosity kept me in conscription. I tried not to be caught between the trenches. Missy Sully had known about Lindy Briggs from a time long before my entrance into things. Eldon Odom had worn Lindy like a bright jewel. They were seen together, the two of them glowing with the conspiracy of mutual possession. And still, Odom kept up the pretense that they were teacher and student, and thus, he needed me. I was Lindy's boyfriend.

In public, Eldon Odom pushed her toward me, spoke of us as lovers, made sly references to my sexual prowess, pimped for me, and Lindy learned her part. She learned to smile at me, to stand by my side, to stroke my forearm in moments of distracted repose, and after a while even Shine and Hubbel, who were Odom's brothers in deception, were confused. We were all devices in Odom's plot.

One day late in spring, Eldon Odom came to my room. He had never crossed my grimy threshold, and I was suitably impressed. He walked to the table where lay my pages, picked one up, read it, and put it back down.

"Toad, you look like shit. We got to get you shaped up, son."

I knew him well enough to know what he meant. The gut that hung from his belt was beginning to smother his vanity, and it was time for him to suffer for it. He wanted company in suffering. Shine and Hubbel, who were already made of stainless steel, would not do. As sculptures in flesh, they were too far ahead of us both.

It was four years since I had swung a bat, run windsprints, and done sit-ups in the outfield grass while a pustle-gutted coach counted cadence over me. I was getting a little soft around the middle. But it was not health that made me agree. I said, "What do I have to do to get myself back in shape, Coach Odom?"

"*Head* Coach Odom." He grinned.

"Head Coach and Athletic Director Odom," I repeated

according to formula.

"Thank you, Assistant Backfield Coach Turlow. Now then, what you got to do is go down to enroll us in Bud's Gym. We gone go down there every day stead of eating lunch and grind that goddamn iron until we turn you back into twisted steel and sex appeal. You understand me?" I had to laugh at the tall, red-faced, gimp-legged man standing in front of me. I said I understood him. I rarely had funds for lunch anyway. I went down and signed us up.

Lifting weights is about as exciting as library research, especially when you are surrounded by subliterates whose idea of delight is to clean and jerk five hundred pounds, then drop it from shoulder height onto a concrete floor. You are in danger of shrapnel wounds. Your ears ring. Conversation is impossible. As the two milkiest guys in Bud's place, Eldon Odom and I were usually ignored. Occasionally one of the beasts would discover that Odom was famous and come over and ask him if he wrote books.

"You rat books?"

"Yup. Do." Odom would say.

"Hum," the lifter would say, or maybe, if he was gifted, "I be dog. I be god dog."

Odom might ask, "You read books?"

"Hail, no. Ain't got time. Got to keep these pecs pumped."

"Right," we'd say, or he would, for I usually kept out of it. I liked it in Bud's Gym. Things were simple there, except when Eldon Odom was talking to me. Then they were wonderful.

Sometimes, as I spotted for him and the iron rose and fell from the bench, or as we sat in the steam room after our workout, swollen and feeling as though the hot air in our lungs were encased in boiler plate, he would tell me things. Sometimes he talked about his North Florida. The population of his memories were the cripples and amputees of a feudal agrarian society.

He was a fugitive from the land of the dismembered, of rickets and ground itch and pellagra, from the world before wonder drugs when infection meant death. Sometimes he talked about the price of fame. The critics gunning for him, the university's demands, and those phone calls late at night from the disguised voice threatening violation. "I know where you live. I know where the boy goes to school," the filtered voice crooned, an echo from a too-familiar dream.

Eldon Odom lay awake nights wondering what slight, what insult real or imagined, had caused the phone calls. Then he lay there knowing the world was such that no cause was needed. The world of his books was the world he lived in. It threatened him, wanted his death and the deaths of his own. So he rose and walked the dark house checking locks.

Once he told me about courting Missy Sully when she was a rich man's daughter and he was a young, unlettered, unpublished Marine Corps veteran living alone with his dream. She had come to him at night in his rented room, a foul place where unwashed laundry lay in piles and candled whiskey bottles lit his manuscript pages. She slept with him there in that sty and shared the dream, and they made the boy Presley within the aura of the dream and the odor of the laundry. And he told me he would always love her for that, his voice full of soft regret, love her for coming to that poor boy who was nobody.

Yes, it was sentimental, excessive. It was not the stern and mournful recollection which is the past in Odom's work, but it moved me and I knew he could not have told it had we not been alone in the heat, suspended from earth, obscured from each other's eyes by white clouds of steam.

I visited Eldon Odom's house frequently, meeting him there for trips to the gym or to do odd jobs for which I was paid more than I was worth. One long night he dictated a screenplay to me, stalking up and down the deck while I typed, my fingers flying, the night insects buzzing us and the whiskey rising and falling in his glass. That night he offered me crystal methedrine and I refused it, but I watched him cut it with a razor blade and arrange it in lines and inhale it through a rolled dollar bill.

Bent over the white powder, his hands trembling, he said, "I'm a wire, did you know that?" I said I did not know it. I spoke casually, but the white powder frightened me. It made him walk faster and speak louder. He tore furiously at the pages of *Naked in Church* as he adapted it for the screen. The only drugs I had ever taken had been given me by trainers and team physicians. I had grown up among people who believed the use of drugs meant instant and complete dissolution. It was breaking bad in the worst way. My sister, whose vices had been alcohol and despair, had been the town's example. If a little whiskey could burn Patricia Turlow, what might the more insidious forms of delight do to a farm kid?

Missy Sully watched us as we worked. All night long she visited the sliding glass door. Her dark nipples came to the surface of the sheer fabric of her nightgown like dark eyes as she lifted her arms to pull aside the drapes. Was she afraid we would speed to nothingness? She did not sleep while her husband was in his crystal meth frenzy. She watched the typewriter as though she knew it was money but hated its constant blather, that lunatic voice she had heard sing until her brain ached.

Once, when I had been typing steadily for an hour and my bladder began to burn, I interrupted the mad flow of words to go to the bathroom. When I emerged, Missy Sully was standing by the bathroom door, a drink in her hand. The light was behind her and her body was dark in the white mist of the gown. She said, "Have some," and I took the glass from her and drank a little bourbon.

"You still a nice boy?" she asked me, inclining her head to the side like a musing cat. "It's been a while."

"I guess so."

Eldon Odom would be coming soon. We could hear his tread on the deck, manic and expectant. He would be coming soon to find me. I made to pass by her in the narrow hall, but she shifted to block me and her breast pressed my shoulder. "Be good," she whispered.

My throat was dry. "I'll try," I said. All I could think was to get away from her, his sleepwalking Lady Macbeth. I stepped back and stood before her again. "Mrs. Odom?"

"Call me Sully, like *he* does." She smiled. As she said, "he," she gestured toward the deck with her drink. A little of it slopped onto the flagstone floor.

I said, "OK, Sully." I knew my voice betrayed fear of her and of the man whose pacing we no longer heard. At the same time, I was angry at myself. So thin was the skin of sophistication I wore. I had played this scene in imagination and much better. I had been the worldly man.

She caught it from me. I could see anger rising in her dark green eyes. She hissed, "You're the boyfriend, are you? Why do you do it?" Her face was old with anger. "You tell Lindy Briggs . . ." She struggled for the right words. She knew it could be a scene from a bad book. "Tell her I said it won't be easy." I was grateful. She had not said, "that little slut," or anything at all about Odom.

I nodded. I said nothing. Not even, "I'll tell her." She let me pass, but only slowly and very close. And as I did, she ran her finger across my cheek where Lindy's boot had marked me.

Seventeen

ELDON ODOM WAS NOT the pinnacle. In the lore, there was someone else. I had come from the pig and pulpwood country by way of the antique shop and cowboy bar, from my diamond dream to the rented room to study with Eldon Odom. Now I learned there was someone else. There was the Old Man.

He was coming, and soon. There would be a competition. In Eldon Odom's class we would all sit as usual, and the Old Man would sit with us in that airless egosphere and listen to someone's story or chapter. I wanted it to be mine.

The Old Man lived in retirement near Vanderbilt where he had been a professor for many years. His books were not retired. They lived in classrooms and libraries. He had founded the writing program in Bainesborough in the late thirties. Eldon Odom was his most famous student, but there was the famous rift. The Old Man was of the patrician Southern tradition. His was a courtly prose that made Eldon Odom scoff. Odom's was the vulgar work that sharecropped in the Old Man's fields, and the two had broken over this. Slowly the wound had healed, but the scar was there. The Old Man was making his yearly visit to greet old friends and to listen to the words of the sons and daughters of the lineage, even though Odom was now their master.

I worked hard at my stories. Sometimes I saw light, heard the voice singing in the tall pines, other times it was dark and not the bottle nor any amount of long walking and long thinking could bring daylight. Finally I put aside "Chatter" and my untitled ode to the convenience store and started something new. It was the story of the short, experimental life of my sister, Patricia Turlow. I wrote about the Price twins, the honky-tonks, and the cowboy bar and the stomping I had taken there, and about that day in Trish's room when I had held her in my arms and said nothing, knowing nothing to say, and of the black face at the door that night, the deputy sheriff immaculate in uniform and bereft of help, and of the solemn drive to the place where the wet black timbers stood as sentinels before the land of the dead. It was called "The Heart in the Fire."

My story ended with that kiss I had seen, as Ardis and I drove away the day of our visit. It was transposed in time and place, but it was that sweet and solemn kiss, a renewing of the promise my parents had always made.

We all submitted our work and after the heat of writing and the euphoria that followed, and the stinking black depression that came after the euphoria and the drunken stupor that was its cure, I knew I had failed. I could not imagine Eldon Odom selecting my work above that of Sarah Fesco or Shine or Hubbel, or even one of the better younger students. Life, I had learned, was not like that. Only dreams were.

The day of the Old Man's visit came round at last. The newspapers had prepared us with learned commentary. The local bookstore was giving an autographing party, and even the English Department had softened its dislike of writers not yet deceased. The Old Man had been asked to read before the entire senior class, but the writing class would be most privileged of all, for we were to have him with us in a small room for an hour.

He was fragile, the word went out, an old man of some seventy-six years, who tired easily. When he tired, the wisdom was, he could be snappish or simply go silent. He liked his whiskey still, they said, though his capacity had diminished. On the day of his arrival, the very air seemed freighted with vibrations of significance.

Lindy Briggs and I sat with the rapt hundreds listening to that sonorous voice. I saw the light glint from the broad forehead, the squint of those exophthalmic eyes, the strong teeth of the famous grin. The Old Man read his great story. "Pillars of Salt" is a tale of lust and vengeance, of a young man's need to own the land in which his ancestors' bones are buried. That need in conflict with the urge to strike out for new places, own new things or nothing at all. It is a story that speaks to me. I had studied it in school (so had every Southern child of my generation), and now hearing it in the Old Man's ringing voice moved me. Lindy Briggs touched my hand from time to time as though to say, It *is* really happening.

When it ended, I hurried with the others to the front of the auditorium. I was compelled forward by love and kinship and probably would have stood rigid and wordless as a tree, had I found myself before the Old Man. But Eldon Odom, who had introduced the Old Man eloquently and with an uncharacteristic self-effacement, spirited him away. The reception would be that night at Odom's house. My engraved invitation was tacked to the beaverboard wall of my room.

I did not own formal clothing, so I went to the local Salvation Army store and purchased for three dollars a used double-breasted blue blazer with real brass buttons, and a blue tie whose white polka dots were understated. At a distance, I looked prosperous. Close up, you could see the gravy stains on my yachtsman's tie and the moth holes in the navy wool. When I had shined my old cordovan oxfords and donned a pair of good gray slacks and a button-down shirt, I was as ready as I ever would be. I fortified the inner man with a long shot of bourbon and, light-headed and hungry in the summer twilight, set out for Lindy's house.

It was a short walk, and by the time I got there, the whiskey was glowing in my blood and the world was a fine and fancy place for a young man to wend his way. (I was an alliterative drinker.)

Lindy was the portrait of debutante chic in light white summer linen, scooped at the neck, and a navy blazer with white piping. She had pinned a magnolia blossom of silk to her lapel. We toasted ourselves from stock whose age was written in years and strode into the gathering dark, a nautical couple.

Walking beside her, I marveled at the athlete's grace loose and shifting in the lines of her clothing. She was Whitman's American Girl. She was Fitzgerald's dark Jordan Baker, and like Jordan, a cheater. There was a honed intensity to all her surface — calves beneath the white hem, wrists, long neck — all bespeaking clarity and discipline. And yet, somehow on her also lay the burden and fatigue of love. I did not let my thoughts wander to the bluffs above the Savannah, where Ardis Baines, a different kind of girl, might also be venturing into the evening.

As we walked down Odom's long drive past the kerosene flares that lit the ivy walls, we heard Leviathan whining from the garage and saw a line of people at the front door. They were deans and department heads, professors and their wives, and at the front was Robert C. Johnson, president of the university and former justice of the state Supreme Court.

We took our place at the end of the line and soon were sandwiched between couples who spoke in hushed, expectant tones, expensive people, older than we and more important.

Just as we were about to enter, Hubbel and Shine swaggered up and pushed in behind us. Hubbel wore a flowered shirt daubed with palm trees and swaying grass-skirted maidens. His large, orange tie was knotted so that its wide end hung at his crotch. He wore jeans and sneakers. Shine wore the usual green fatigues and the usual angry look.

"Coach Hubbel, Coach Shine," I said as we made room for them.

"Assistant Coach Turlow, Missy Briggs," they said.

Hubbel hustled his crotch and picked up the tie and sniffed the end of it. "Butt-rash," he said.

"Yup, butt-rash," said Shine.

The wife of the dean of Arts and Sciences winced, then stared a turd at Hubbel. He hustled his crotch aggressively and stared a turd back until she looked away.

He turned to Shine. "I like a woman that loses her shit easily."

Shine said, "Her shit is weak. Very weak," just as we reached the doorway.

It was an honest-to-God receiving line. I hadn't seen one since the senior prom. Rebecca Sullivan Odom, lovely in a black tulle cocktail dress and black lace shawl, stood beside her husband who inhabited his only suit of clothes, a blue pinstripe. Beside him stood the Old Man, pale, squat, and noble in a white dinner jacket with a pink carnation. I don't know what Lindy had expected, but when she saw Missy Sully, she stopped moving.

I gently put her in front of me and raised a clenched fist to my face and coughed, readying myself to shake the hand that had written "Pillars of Salt." Missy Sully and Lindy Briggs shook hands, and Missy Sully said, "So glad you could come," in a tone that was acid and ice. Eldon Odom pried Lindy's hand away from his wife and passed it to the Old Man, who gave a courtly bow. I took Sully's cold palm. I guess I felt sympathy in that moment, and I said something asinine about still being good. She said, "You don't keep very good company," and reached for Hubbel, who was behind me.

I shook Eldon Odom's hand, and he held mine in his and leaned to the Old Man, who looked up, his face brightening, and said, "Ah-hah, the young blades! Glad to know you, Mr. Turlow. A fine night."

"A fine night, indeed, sir," I said to him, taking his old bird bones in my hand and pressing them like the talisman they were.

I tried to meet his eye, but he was noticing Hubbel's shirt. I passed on into the living room, following Lindy straight to the bar.

A black man in white sleeves, a red vest and an ivory grin was pouring drinks with a jazz drummer's flourish. Already business at the bar was good. I asked him for three fingers of Jack Black and a short one for the lady. He handed them to me with a wink and said, "Be a long night, this one."

I said, "Don't you know it," and raised my glass to him. The whiskey burnt down some of my nerves. I turned to Lindy, who was already handing her empty glass back to the barman. "Times two," she said. He raised his eyebrows and poured her a double. She looked sick under the paint, and her hand shook as she took back her glass. I touched her elbow, "Let's go outside."

We took a corner of the deck and sat on the railing, sipping, staring out at the night woods. "Pretty rough?" I asked after a space.

"Yeah," she said. "On her, too. I feel like a shit."

I started to say something like, "You look like a million bucks," but bagged it. Across from us in the woods, the night world was loudly wondering what was going on. The frogs and the cicadas were discussing us. The kerosene flares lit the trees a lurid orange, and the music rolled and reverberated down the ravine toward the Baines Creosote Works. "She sure as shit hates me." Lindy said, taking a big drink.

It was then I told her what Missy Sully had said to me the night I had typed the screenplay.

"Nice of you to let me know *now*."

"You would have come anyway." I was going to tell her I hadn't been punching a clock as anybody's messenger boy but thought better of that, too. In fact, I had been the go-between, the fifth business, that most needed and least appreciated of dramatic devices. I was not proud of myself.

After we had sat on the railing for a quarter of an hour drinking Lindy's courage back into place, we wandered inside again, into a room suddenly crowded with overdressed, under-intoxicated English professors making one another uneasy. I looked for Hubbel and Shine but didn't see them. We circled the fringes and ended up back at the bar. Lindy excused herself to the powder room. It was only nine o'clock.

I hadn't promised myself anything, but I was excited. I hoped to stand next to the Old Man and listen to what he said. I had even imagined myself talking to him. But the Feds and their footnoting acolytes had him trapped and were firing notes and queries at him, and there was little chance of getting close. I drifted back out to the deck, figuring Lindy could find me if she wanted to. I stood there drinking and letting absolutely nothing, its cousins, heirs, and assigns, float through my head. Then I heard a muffled, suppressed cough, a familiar sound, and looked down to my left. A match flared briefly in the darkness against a background of palm trees and grass-skirted maidens. A cloud of smoke that smelled like burning autumn leaves drifted out toward the creek.

The way down under the deck was by a steeply angled cypress ladder. I started down the steps, knowing what I would find.

Hubbel and Shine and Sarah Fesco were passing a joint and looking at the boards above with serious speculating faces. "That one," Shine was saying, "right there. The one by the post."

Sarah Fesco shook her head, "No, my young friend," she said, "I don't think so." Her tone was superior, aloof, stagy.

I took the joint from Tory Hubbel, who was wheezing a monstrous toke, and asked. "What?"

"Sure enough ain't," Shine said.

"You'll have to prove it to me, boyo," Sarah said; her accent was a little Irish, in honor of the Old Man's ancestry.

"Come on then," Shine said, walking off.

"What?" I asked, following them. The deck was about thirty feet by fifteen. We walked to the corner and stared up between the boards. A woman stood above us in the tent of a long skirt. It was difficult to see in the darkness.

"Look," whispered Shine, "just look."

Sarah looked up. We all did. Nothing. Finally Hubbel blew a huge plume of smoke into our faces and said, "Goddamn it, get out of the way. Let me." He took out a book of matches and lit them all and raised them like a torchbearer. We all looked up. Then we were laughing. Shine said, "I told you so. Didn't I tell you? Hot damn!" The dean's wife wasn't wearing any underpants.

We moved back to the black darkness in the lee of the house. After a space, Hubbel said, "Pretty good pelt, all in all."

"Nice bush," said Shine.

"Burning bush, almost," Hubbel said.

Sarah Fesco pulled up proper. "You all are such adolescents, I swear."

"I didn't notice you hanging back, Sarah. You was right underneath."

Sarah said, "Oh, piss off."

Shine turned to Hubbel. "Let's turn it upside down and see what color it is." Hubbel caught Sarah before the words were out of Shine's mouth. I stood wondering what to do. I didn't think they really would, then I thought better. They had cancelled all rules. Everything was permitted.

Hubbel handed Sarah to Shine, who held her shoulders while Hubbel bent to her ankles. She struggled silently, kicking, breathing hard. They laid her out flat, then upended her, and Shine rubbed her skirts down. Hubbel stood, muscles bulging, his arms above his head. Sarah Fesco's head hung between his knees. "Look at these, Toad," Shine said to me. "Ain't that something?" There were little drawstrings on her underpants.

I said, "Mike, you don't want to do that."

"Hell I don't. Don't I, Tory, old buddy?"

"You better do something quick," Hubbel said. "This thing is heavier than it looks."

I said, "Come on, Mike, don't. She's had enough." Sarah hung down silent, too tired to kick anymore. I wondered what her face looked like. I knew they were going to do it, and I knew I wasn't going to the wall for Sarah Fesco.

With a gentleness I had not thought him capable of, Shine undid the drawstrings and drew up Sarah's underwear. His claw hand was precise in its work. Hubbel was breathing hard, his arms beginning to shake. "What color of a prune is it?" he asked. "I can't see nothing back here."

"Just a minute," Shine said, lighting a match.

In the bright burst of light, Sarah's pudendum seemed to flinch. It was decorous, thinly haired and quaintly sweet like the clothing and accents she affected. "It's brown," Shine said, his voice full of regret." "Brown 'uns is common as dirt."

"I had my hopes," Hubbel sighed.

I said, "Mike, let me help you," and lifted her head. We set her on her feet and she stumbled away a few feet. She stopped and drew her underpants up, and we heard her furious fingers at the ties.

Shine said, "Sarah, we like it all right. It's a vertical smile, and I ain't never seen a bad one, but brown is just common as dirt."

Hubbel was shaking his arms at his sides in the manner of a swimmer standing on a platform before a race. He drew a deep breath and sighed. The flesh on his arms rippled in the moonlight that filtered down through the deck. "Next time, Shine, you hold and I look at the furburger."

"Sure," said Shine. "Fair's fair."

"Toad," Hubbel turned to me, "what do you think?"

I watched Sarah, who had said nothing. I was surprised. Often the reaction was humor. People laughed when they were violated by Hubbel and Shine. Later they got angry. I said, "I think you just lost a friend."

"Sarah?" Hubbel said, his eyes large in surprise. "Oh, she'll be back. Don't underestimate Sarah. She's with it and for it. She's for the group."

"Right," Shine affirmed.

As I left them, giving Sarah time to go ahead of me, I heard them mumbling about how common it was to have a brown beard on your clam, common as dirt. When I reached the glass doors, the bright light and loud music, Sarah was gone.

I surveyed the room and decided on the bar and another light bourbon. Then I noticed Missy Sully. She was walking fast with a drink in her hand and spilling some. She walked in a stright line and with a hard determination in her face. I

looked for her destination and spotted Lindy Briggs sitting on
the stone hearth under the big metal hood of the fireplace. She
was talking to Frank. His flat, earnest face was inclined
toward hers, narrow and tense and beautiful. I started walking
fast, knowing I would not get there in time.

Missy Sully went straight to the hearth and tipped a tall gin
and tonic into Lindy's face. I stopped where I was. No one
could enter the circle of that hate. Missy Sully stood erect,
and said, "Oh, I'm so sorry. Let me help you." She spoke
loudly, putting spaces between the words. Quiet spread
across the room. The last few voices from the party sounded
impossibly loud, then their owners ducked in embarrassment
and followed sightlines to the hearth. Lindy sat cold and rigid
and silent, staring into Sully's eyes. Sully leaned down and
with the black lace shawl began mopping at Lindy's breast.
Her strokes were rough, almost blows, and Lindy stood them
as long as she could. Finally she wrenched the black cloth
from Sully's hand and stood up. "*Thank* you," she said. She
walked toward the bathroom, changed her mind and turned
toward the front door.

As she passed the hallway that led to the bathroom, Eldon
Odom emerged from it. His eyes were alight, his nose was
red, and he held a handkerchief in his right hand. I knew he
had been back there with his vial and mirror and razor blade
and a rolled dollar bill. He took in the scene, and as Lindy
rushed past, he fell into step behind her. In some ways, he
revealed more than Missy Sully had just revealed. The crowd
watched the two of them go out, and I heard the Old Man's
voice, droll but with iron in it: "Great goodness me." And
then the whole room watched me leave too, because I was
Lindy's date.

In the driveway, under those warm stars, Lindy Briggs and
Eldon Odom were wrapped in an embrace. When they parted

from it, Lindy's eyes caught mine and I knew the date was over. I went back to the house. I would have walked on home, but they were in front of me, their love impassable.

Eighteen

AS A COURTESY to Eldon Odom, I did not enter through the front door. I walked around to the back of the house and stood by the deck, watching the woods and the stars for a space. Our audience would think the three of us were still together, at least for a time, and maybe it would save a shred of someone's reputation. That was my old Alligood County way of thinking. I heard Eldon Odom's car start from the front of the house. Leviathan whined from the garage as the engine labored up the drive. The roar of voices above me increased and the music rolled over the trees and the water and was transformed into something strange and sinuous. After about twenty minutes, I walked up the steps to the deck and into the light.

The bar seemed the best place for an unattended gentleman to anchor himself. With one foot on the brass rail and an elbow in a pool of beer, I was rooted and able to deflect the occasional inquiring glance. From here and there, eyes cut to me and then flickered away, and I imagined what they wanted to know: Which side of the triangle was I, or was it a square?

As it turned out, the bartender was from Lake City. His daddy had owned a cane press and had bottled his own syrup. A vague recollection was rolling in my head of driving past the place and stopping to watch the mule pull the press in its eternal circle. The Negro flourished drinks like drumsticks and told me the mule's name: Franklin Delano. We agreed that you just about couldn't find a mule in Alligood County anymore, and that it was a pretty sorry state of affairs, all in all. When I began to wonder if the bartender had been drinking, I knew it was time for me to slow down.

After a space, the party began to thin. Those of us who stayed knew the real celebration might last all night long. There were all sorts of proper good-byes, and Missy Sully was back at her best, pressing the flesh and even hugging and kissing a little in the pristine, giddy way of the Southern hostess. She had managed to process three deans, two department heads, and a vice-president for development before Eldon Odom came back. By my watch, he had been gone forty minutes, long enough to take Lindy home and get back and then some.

Eldon Odom came in though the kitchen and glanced at Sully. He knew where his duty lay. On his way to do it, he stopped at the bar and smiled hugely at me. We stood there in the beams of all those eyes, acting out our scene.

"She wasn't feeling too good, Toad, so I run her on home. Hope you don't mind."

"No, hell," I said, standing in front of him, grinning like a dog passing peach pits. "I don't mind."

Odom was at the front door with Sully getting rid of official guests when Ardis came through the kitchen door on the arm of Tommy MacEvoy.

MacEvoy was the kind of grit who had always made me uneasy, the kind you see in bars and roadhouses drunk and wobbling, or dancing with himself, stuffed into jeans as tight as any my sister ever wore, and always leering. He saw the world through an ogler's eye. I didn't like it that he had come into the group without ever writing anything, or even showing much interest in writing. For whatever you thought of Hubbel and Shine, they were serious. In their ways and to the degree they were capable of, they loved words, heard the voices, wooed language. MacEvoy was among us because he could supply drugs and because of his Viet Nam connection to Shine. As I stood there, a little unsteady from the whiskey, watching Ardis come smiling toward me with her fingers tangled in MacEvoy's, I asked myself who I was kidding. I didn't like him because he was with Ardis.

As he walked across the floor, taking for granted what I had taken for granted the summer before, I endured an instant when violence seemed inevitable. It came and went and left only white knuckles wrapped around an empty glass. I put the glass on the bar, the drummer filled it for me, and I heard him say, "Take it easy, home boy. Remember that long night."

I lifted the bourbon and turned to Ardis and said, "You look very nice." I don't know what was in my voice or in my face. Probably it was some mixture of sad delight and drunken anger, and any number of the thinnest pretexts for self-pity you can imagine. Ardis, on the other hand, seemed completely at her ease.

"Thank you," she said, turning in a graceful circle. "I just got this at McDougald's. It cost too much, but I said, Ardis, treat yourself nice." She looked up at me, waiting for my response. Her eyes were lit and her hair was auburn with its own lights. I shook my head and smiled. I said, "Treat yourself nice, Ardis.

Do that."

"Somebody's got to," she said.

Tommy MacEvoy had negotiated a glass of white wine for Ardis and a bourbon for himself. He turned to us and held the wine glass in front of Ardis, his eyes covering the party.

"Anything doing?" he asked.

I remembered the dean's wife in her tent, and Sarah Fesco's flinching private parts, and the sparkling cataract of gin and tonic at Lindy Briggs's beautiful neck, and said, "Naw, pretty dull so far. When all the suits leave the real party's gonna start." I was well withdrawn into the armor I had learned from Hubbel and Shine. Ardis looked at the glass in my hand. "You going to do the *real* party from a prone position?"

MacEvoy laughed. I turned to him and we regarded each other for the first time. He had the look of a crow. A long, hooked nose with a translucent hood of skin stretched over a prominent crown of bone. His brow was overshot and his eyebows were dark, and above was a shock of black hair. He had fine bone-white teeth, and when he grinned, his head thrown back a little, the light glinted from his teeth and those dark eyes. His was the face of a country man and lounge lizard — somehow both at once — and it bespoke the long road with the tobacco allotment at one end and a bottle at the other. I hated him, and I saw his eyes search some essential thing in mine. It was my hatred they found, and he calmly gave back his own with a leer.

I turned to Ardis and said, "You take care now," and nodded in the direction of MacEvoy, who laughed again.

Ardis did not laugh. Whatever piece of regard she still owned for me kept her from it. She followed me a few steps and took my arm. "He's all right now, Toad." She smiled up at me.

"You cured him, did you? You and the halfway house?"

Her face set hard, and the smile slowly gave way to that stubborn Baptist certainty. "I did not cure him, no. But I have tried to understand him a little bit, and it's more than I could ever do with you. He's not as bad as you seem to think."

She waited for something I could not give. I think she half-wanted me to prove to her he was rotten, but I wasn't going to tell her he was a gang-banger and a thief who stole drugs from the halfway house for Odom and Hubbel and Shine, and for me if I wanted them. I wasn't going to tell her that. And she took my silence for her proof, and I saw the glint of victory in those Baptist eyes. I said, "I sure-god hope you know what you're doing." I lifted her hand gently from my arm and left it in the air between us.

I went back to the bathroom and did what characters in novels are never supposed to do. As I stood in the transport of a good urination, it occurred to me that I had almost asked Ardis if Tommy MacEvoy knew the way over her wall. I closed my eyes and envisioned my own midnight journeys to Ardis's door, and I was glad that I had possessed the restraint to stop short of that question.

As I was coming back down the hall toward the party, which was beginning to sound less like an undifferentiated roar and more like an argument, I heard Eldon Odom's voice: "I never read her. She's about as much use as tits on a man." And then the Old Man's droll, scolding tone: "You'd have done well to read her a long time ago, Eldon." I had never heard anyone speak to Eldon Odom in that tone, using his first name to his face. I was hurrying toward their voices when another sound stopped me. It was a long, aspirated sigh. I paused in a doorway and was instantly sorry, for it was Missy Sully who said, "Come in, Toad."

She was sitting at a little vanity, watching herself in a gilt mirror. The room behind her was ordered, but the bed held her imprint. She had put on fresh lipstick. She was prepping for the second round, I supposed. The lace shawl lay in a sodden heap on the vanity in front of her, and her right hand rested on it. As I came into the room, she picked up a gold chain with a locket depending from it and held both halves of the clasp at her shoulders. I stood behind her and took the clasps and fastened them as best I could with my clumsy fingers. I remembered how quick and sure Shine's fingers had been with the tiny drawstrings of Sarah Fesco's antique drawers, and then, for some reason, I remembered my sister's charred heart.

"Thank you," Missy Sully said quietly, keeping her eyes on her own reflection in the mirror. I nodded, "Sure." I moved toward the door, but she said, "Wait," and I knew what she was going to do. She rose with another tired sigh and came to me. She took the lapels of my three-dollar yachtman's jacket. "Know what I want to do?"

I thought: *If you've got sense, you want to get back to the light.* I leaned toward the door. "It sounds like it's getting . . ." With a strong grip, she shook me a little. "No," I said too loudly.

My face must have been crimson. The bourbon singing in my blood was loud, too. She said, "I want to keep you right here. I don't want to go back there, and you don't either." She held my lapels and looked into my eyes, and something happened to me then. I realized that a woman almost old enough to be my mother was a woman nevertheless. She pulled me down to her, using that strong grip, and kissed me. My mouth was slack, and when she felt this, she took my right hand and pressed it to her bosom. My mouth became just as demanding as hers. When we finished, both breathless, I heard Eldon Odom shout from the party, just a noise across the noise in my blood, and it brought me back a little. She let go of me and walked toward the bed. She stood by it as though to say, Here it is. I shook my head slowly but my heart was not in it, and somehow a promise came into my eyes.

I stood in the dark hallway, straightening myself, knowing the disorder was on the inside. While the swelling below my belt abated, I considered the symmetry of events. Eldon Odom had taken Lindy home, and I had kissed his wife in their bedroom. He had pushed me toward Lindy, and now I was being pulled by Sully's strong white hands. My geometry got skewed somewhat when I began to think of Ardis, out there with Tommy MacEvoy, doing what came naturally to her — good works.

Nineteen

AFTER THE FEDS went home, the writers came to the light. One late-comer was a New York editor, Merit Norman. He was very young to figure in so many of Eldon Odom's stories and to wield so much power. His was power over the lives of writers, and it made me a little milky to notice the bald spot in the middle of his curly head and the button missing from the sleeve of his blue blazer, signs of human frailty. He looked tired from the long flight, but his eyes were quick to spot Odom and next to find the Old Man, and he walked straight from the door into the heart of the circle as though it were the most natural thing in the world to fly two thousand miles for a party.

Sitting in the steam room after our workouts, I had heard Eldon Odom's tales about Merit Norman. Odom called him a smart Jew up from the garment district. I knew what smart was, or so I thought. It wasn't wise. I had no idea what a Jew was, or what it meant to be up from the garment district. Odom had said

these things with tough affection. He had told me stories about
his trips to New York and their meetings, of how little Norman
knew of the voices and habits of country people, things Odom
and I wore with our skins. And there was the great city of which
Odom had little knowledge. He spoke fondly of Norman's
advices about neighborhoods and restaurants, of their sallies
into Little Italy and Chinatown, of the entertainments, licit and
otherwise, of the Big Apple. I sat there in the steam listening as
the words unreeled, counting myself among the lucky of the
earth and Merit Norman among the chosen.

Norman greeted Odom with a bear hug. His coming seemed
to us a large and generous gesture, even when we saw that he
had come to do business. He was trying to promote a collected
edition of the Old Man's works, and the way he went about it
was masterful. After Eldon Odom had introduced them, noble
in his humility, calling the Old Man his mentor, the editor spoke
of their two bodies of work. Then the Old Man talked, Odom
deferred, and the young editor listened, and just when the Old
Man was warming to exegesis in his grandiloquent style, Norman abruptly said, "It's just too bad these students (he swept
quick, fervid hands at us) can't get your books anymore."

The Old Man halted mid-sentence, perplexed, his eyes a
cloudy blue, his hands agitating the drink they held. "But
surely, sir . . ."

"But, no," Norman insisted. "I'm up there. I know what's
available. Those . . . those guys at Corwin and Sons aren't
pushing you like they should. New York is half the market, and
you're not *on* the market in New York. See what I mean?"

We were all quiet. The Old Man's eyes narrowed to a dark
geezer's squint. Gentility, which forbade talk of business, was at
war with enlightened self-interest. He sipped his drink. Eldon
Odom looked on, smiling weary admiration for Norman. He
shook his head as though to say, You bastard, you're doing it

again. The Old Man sipped bourbon and we saw what concentration it took to lift the glass to his lips. "What do you propose, *Mr.* Norman?" His old voice underscored the "mister," issuing a warning. He would brook nothing crass here among the literary lights, under this poetical moon. Norman knew what to say. "Later on, when we can get by ourselves, I'll tell you what I propose. It's a big project and a little dangerous for both of us, but we both stand to gain a lot. What do you say?"

"We will talk," the Old Man said, and then he turned to us all and winked, and we saw his horse trader's gleaming eye and knew it was the match for New York, and we felt included. Beside me, Hubbel dug an elbow into Shine's ribs and the two of them nodded to each other as though to say, "See, see. There *is* control." Sarah Fesco had returned, unable to stay away from the light of the Old Man's eyes, and I stood with her and Hubbel and Shine and Frank. The group pressed against the three big prey and divided them, and before an hour had passed, each celebrity was the nucleus of his own cell, and each dispensed wisdom or glory or smart. I stood on the fringes of the group that had captured Merit Norman, listening to him tell young writers what New York would buy. I heard him say, "You gotta harelip'em. You know, harelip'em a little," and then grin in an irrepressible street kid's way. I circled around to the Old Man. I understood him by simply looking up. He was from just above the place where I had been born.

The group that surrounded him was the smallest of the three. Near me, Ardis stood with Tommy MacEvoy. She was rapt. The Old Man's courtly manner, his grandfather's wit with a dash of the most gentlemanly lechery, even his Mark Twain linen coat must have seemed to her precisely right for an inhabitant of textbooks. MacEvoy, his hand on the small of her back, looked on with unconcealed boredom. Ardis did not acknowledge the touch of his hand, just stared at the Old Man's mesmerizing eyes and upsweeping Elizabethan gestures and that old-leather face with its repertoire of winks and nods and sighs and wry grins. Was this what Ardis had wanted to see when she looked at me?

In my mirror, I had wanted to see Eldon Odom. Once Ardis had told me Odom was no different from any of the grits who passed through her daddy's creosote works — drinking too much, punching in late and out early, wrecking his trucks, and maiming one another in the bargain. Ardis knew from grits. Her halfway house clientele was a legion of bent grits, all drunk and maimed and unproductive. But Ardis *recognized* the Old Man in some deep sororal way. They were of the same stuff, and it was good old tough stuff, and she could see it as clearly as she could see good works.

The Old Man was talking about his family. Modestly, he told us that he was the least of its storytellers, just the strange boy who cared to write things down. The others were all busy *making* stories, living plots and generally plowing a furrow though the human dialectic. He made them epic, brother, uncle and son.

"We are the sad ones, my young friends," he said. "The pen may be mightier than the sword . . ." He lifted his hand and gripped the air between us, his fist an oaken club which sprouted fingers. There was a puff of inky smoke in the air before us. ". . . mightier perhaps, but the heft of it, the feel of it, the way it stirs the blood. Nothing like the sword, and we know it, don't we?" His eyes searched the crowd. They found mine. "Don't we?" I nodded, for it was true. His eyes swept on. "We are a sorry lot of watchers," he concluded, "and I love us every one." He raised his glass to us.

I thought Ardis would faint dead away from the sheer sacramental power of that hand in her face, but she was not mine to worry about anymore. We had turned ourselves into nothing months before.

We would have kept the Old Man until the sun rose had he let us, but he was tiring. Now and then he cut his eyes to the group where Eldon Odom shouted and gesticulated in the usual fashion. He seemed to wish for rescue. At last, Missy Sully came from the house, walking straight and erect and with a purpose we understood. The moment we saw her, our groans rose. The Old Man was pleased to hear our regret. We stood on the deck watching his bedroom light come on. The place where he had stood against the railing was empty and begging. No one stepped there. We were a priestless tribe. I looked at the drink in my hand, hefted it and considered the day's writing ahead. It was what the Old Man meant to us. We wrote for him.

Twenty

I THOUGHT OF THE Old Man often during the hours that interceded until we saw him again in Eldon Odom's Tuesday night class. I knew he was in repose there on the cypress deck by the lake under the administering hands of Missy Sully. I imagined him there in a clear and pure summer sunlight, always in the white linen suit, and holding a glass of some clear medicinal liquid. It was a picture from the corridors of my dream museum. The Old Man in repose, in restraint learned from the long years of struggle with demons. The Old Man in serenity and certainty of accomplishment, of having outlived the besetting furies, the bastards and the smarts. I needed him more than I had ever known, and if I needed him more, I needed Eldon Odom less.

On Tuesday night the group assembled in a crystal quiet so fragile that its breaking would alter all our histories. I looked around me at the faces. They were Hubbel and Shine and Sarah Fesco and Frank Lagano, and they all hoped hard and tried not to show it. And I knew what they saw written on my face. Merit Norman had come, too. Dressed like a college boy, he sat smoking in the furthest corner, an expression of tempered interest on his face.

It was my story that Eldon Odom withdrew from his bag of manuscripts. His red-leather face was careful, alert to our misery, even compassionate for once. I wondered, as the significance of what was happening came to me, whether he had once sat where I was sitting, had been chosen by the Old Man. Or was he doing something for me which had not been done for him?

Mine was the story of my sister Patricia and that sad black face at the door, and of that long night ride with my parents to the place where the only thing left was to identify. In the end, for the boy in the story, identification is more than a hateful formality. It is acknowledgement and claiming. As he lifts the soaked and smeared sheet to see the heart-shaped locket, the heart in the fire, he is taking his sister to his heart again as once he did in an embrace, tender and embarrassed, by the vanity in her bedroom. She and he are of one lineage, the same blood though always separated now, and he knows it.

I sat in the armature of an unaccustomed calm and watched the Old Man as the words began to rumble out, my words. He sat through it all with his chin lifted, balancing some priceless object on the bridge of his parchment nose. His eyes were closed and at times I could not distinguish deepest concentration from sleep. Two or three times, he seemed to awaken and nod, whether in approval or surprise I could not tell. As I watched him, only half-listening to what I knew by heart already, I marveled at the delicacy of his frame and face, at their honed fineness; he was like an old blade, hollow-ground and tempered to fine cutting.

When Eldon Odom finished, Hubbel and Shine and Sarah Fesco were silent. I watched them, thinking of the Old Man's words from the night of the party, "I love us every one." The silence gathered mass until I thought not even the Old Man could move it. At last Eldon Odom said, "Well, now." The way he said it told me that my words and the voice had become one. I waited in their silent awe, suddenly wanting to show them all the flaws I knew by heart, all the struts and the hastily puttied places and the slick spots where a hard mind dare not stop. I was the happy fraud whose words had struck this room dumb.

Odom stared around, his eyes tracking each face, seizing each for a moment, each except mine and the Old Man's and Merit Norman's. Norman sat in deep thought, his fist pressed to his chin. The Old Man still stared upward. When Odom's eyes had made the whole circle and met only silence, they came to Lindy Briggs. There they paused, but briefly, for she never spoke in class. Odom turned to place us in the hands of the Old Man when, unaware of herself, Lindy said, "It's beautiful!"

The Old Man's chin snapped down, and we all watched the priceless thing fall and shatter. "It *is,*" he said, and he reached out to touch Lindy's shoulder. It was a petting and a reigning in. "It truly is, but it is other things as well, and some of them we need to talk about."

Eldon Odom recovered himself and became once again the impresario. And I knew, as the talk began and the simplicity of what Lindy had said began to sink beneath the surface of reasonableness, that I had done something I might never be good enough or lucky enough to do again. I had moved a simple heart.

"Toad, get over here. I got a job for you."

Eldon Odom's voice on the phone was a mock growl, and I knew from tradition what the job was. The student whose story had been read always drove the Old Man to the airport.

These were not always glad occasions. There were tales of solemn rides in the dead of winter when the student driver could recall only the smarting things that had been said in class and was only too glad to see the back of the Old Man in the doorway of the Jacksonville-bound 727.

It was, I knew, the Old Man's part to ride in silence until I spoke, and if I found that temerity, then he might give me some last word. Might. The stories ran both ways. I had stood in the kitchen of the Thrash Palace drinking and listening many nights to Hubbel and Shine, who were stewards of the lore; they told of graveside silences lasting thirty miles and even unto the departure gate, finally broken by the dropping of some unimaginable pearl from the Old Man's lips, a key to many doors. Or there were pilgrimages which came to nothing more than good company. And there were the few during which the silence was never broken at all. But always, I knew, it was the apprentice's place to begin.

We loaded the Old Man's luggage, Eldon Odom and I, while Missy Sully stood at the doorway letting her fingers play in the ruff at Leviathan's neck. She watched us, seeming neither happy nor unhappy. It was a brilliant summer sunrise of bird song and cool breezes in the tall pines. The Old Man's traveling outfit was a pair of wool trousers and a plaid preppie sport coat. He stood in unseasonable clothes, in the winter of his life, cool and immaculate, watching Eldon Odom and me in shirt sleeves sweating his baggage into Odom's Mustang. When we finished, I stood back in deference to their good-bye.

The Old Man kissed Missy Sully lightly on the cheek and

said, "Thank you, child. You are a nurturing angel." Sully did a shuffle that might have been a contracted curtsy. The Old Man turned to Eldon Odom, and the old rivalry came alive in the grip they joined. The Old Man said, "Eldon, you need to slow down." I winced at this intimacy and backed another few steps. "You're going too fast and it shows in your work, as well as in your . . ." His voice dropped an octave. ". . . domestic affairs."

Eldon Odom let go the Old Man's hand and in a cold tone said, "I appreciate the concern." That was all. The Old Man cast a backward glance and a smile at Missy Sully and walked to the car, motioning me toward the driver's seat. I muttered, "Yes, sir," wanting to get my voice in order.

The driving was easy — all good county secondary roads, then a short stretch on US 441 just before the airport. I had resolved to be cheery, like any good ferryman. I was damned if I would ride thirty miles in brooding silence, waiting for the perfect configuration of highway and horizon before making my one gesture at destiny.

We turned north, through the university's agricultural station where the county hardroad crossed rich pasture land. We passed a small herd of sleek black-and-white Jerseys. The animals stood at corn feeders, and in the cool morning air their combined exhalations made a tall column of steam. A few of them bolted as we passed. "Nice-looking stock," I said. "I guess the university can afford cornfed beef." I looked over at the Old Man and smiled, as though these elliptical ruminations on feed costs since the Russian grain deal were plausible fare for a drive in the country. I couldn't tell whether he nodded; if he did, it was subtle. I said, "Back home, the best we do is plant a couple of eighties in rye in the wintertime and rotate the herd. In the summer they just go grass belly." I looked over. Cold stone. I looked again. Granite. The Old Man's head lolled a bit with the motion of the car. Were his eyes actually closed? I felt my resolve softening.

Five minutes later I was staring up the long stretch of back road, thinking: This is it, the long way I have chosen for myself, lonely and desolate. If I have companions, at the very best they are sleeping. We plunged ahead in silence, through the pine canyons of an old New Deal tree farm. The trees rushed at us in green ranks, a uniformity of vegetable life, grudging open, crowding against us, closing behind us.

"You have to do more with the mother."

The Old Man's posture and the way he rode in the seat beside me were the same. His words, though his body contradicted them, were fervent. His hooded eyes blinked and he said, "She is the key. You haven't got her up and walking yet. That man does not allow his daughter such freedom unless his wife took those same freedoms as a girl. Don't you see? That man's daughter is his wife in every but one essential way, and despite himself he raises her up in the image of the woman he married."

I nodded, wishing I could stop the car and turn to him, protest, agree. Wishing I could write this down.

I said, "But I don't see where there's room for more about the mother."

"That's because you think your words are chiseled in granite. They are not. You are too young for that, and always will be, and your story has not been worried and haggled enough for that. Ransom once told me he judged a writer by his capacity to revise. The more I see of writers and writing, the more I know we are all, God help us, so judged."

We swept on in that thundering canyon of pines, and after a space I stole a glance at him, and he was the same as before when I had thought myself completely abandoned. We broke from the trees into a rush of silence, and in the rearview mirror I watched the aperture in the woods, the long way, close behind us.

The Jacksonville shuttle was late. I stood beside the Old Man, his leather satchel resting by my leg, staring with him off across the tarmac into pine barrens and the azure summer sky. He was wrapped in his plaid prep school get-up and in silence impenetrable. He was about to go, taking with him that glowing rind of the eternal he had brought to our little sump of time. He had conferred upon me the campaign ribbon of the lowest order of the legion of art, and now, tired, constricted, another weary traveler, he was going. I wanted to reach across the few feet that separated us and touch him, to seize a piece of history, a scrap of his gift. I wanted to take it home with me to the shadowed room where the dream was poised between rot and fecundity. But we only waited, gazing at the empty heavens, and I knew I had already been given more than many in the lore received.

Someone pointed to a smoky dot on the western horizon, then we saw a silver flash circling westward. The gate was opened and we began the fifty-yard walk across the tarmac. Halfway, the Old Man turned to me and smiled. It was the smile of that night when he had held us all in his hand and spoken of the pen and the sword. "I hope they've got whiskey on this ride. I'm a bit of a white-knuckle flyer, I'm afraid." I nodded and smiled. He was scared.

At the foot of the metal stairway, he took his bag from me. We stepped out of line while businessmen and vacationers pushed past us, and the Old Man offered me his hand. "Take care of Eldon Odom, son. He needs you." He turned to go, then turned back. "If you do some more work on that story, send it up to me for the magazine."

A week later he was dead.

After a decent space, I sent the revised story. It was as good as I could make it using the Old Man's advice. I received a polite note. The magazine wished to honor its late editor's commitments, but it must also look to the establishment of a new editorial voice. All commitments could not possibly be kept.

Part IV

Twenty-One

THAT MORNING, as I returned Odom's car, I was still with the Old Man. I was conjuring the *Nashville Review,* the literary quarterly he had edited for some forty years, seeing myself in print for the first time. I stood at Eldon Odom's front door for some time before I noticed that I was not being met. I went to the back yard jingling the car keys and whistling to give warning. It was a country habit; you didn't walk up on people in Alligood County. The distances there were far and the silences deep. You were liable to come upon a woman singing hymns or a shy man in lively conversation with himself.

I began climbing the deck, still pondering the Old Man, the magazine, and the lore. As far as I knew, no student before me had ever been asked to send work to the *Review.*

Missy Sully was standing on the deck in her karate GI. As I came toward her, smiling abstractedly, she executed that brisk kick, the one she had aimed at my face the day I had met her.

With a reflex, I snatched her foot from the air and held it, making her hop. Then, in the pride of my quickness, I raised the foot and dumped her. She lay sprawled, breathing hard. Her face was the high color of exertion and hurt pride. She was angry. With time to think about it, I was angry at myself. She would have hurt me only by accident; why had I shown her the uselessness of the weapon she had learned?

She got up and walked to a canvas chaise, picked up a towel and turned back, mopping her face. "Did you get the old bastard on the airplane?"

"Sure," I said, and she smiled. "Child," she muttered. "The rest of you can be his children if you want to, but I'm damned if I will." I held the keys out to her, but she threw the towel to me and walked into the house. She used a precise and pretty gait, slightly pigeon-toed, crossing with each step like a model. I thought of Lindy's walk, the toed-out, sweeping walk of a dancer. Leviathan was waiting at the glass door. As I followed his mistress into the house, he speared me with a blunt snout and drew my scent.

Inside the gloomy living room, I watched Missy Sully disappear down the hall that led to the private parts of the house. I was about to put the keys on the hearth and go out by the way I had come when she called to me, "Toad!" in a small voice that barely carried to the spot where I was standing.

She was sitting at the little vanity again, still in the white karate GI, damp hair lank at her neck, and her head bowed as though in meditation.

"Do you have a middle name?" she asked from under the fan of that black hair. I stood in the doorway, trembling a little and trying to control it. I had one, but it was as unlikely as my other two names. It was the family name of my maternal grandmother: Jedeco. I said, "Yes, but you don't want to know it."

"Yes, I do. I won't call you Toad anymore. And I don't want

you to call me Sully or Missy Sully like he does."

Eldon Odom had been mentioned. Relieved, I said, "Where is *he?*"

"Gone," she said. "For good this time." Still she looked into the mirror. "Left right after you did. He's probably off with her."

It was Lindy's day off from the dance studio, and Eldon Odom never went to faculty meetings; the prospect was good that she was right.

"What's your middle name? Please tell me." I was still in the doorway and still trembling and damning myself for it, yet in a strange way unsurprised. In order to surprise myself, I tried to hand her the keys.

"Keep them." She looked at me, then hard at the room behind us. She had turned down the comforter on the bed. The sheets were white and lace-trimmed, and I could see Eldon Odom's red-Indian skin against the white.

"Not here," I said.

"When I was a little girl, they called me Reeba, short for Rebecca. Can you say that . . . Reeba?"

"Reeba," I whispered, thinking she would never be a little girl again.

She stood, "Where then?"

I wanted to say I didn't know, I wanted to tell her it was her house, but it was Eldon Odom's house, too, and I was not going to lie in his bed. I felt the doorway, the room, the house closing around us like one of Eldon Odom's lesser works. She came to me in the doorway and took my face in both hands tenderly and kissed my lips. She whispered, "I don't want to hurt you." It was the same thing she had said to me that night at the Thrash Palace, sitting by me on the screened porch, knowing what her husband was going to do upstairs.

We stood very close while she kissed my lips and whispered

to me, but I gave nothing back. Finally she stopped and looked at me; something broke free inside. I accused myself of the hypocrisy that withheld half of our embrace. I kissed her hard. We struggled in the doorway for a moment, deep in each other until she broke from me and took me by the hand and led me to a small room with a daybed and a desk and framed copies of Eldon Odom's book jackets on the walls. Yes, I thought, this is it. Eldon Odom's study.

There were no fumbling uncertainties, no embarrassed or guilty surprises. I was with experience, a woman who had invented pleasures to hold a man through anxious years. I closed the door of the study. It was the last thing I did without guidance. She was all help and all sustenance. At times she gave almost wearily but never without gentleness. Somewhere in it, I told her my middle name, and loudly. As she blurred before me in the frenzy that held us together, I saw her lips memorize me, a new name, "Jedeco, Jedeco." And later, when we cried out together, my cry was "Reeba!"

We lay together in cooling sweat and warm swampy odor, and Leviathan came whining at the door. His voice was feminine. She lay with her head over my racing heart while I stroked her black hair. She whispered in soft, weary contentment, "Thank you." I remembered her voice — acid and ice — the night she had thrown the drink in Lindy's face. She lifted her head and kissed my cheek, and it was precisely the place where Lindy's boot had put a hard lump under my skin.

Sometimes I could feel her smile, her lips moving against the rhythm of my heart. I wanted to talk to her, but I did not want to say any harmful thing. And there was the literary scientist in me, careful of cliché. I lay silent.

"He never loves me anymore," she said.

When the telephone startled us awake, I realized how fragile our secret was going to be. Lying in that little room, I counted seven rings from somewhere in the house and watched her all the time. She lay rigid, staring at the room as though its only meaning were that ringing phone.

I ate what I could of the breakfast she prepared, mostly to please her. The biscuits were good, but they were dust in my mouth. I drank too much coffee, and finally we sat watching the late morning sun spread across the lake. It took the mouth of the creek, the far bank and the features of the trees, and those huge clots of driftwood and debris which were osprey nests. We watched the big raptors make their skimming passes over the lake.

I helped her carry in the breakfast things and fed Leviathan, who whined and sniffed at my feet and then ate listlessly.

"He misses Eldon," she said. "He hasn't danced in weeks." We both had to laugh. We were almost comfortable together when the telephone rang again. She looked at it there on the wall, then at me. "Would you?"

I hesitated, foolishly miming my confusion at her. I couldn't answer her phone.

She clapped both hands to her temples. "Just . . . *please!*" And the phone rang a third time. Those hands, that gesture of distraction and panic, forced me to the phone. I picked it up thinking I could always just put it back down.

When I noticed the breathing — that it was heavy — I smiled.

"I haven't seen the boy in a week. Where is he?"

The smile began to stick to my teeth. I said, "Who is this?"

"Ah, but who is *this?*" the voice crooned. It was distorted as though spoken through lips always pursed, and there was something oddly familiar about it. "I'm going to need that kid. I've waited. I can find out where he is. Sure I can."

"Look you . . ."

"What I'm going to do with him, I'm going to take my . . ."

I slammed the phone against the wall but it fell and dangled, and faintly we could still hear the crooning. I reached down and picked it up and cradled it. My hands were shaking. Reeba was against the far kitchen wall on her toes, her chin lifted as though someone held a knife under it. I stepped toward her and she flinched. I started to say, "It's me, Toad," but stopped, remembering I was not Toad anymore. I held my arms out to her.

Slowly she lowered her chin and came to me. "Presley's at summer camp," she sobbed into my neck. "What if he . . . What if they . . . He *knows* things. How could he know?"

"Look," I said, having no idea what I would say. "Look . . . these guys, they don't, they don't know what the hell they're doing. They just say what will scare you. He hasn't got any idea where Presley is." I took her by the shoulders and held her away from me. "Come on, Reeba. Don't worry." But all the time I was thinking, Jesus, what if he does know?

I took her out of the kitchen, away from that black malignancy on the wall. Leviathan padded along beside us, growling at the hands which held Reeba. We went back to our room, the little study where we had made love, and lay down listening to the morning world outside. After a space she stopped crying, but for her it was night again, black and hopeless.

I asked what they had done about the calls. She told me, nothing. Eldon Odom would not allow the telephone to be tapped.

I held her and maybe we slept. She placed her head over my heart again, and I gave back the rhythm that beat in me. Finally at mid-day, stiff from the weight of her, I touched her hair. "Mmm," she said, and raised her head. I went to the bathroom, and when I came back she was lying on her back in the center of the small bed, her clothing in a pile on the floor. "Look at me," she said. Her face was calm, serious. "I'm old."

"You're beautiful," I said reflexively before I had really looked at her. She threw up her arms to me, and I leaned and she pressed me to her warm breast. When she let go, I did look at her. She was beautiful, though not in the way I had learned beauty from the dream collective, those magazines in the convenience emporium. Nor was she like Ardis; there was something used and useful about her that Ardis had not yet achieved, a stressing as from the secret necessary shifting of parts into painful alignment. Old houses have it, and so do firearms which have been used in anger and necessity, and so do the hands of the people who have made and used these things.

Her frame was small, even delicate, her breasts not large but large-seeming because of the size of her. They were traced by delicate blue capillaries, and as she lay on her back looking up at me with that serious calm face, they pooled toward her arms with a blue-marbled hue, leaving a hollow at her breastbone. I could see her heart beating at her throat and in the center of her left nipple. Her fluted hipbones were pushed up sharp by the hard bed beneath her. In the hollows between them, her belly was all cross-cut by childbirth, even to the edge of her pubic hair, which was lustrous and coarse. Suddenly I buried my face in it and she gave a surprised, pleased cry. I was thinking of the words Shine and Hubbel had used that night under the deck to describe Sarah Fesco's flinching private parts. None of them fit now, and no word formed in my mind until — mystery. I heard her say, "Now, let me see you."

I stood and she motioned me away a few steps. "There," she said, as though I had found center stage. I was drunk. She turned on her side and propped an arm under her head, and I watched her breasts roll with gravity. "Go ahead," she said.

I did not know what she meant, where to start. She pointed at me, drawing a dot somewhere near my middle. I tugged at my shirttails, bent to one shoe, then straightened up and she laughed, and so did I like a fool.

Finally, in an embarrassed and euphoric fury, I got out of my clothing. I stood before her, a little chilly, looking down at myself, then down at her. She motioned me to turn around, and I did, slowly, feeling like a statue on a dais. "You're beautiful, too," she said, and I could tell that she meant it. She motioned me toward her and reached out and touched the two scars on my right knee, tracing their corrugated surfaces. Then she began finding other hurts and blemishes and gnarled places, all the signs of collision and hazard. I looked down at her and oddly knew that she could make them go away. If not in fact, then in this secret, the one we were making. She began kissing them, first the long scars, then the smaller places, and finally she pressed her lips to the clump of practical, ugly flesh that hung between my legs. I was straining for her to take me and yet was shy, for I could not believe a woman could find beauty in that part of a man.

When I was inside her and saw the fan of that black hair spread over my thighs and saw its loving, waving movement, I knew that I had been wrong. I took her head in both hands and helped her.

As I was leaving, she turned a hard face to me in the doorway. "Tell me about her."

"About who?" I knew full well she meant Lindy and knew it was exactly the wrong thing for us to talk about.

"Eldon's little cunt. You know her, don't you?"

I winced at her word, for it was from that night under the deck with Sarah and Shine and Hubbel, and it had no place between us. Still, I answered her, "A little."

I was about to ask her to please let me go, to cancel this before it started. I wanted to take with me only what she had given, but she thrust her face fiercely close. "I need to know," she said in a voice that was twisted and artificial like that one on the phone.

Angry then, I set my own face hard, for hers was no longer the face I had known. "All right, I'll tell you. What do you want to know?"

She stepped back. "Good." We stood in the doorway. "It's funny," she mused. "I don't know what I want. Maybe just what he sees in her."

"She's young," I said brutally. I remembered her saying earlier, "I'm old."

"She's that," Reeba said. "And pretty, too, like I was when I was her age. I was pretty. Did you know that?"

"And now you are beautiful," I said, and I meant it. I added, "Maybe she *is* you . . . to him. Maybe she's just the past." If crystal methedrine made you feel the way you used to feel, I reasoned, maybe Lindy Briggs did, too.

"Is that supposed to make me feel better?"

I shrugged. "You didn't ask me to make you feel better." But I hoped that I had done so. I knew I had.

I continued about Lindy, but I was tired of it. "She's a dancer, a pretty good one I've heard. She's interested in writing, but she doesn't write, at least as far as I know. She's . . ."

"Does she buy his goddamned act? Is she that stupid?" She was angry again, her face and neck hot red, and suddenly so was I, for his *act* was something I had bought. In my thinking, it was more appropriately entitled: The Life, The Work, and The Difference.

"As much as anybody does, I guess. Maybe a little more." I did not say what I was thinking: As much as you did for twenty years.

"She thinks he's The Great Writer, like you do?"

"I don't think she cares much about that," I said, and too late realized how much it would hurt.

"She's just a little powerfucker," Reeba said hollowly. She was trying to convince herself, not me. I nodded, shifting out of the doorway.

"He's been powerfucked before. It doesn't last. It never does." She looked up at me, lost in her own sour logic.

I stepped close again and touched her face as gently as I could. It was the way she had touched me that first night at the Thrash Palace, saying, "Why don't you go home? Why don't you leave?"

Twenty-Two

I DID NOT ACCEPT Eldon Odom's every act with a ready heart. His rise was my decline from innocence, and I knew it. The night he had climbed the stairs and I had climbed the trellis with Lindy Briggs, I was appalled at what my night sight revealed. And yet I was fascinated and believed the power of this fascination was worth far more than the safekeeping of innocence. Somehow I knew that the clash of my past and this future, earned by pain and disappointment, would be the source of my voice.

After the Old Man's visit, I was elevated. I became the third lieutenant. And by the slow accretion of works and days, Eldon Odom was rising, too. His career was taking off again. He had flown before, but now he soared. With the publication of *Sojourners Under the Mountain*, his epic of Atlanta in the years after World War II, he was raised to national prominence. The time he spent in Bainesborough was telescoped; he kept office hours and taught only two days a week. He spent more time with Merit Norman in New York and at writers' conferences and on television talk shows and on assignment for national magazines. That astonishing physical vitality and that cruel single-mindedness and that country charm all shone at us from the television screen when we gathered at Moby's without him. Eldon Odom, who had been ours, was now the public Southerner. He had told us at the beginning he would ride this thing to the end of the line. We had ridden his coattails, whipping him into the future. Now he was escaping us.

One afternoon in late August, I met Eldon Odom on the street by the Old Barracks. He had been gone for a month, during which the class had been cancelled. For some of the group — Frank, who drove each Tuesday night from Jacksonville, and Sarah — the core of life had been pared away. And I will admit I missed the class, had found myself in Moby's those Tuesday nights hoping the remnants would collect.

"Ho, Toad!" he called to me, reaching for my shoulder. "Been hunting for you." I looked closely at him. He was tired and sallow and thin, his eyes puffy and unlighted. I had slept a month of nights with the fear that he would discover my afternoon with Sully. Now I knew she had kept our secret.

"You look like shit, big'un," he said to me, meaning of course that he knew how bad he looked.

"I feel like it, too," I said, true enough.

His laugh boomed out. It was the first old sign of him. He wasn't thinking about me. "Been riding the goddamn blue lightning bolt across the milky retina of the public eye. Flew in from Nuebe Jork last night on the midnight special. They had me on 'Meet America.' We were alone on the sidewalk, but he leaned toward me conspiratorially. "Got into some very fine genius powder with Merit Norman." He showed me trembling hands and stuck out a furry tongue. "The payback is very bad."

"Genius powder?"

He drew back in disappointment. "Crystal meth! Them fuckers up in Nuebe Jork keep it in salt shakers. We tooted up right in the middle of Elaine's. Then I went to tape the show. Jew see me? Did I pontificate or what?"

"What," I assured him.

He laughed and suddenly, strangely, I was ashamed of us. We were performing, we were children, exchanging gleeful secret looks that revel in complicity. He took my shoulder again. "I'm having a little thing for the group. I want you to come."

We walked to his car while he rambled on about the talk show host.

"That fucker is godawful short. He's almost a midget."

"Gives good talk show," I commented.

"I guess so. Did you know the audience is scattered all around out there in a big warehouse-looking place, sitting on cables and tool boxes and heaps of equipment? When they say studio, they mean it. That little room you see on TV is nothing but a two-walled fake on wheels." He paused and grinned, "Come to think of it, so is everything else."

He wiped his nose. "Smarts," he said. "That meth'll burn up your septum. Norman told me about a guy that got an encysted crystal in his snot locker. Didn't cut the stuff up fine enough. Anyway, they had to go in there and carve the fucker's nose all up. Went around wearing a bandage the size of a grapefruit with tubes running out of it. Looked like Bozo the Clown. Some bigtime fucking Nuebe Jork editor. Everybody knew what he'd been messing with." He shuddered. In his car, we took US 441 toward the Savannah.

"Grab your ass in both hands, Toad. You're about to visit the illicit love nest of Eldon Odom."

We had traveled a maze of secondary roads, and I could not have said exactly where we were. By certain landmarks — the radio tower at Crossland and the prison farm — I knew we were not far from the Thrash Palace. We stopped in the dooryard, next to Shine's Karman Ghia and Tory Hubbel's van. Ardis's blue Mercedes was parked in the yard. It was an old tin-roofed cracker house, perched on the edge of the Savannah. Inside, a radio was pouring out "Layla," which was that summer's rock lament. Lindy Briggs opened the door to us.

"Oh . . . it's you."

"Yup," I said, inoffensively. "Me."

Eldon Odom shouldered past me into the screened porch. He stood by Lindy whispering something I could not hear. She listened, keeping her eyes on me. I followed them down a hallway. Eldon Odom pulled her to him as they walked; it was, I knew, his way of taking her back from me and from the pretense he had labored to create about us. It was the reason he had been looking for me.

Hubbel and Shine were sitting on the living room sofa. Ardis and Tommy MacEvoy stood in the little kitchen. They stopped laughing when they saw me, and Ardis turned away to the window. I looked around at the boxes of books and unpacked suitcases and said, "Looks like some serious homemaking."

Hubbel nodded at me from the sofa while Shine kept his eye on MacEvoy. Hubbel said, "That was some story you wrote, Toad." His high voice came compressed from that great bellows of a chest, and despite what I thought of him otherwise, I knew he was capable of generosity.

I said, "Thanks, Tory."

"How'd you like to come out to the Gash Palace some time and read my new chapters," Hubbel said, his voice honest, fervent. He was being a good sport, a good loser. They were all ready to let me in, and this place, new and secret, was the next privilege.

From where he stood with Lindy, still in the mouth of the hallway, Eldon Odom said, "Sure, Toad, do it. You got a better eye than you know."

Shine looked at me for the first time and nodded.

MacEvoy ambled to the center of the room, grinning that black crow grin and bringing the only thing he could contribute. He unwrapped a piece of old-fashioned waxed paper, revealing a mat of white powder, a single-edged razor blade, and a rolled cardboard matchbook cover.

Eldon Odom walked over to the coffee table where MacEvoy had placed his wares and looked down. Through his bad boy grin, he said, "Up in Nuebe Jork, we don't toot through nothing less than a twenty, but I guess this'll do in a tight."

Mike Shine leaned forward and said, "You so damned New York, maybe you want to sit this one out."

Odom drew back and grinned harder. "I ain't *that* New York."

Through all of it I watched Ardis. She stood a little behind MacEvoy observing with a serious, clinical look on her face. I remembered the two of us sitting at my parents' supper table while my father prayed for my sister's soul, and this room and that one formed an incongruity that overloaded the wires. I shook my head.

"How you doing, Ardis?"

MacEvoy stopped cutting the white powder on the glass table top.

Ardis smiled at me, the old slow, Ardis Baines smile. "Grabblen," she said. "Some days chicken salad, some days chicken shit."

I had to laugh and my laugh was friendly, and with it I offered half of a bargain. You can't die for love forever.

She watched my face carefully, and still MacEvoy's razor was poised above the crystal meth. I said, "Treat yourself nice, Ardis." My voice was soft. They were all listening to us, but I didn't care. She said, "How *you* doing, Toad?" In her tone there was something indecipherable except by me, and I suppose by MacEvoy. It was a cancelling of hostilities and a recollection of things, things we had done. I sued for peace. I said, "As good as I can in an imperfect world."

Shine, who had been watching us from the sofa, said, "Jesus, what are you two assholes co-authoring?" Everyone laughed and MacEvoy started chopping again.

I turned away to the window and let my red face burn into the summer air. A seagull, gray and white, drifted over the Savannah, and I wondered what it was doing so far inland. Then I saw a whole raft of gulls in the pasture below me, all lost. I thought of Reeba, for that was her name, just as mine was now, improbably, Jedeco, and I wondered what it was like for her now that Eldon Odom had made public his abandonment and all of us had been invited to it.

"Hey, bud, it's your line."

MacEvoy was calling me to his delight, but I hesitated to turn from the window. They were all behind me, some of them sniffling already, some waiting, and all wondering if I would go the next step with them.

I turned to MacEvoy and smiled my dislike. He gave back an impresario grin, generous and certain of his gifts. I leaned to the white powder and took half a line in one nostril. Before long, my head was singing a dark song, and I was back at the window watching the lost world grow more familiar.

An hour or so later, with a singing head and grinding jaws, I was telling Tory Hubbel exactly how to write a story, absolutely.

"Understand? Understand?" I kept asking his big red face, which kept nodding, yes, yes.

Ardis and Tommy MacEvoy were playing what she had called a balls-to-the-wall game of backgammon, and Eldon Odom and Lindy Briggs had drifted out of sight. We were all happy, and light was bright and objects were hard and definite and came to the hand with a certainty that was from our very best moments, which seemed to repeat themselves now one after another. I was talking better than I had ever talked, and it was clear to me that Ardis and Tommy MacEvoy were playing the best game of backgammon they had ever played, and Mike Shine was reading album covers with a concentrated intensity that would have been frightening had it not been so precise. Crystal methedrine is distilled nostalgia, though none of us could have said so then. We were all doing exactly what we wanted to do when the doorbell rang.

We might have waited forever, stuck, unable to identify the proprietor of our spaceship, if Reeba hadn't pushed open the door. She stood in it looking at us, her eyes adjusting to the dim interior. Behind her in the white corona of the summer afternoon, the boy Presley stood hugging a cardboard box. It was too big for him and he was beginning to wobble and to search past his mother, who stood impassive in the doorway, for a place to disburden himself. I don't know what the others were thinking, but there came to me the recent image of Eldon Odom and Lindy Briggs drifting slowly along my peripheral vision to the narrow hallway that led to the bedroom, the sound of the door closing, and I wondered how long they had been gone.

Reeba moved into the room, shading her eyes with a white palm that I admired because it had once touched me and because now it held steady along her brow. The look on her face was grim hospitality. Was she still so connected to Odom that she believed she had to welcome us? Some of us must have been watching the

bedroom doorway, for without saying a word and followed by
the boy, she walked through us and slowly opened it. I stared
past her shoulder and a tilting box of underwear and shirts. On a
bare mattress, I saw tangled together the red and the tan of Eldon
Odom and Lindy Briggs. First the sounds from the room were
common, animal and wet, the undignified noises of love, and
then came Lindy's cry of anguished surprise and Presley's
choked sob.

Reeba turned and bent to Presley. She took the box more to
shield him from the bedroom than to relieve him of it, and using
it as a partition, pushed him toward the nearest chair. "Sit down,
sweet," she said. Presley resembled his father, and now his
expression was one of Odom's habitual masks — detached
curiosity and comic outrage. He sat down heavily, and Reeba
slid the box from his lap. She turned, her back to the boy, and
watched the doorway.

Eldon Odom broke from the bedroom in a stumbling run with
an angry, grinding look on his face. He rambled at us, red,
naked, half erect and smelling of whiskey and musk. I saw
Lindy Briggs's perfect body in the dim rectangle of the bedroom
door. She was sweat-glistening, matted, suffused, and it is to
Reeba's everlasting credit that she was the only one of us who
did not gape. She kept her eyes on Eldon Odom, who had
backed to the window and was beginning to tremble.

Reeba moved slowly to him and reached out. He slapped her
hand away as though it were a striking snake. "No," she said.
"Let me." She reached with the other hand, the same slow,
ministering gesture, and a storm of misery crossed Eldon
Odom's face. This time he let her lead him back into the
bedroom. We watched them go, the woman supporting the man
whose naked red limbs swam in our altered vision. Reeba's
hands on him were tender and learned, and we heard her
whisper to him as they passed the doorway. "Easy, Eldon. Just a

little longer. Come with Mama."

Ardis walked quickly to Presley and said, "We need to talk," holding out her hand to him and smiling. Presley looked at the doorway, his eyes full of his father's misery, then took her hand. Afterward the only significant thing in the room was the cardboard box full of underwear and shirts. Tommy MacEvoy was gone. Shine and Hubbel were looking at each other with expressions that said good-bye.

After what seemed a long time, Reeba and Lindy came to the door. Lindy wore jeans and one of Eldon Odom's khaki shirts. She watched Reeba in complete confusion. Reeba handed her something. "Two of these," she said, "no more than two." Lindy's eyes were wide with concentration. "Can you remember? No more than two," Reeba said. "It's on the label."

"Yes," Lindy said. "Thank you." They might have been mother and daughter.

Reeba crossed the room to me. "Where is Presley?"

"Outside," I said.

She stepped out, and I followed her. On my way out, I heard Hubbel say, "Marriage is a trick of shit, ain't it?" His voice was sad and sorry.

Ardis and Presley were sitting on a patch of grass under a jacaranda tree. Purple blossoms lay all around them on the ground. She was sitting cross-legged and plucking up the purple flecks from the grass and popping them and talking earnestly to Presley, who, by the look of him, was rapt. I watched Reeba go to them and lean and take Presley's hand, and heard her say a formal thank-you.

"I guess I never should have brought him with me. I don't know what I was thinking."

"How could you know?" Ardis said, and that ready pioneer kindness was in her voice and in the way she inclined her body sharply toward Reeba. They were two stoics there under the trees and, though it was pretty to see in the aftermath of what had happened, it was also somehow forbidding. I had never felt so excluded. Towing Presley, Reeba walked to the car and got in but did not start the engine. She stared at me while I stood useless on the porch. We were a triangle. Ardis, under the jacaranda tree on the carpet of fallen blossoms, Reeba, and I. Reeba called out to me, "Good-bye, Jedeco!"

It was then that I felt gravity in the pit of my stomach and the first nausea of a hard return to earth. Where would I go? What would I do with the rest of the speed voyage? MacEvoy emerged from the trees at the side of the house. Casually he stubbed out a cigarette, and I watched him go to Ardis's expensive car and stand waiting for her, and I watched her, reluctant to leave that carpet of flowers where she had committed an act of kindness. She decided to go to him, but not before calling out to me, "Good-bye, *Toad*."

Hubbel and Shine emerged, talking about the new national indoor record for marital bliss that had just been set. Then they began to talk about seeing Lindy naked. Hubbel advocated the position that Lindy had rat-nose titties, whereas Shine was not so sure. It seemed to Shine that they were not honest-to-God rat-nose titties. They had potential, he was willing to admit.

I rode with them. We flew fast across the gulf of the afternoon, singing a loud and raucous song, hoping to delay as long as possible the fast descent and hard methedrine landing.

Twenty-Three

IT WAS TYPICAL of Eldon Odom that his antidote for humiliation was the weight room. It bespoke his optimism and sen-
sitivity to the heightened moment. In the weight room,
epiphany and transformation are possible. This hope was his
higher nature. He knocked at my door early, and when I opened
it, shrunken and dried and at the ragged end of the black
depression which is the payback for a few hours of nostalgia, he
looked at me levelly, showed me his gym bag, and said, "We got
to go to Bud's and sweat some of the shit out of your system."

There was a blue mouse under his right eye. I guessed he had
got it thrashing in that room with Lindy and Reeba and his
demons.

"You ought to seen the other guy," he said. He gave me a
grim, one-eyed grin. "I hope *I* never see that sucker again."

I said, "Me, too."

He stalked up and down my narrow room while I pulled on

some clothes. Once he picked up a page from the desk and read it.

"What do you think?" I asked him.

"About what?"

We struggled through our usual workout, but the energy was not there, and worse, the sweat wouldn't come.

Through a nose that was swollen and running, Eldon Odom said, "That meth'll dry you out, won't it, Toad?"

I was spotting him while he pushed a measly two hundred pounds through the usual three sets of ten bench presses, suffering like only he could suffer. He had lost weight since the publication of *Sojourners,* and the weight he could push up to me was consequently less. The deep red color that lived in his skin seemed to have paled, and his dry odor was ammonia as he worked the weight.

After we had done our drill, we sat on the hot tile tiers in the old steam room, watching the white clouds fulminate and listening to the drumming, dripping pipes.

"Toad," he said after a space. "Missy Sully and Lindy stood over my corpse in that room."

"Yeah, what did they say?" I thought of him lying there, unconscious as dirt, with his two women watching for a sign.

"I don't know. Prayers for the dead, I guess. Dithyrambs on the blue vein in my dick. I don't know what they said."

Behind my cloud, I nodded.

"It gives a man the fantods to be laid out in his own stupidity and excess and unaware of himself, and . . ."

"And?" I asked him.

"I got to get further out. When you break, break clean. There's a place out on Lake Searl. Some culture vulture offered it to me for a 'retreat,' if you can believe it. Maybe I'll take my ass on out there."

I could believe it. "Take Lindy's, too," I said. He looked at me with a severity that was hard to maintain. We were naked and exhausted and shriveled. In the steam, it was common denominators.

"Aw, I'm sorry about all that with you and Missy Briggs, Toad. You know how it goes."

I told him I knew.

"After I started doing that, pushing her off on you, I felt like a goddamned pimp. I knew I had to do something. So I went home and had it out with Sully. God, it was elbows, assholes, and eyeballs. I wish you'd of seen it."

"No, you don't."

"I don't, come to think of it. But you know what I mean. A woman scorned is a formidable thing."

I nodded, but I knew very little about women scorned. I knew Ardis. She had felt devalued by my work and what it had led me to do, but I did not think there was scorn in the equation with us. As I looked back, it seemed to me that I had simply outdistanced her in my rush toward this heat. There were times, too, when I told myself it was my nobility that had put the distance between Ardis and me. Those times, I supposed that her taking up with MacEvoy was her revenge against nobility.

Eldon Odom spread himself out on the white tile across from me, resting his head under a backflung arm. With a free hand, he rubbed the bruise on his face. "That bitch," he muttered.

"She has her rights," I said.

"So do I." But he didn't sound convinced of it.

"They don't cancel hers," I said, remembering my sister who had always spoken of her rights.

"What do you suppose she'll do now?" His voice was small.

"I don't know. But you better be careful with that genius powder. That's where you don't have rights."

"Right," he said. "Toad, did I ever tell you about when I was your age?"

"Some," I said. "Not much."

"I was a poontanging fool." He said it with tired elation. "It's a hard habit to break."

I considered the procession of women and girls bedded by the young stud, Eldon Odom. My reflection took me to the threshold of that squalid room where Reeba the rich girl had wedded herself to the young writer's frustrated dream. Suddenly I was seized by the impulse to confess to him. To sit in the hot white room with the world outside the door, the place where I was closest to him, to the heat, the place where our egos slipped furthest from us, to let my voice begin and let it tell and tell, using the hard details a writer's eye records, and let the words flow across to him and see what he would do. It was a moment of love and insanity, quickly suppressed. It left me with a quickened heart. The sweat broke on me at last. What I said was, "I imagine it *is* a hard habit to break."

"Toad," he said, "what I like about you is you don't want anything. You're self-sufficient, like me."

I didn't speak. I suppose he had embarrassed himself, so he said, loudly, "Bet you chased some pussy in your time, Toad."

And I said, "Yeah, I guess I did."

Outside on the street, we were pumped from the weights and still floating from the steam and tired, but for some reason we lingered. I looked up and down University Boulevard, inspecting a block of commerce either way. I was about to lower my head and plunge into the quotidian when Odom said, "Come on, Toad, I got something to show you."

He took me to his "birding place." That's what he called it. We drove that maze of roads out toward the Savannah, until I guessed we were somewhere between the Thrash Palace and Odom's new place, but he was driving by landmark and luck, and I had no real way of knowing where we were. We stopped at a little hummock just on the lip of the Savannah, a platform almost; in its center stood a tall, graceful cypress. He opened the trunk and retrieved a handsome old leather case and shucked out a pair of Zeiss binoculars the size of two whiskey bottles. Then he walked to the edge of the grassy platform and said, "Up periscope."

He sank almost to his knees, then straightened slowly with the imagined rise of a periscope tube. Before bringing the glasses to his eyes, he mimed the bill of his U-boat captain's cap to the back of his head. "Now zen," he muttered diabolically. "Vot haff vee here? Mine gootniss!"

He was beckoning me, pointing, holding the glasses in place so that I could fit my eyes to them without losing the image they held. What I saw in the rolling air half a mile above that grassy lake was a wheeling red-tailed hawk. "A big old cock," Odom told me in a breathless voice, "king of the air, holder of the highest circle, disdainer of carrion, free-booter, wide-berther, scoundrel and sovereign of all sky hunters and all land dwellers, save the bobcat and the gator." He said that he had personally seen one of these birds, perhaps this very one, kill and carry a rattlesnake as fat around as his arm. "It was one of the most exciting moments of my life, Toad. I don't know why. But I'll tell you this, I'd put it right up against the day I got the phone call about my book, my first one, that it was going to be published. When that call came, I thought I'd die from the sheer rush of it, from the way the world that's real and the one I made up and put in a book seemed to join. But I'll tell you right here and now, the day — it was a morning, a very early spring morning — the day I saw that king bird take that snake, it was the same thing. It wasn't even that he *did* it. We *know* that. It's that he did it and I *saw* it. Somehow, it was life and work, or life as it is in work, which is to say, as it ought to be. Do you understand me, son?"

Holding the glasses firmly on that soaring hawk, so big to my eyes in the power of those lenses that it might have been swinging on a tether ten yards in front of me, I could only say yes, and yes, mumbling in embarrassed rapture. Yes, I did understand. And perhaps I did, and perhaps I do. Still.

We watched the bird, taking turns, until it was only a dot hunting quail above the fencerows at the prison farm. When he finally lowered the glasses, Odom walked to his car and took a bottle of Jack Daniels Black from the glove box. He broke the seal and handed it to me, looking off toward the guard towers at the prison farm, which were nothing but jittery smudges in the noon haze.

I took a deep drink of the sweetest, warmest, cuttingest, most spiritual whiskey I had ever drunk, then handed him the bottle. Absently, he wiped his red palm across the mouth of it, as though to obliterate me from the experience, and then took a deep pull, letting the amber bubbles rise up the neck of the bottle. He walked over and let his back slide down the furry trunk of the cypress tree and drank again and held his head back against the bark, his eyes closed, the whiskey trickling down his throat. "I don't just come here to collect impressions of birds. I do my best thinking here. This is where I got the idea for *Sojourners*. Saw the whole city of Atlanta — people and brick and mortar and muck and mire — right out there."

He lowered his head and regarded me. I was holding the field glasses, still magic, full of that bird and the things Odom had said about it.

"This town's a lot bigger than it was when I found this place. I don't think anybody's ever been here but me and the people I brought here, and there was only two of them. I say I don't think because I'm not sure. If I knew someone else was coming here, I might not come back, I don't know. Might be like a hen hawk and abandon what had been soiled by the human hand. I don't know. Anyway . . ." He took another drink, capped the bottle, and flung it at me. I caught it one-handed and sat down, placing the glasses on the grass beside me. "Anyway, this town is bloating, and this place just ain't . . . it ain't as far away as it once was, and you don't get the same feeling from it you used to get. You know what I mean?"

I nodded, having only an imperfect notion but not wanting to stop the rapture. I looked out over the Savannah, thinking the town could never grow to kill it all. It was protected. And thinking, too, in my ignorance, that the beauty, the power of some things was never less. We sat like that for an hour by my watch, just drinking and saying nothing. And that was the best time, those ninety minutes or so, I ever spent with Eldon Odom.

Odom told me, "When you break, break clean." True to his word, he went farther out. He kept the little cracker house on the edge of the Savannah for only a month, and then he moved to a small cabin on the shore of a wild lake near a little grit hamlet called Hardentown, forty miles from Bainesborough. It was rural, and the locals were known for publicly condemning and privately condoning whatever brought revenue into the county coffers. What brought revenue were cut-and-shoot bars, double-wide—trailer whores, good country restaurants, and little airstrips bulldozed deep in the piney woods and lit by gasoline flares late at night so that a Lockheed Lodestar could get in and out quick.

Twenty-Four

I WAS DREAMING of the Old Man's words when Traymore pulled me from the shallow burrow of my morning sleep. The Old Man was telling me, "Do more with the mother." I wandered to a phone in a hallway somewhere in the precincts of my dream.

"Blackford? Is that you?"

There is only one woman who calls me Blackford. Her voice located me in the cold corridor by Traymore's room. "Yes, Mommer. It's me."

"You better come if you can, son."

"Is it Daddy?"

Silence, punctuated by the windy twang of our country telephone connection, stretched out between us. In her tired and practical voice, she said, "He's hurt is all. It's serious, but you can't kill Delia Turlow's oldest son. I been trying for years."

I laughed, but it was no relief. "What happened, Mommer?"

"Pump got him."

"What?"

"I'll tell you when you come. Drive safe."

"Do I . . .?"

"Don't rush. He's going to get a long rest, and he needs you to help until we can figure something out."

When she hung up, I sank to the floor in my underwear. Traymore, who was standing in his doorway, said, "You all right, Toad? Want some tea?"

For the first time, I said yes.

I parked my calamitous old Toyota under the tall pines of the dooryard beside an International pickup truck I had not seen before. Stretching to rid my frame of the kinks of a forty-mile drive, I watched the house, hoping this truck did not mean more or worse. I walked across the yard and shouldered the kitchen door, but it stopped against the heels of Mr. Frank Arneau, our nearest neighbor. "Pardon me," I said. Mr. Frank turned from my mother's parting handshake and, blushing, took my smooth city palm. "Hi you, Toad?"

I didn't know how I was until I saw Daddy, but I said, "Fine sir, thank you, and you?"

"Now that I seen your daddy, I feel some better," Mr. Frank said.

Mama came to me and hugged my neck and said, "You eat yet, son?"

My stomach was full of anxious hope and herbal tea, so I said, "Yessum."

"Well," said Mr. Frank, turning his hat around and around by the brim, "I better go see'f I can find Sir Alfred."

"Thank you, Frank," my mother said levelly. "And he appreciates your coming over."

"Well," Mr. Frank said, "you know . . . you know. . . ." His voice guttered in his throat, then quit on him. I stood stupefied, heart constricted by a feeling I was not much acquainted with. I had never seen Mr. Frank Arneau, my father's longtime co-op partner, lost for words. He was the cracker wit of Alligood County and otherwise as ready a man as you were likely to meet. He gripped my hand again and gave me what can only be described as a meaningful look. "Take care of your mommer now, Toad." There was cold reproach in his eyes as he let go of my hand. I had left the farm. I was another defecting son, a member of the legions of betrayal who had caused old men to work too hard too long and to depend upon hired labor and go into debt for machinery that could harrow and harvest and grind them into the twentieth century and in the process, take all the fun out of it.

Mr. Frank had said, "Take care of your mommer," so I nodded solemnly, knowing that my mother would get through the next few days by taking care of me. I turned to her as Mr. Frank's new truck started up outside; her eyes bore in on me, then she snapped her head in the direction of their bedroom.

"Is he asleep?" I asked.

"Doped," she said.

Quietly I stepped past her on the toes of the stiff old work boots I had pulled on in my hasty departure from the dream closet in Bainesborough. Try as I might to muffle them, they thumped under me with a familiar clumsiness.

My father's eyes rolled forward from the back of his head as I eased toward him, and after recognition there came a dopey chemical grin to his face that was unlike any real expression of his. It frightened me more than the white dressing that covered his crown and the right side of his face and then disappeared under the covers at his right shoulder.

His left hand began to move under the bedspread. The grin

widened and he said, "Pump got me, Toad."

I nodded. My throat was stopped by the hundred things I had never said to him and by the knowledge that I had almost lost the chance forever. Close enough, I thought. Close enough. Then, hating our code of silence, I said, "Looks like you fought a buzz saw."

"Mought did," he said. The parched, chemical grin cracked at the edges and released an involuntary groan which was the first concession to pain I had ever seen my father make.

I reached down for the hand that had made its way out. It tried to take mine in the usual man's grip, but I held it like I might have held Ardis's hand and did not let go. I saw that to sit on the edge of the bed would hurt him, so I stood over him, watching him conquer the spasm. The crazy grin came back to his face.

His eyes rolled back near unconsciousness at the tops of their sockets and rolled down again, and he said, "What you doing here, Toad?"

The innocence of the question and the reproach, entirely unmeant, ground in me like swallowed sand. "I was in the neighborhood," I said shrugging.

My answer took him funny, and he gritted his teeth and let his eyes sparkle a laugh to pay for my joke. I said, "You sleeping late these days? It's eleven o'clock." Then it came to me. "You must be all caught up."

His eyes gave me an "Oh, *you*" look, their black irises surrounded by a heightened whiteness that was clear and humorous. Then they closed.

The pressure of his hand in mine lessened, and I felt my mother's hand on my shoulder. I crept away from him on the toes of my heavy old boots.

My father had gone out the night before at nine to check the sprinkler system that was watering his peanut crop. The water was pumped by an old Chrysler engine, a 1950 flathead six, mounted on a platform of railroad ties and sucking fuel from a converted aluminum beer keg. The drive shaft that operated the pump was exposed. He was wearing bib overalls that night. They were the last pair of an old lot, faded milky white. He had thrown them on for no particular reason after rising from his Easy Boy recliner and his copy of the *Progressive Farmer,* or perhaps because my mother, for once in her life, was not caught up with her week's wash. Normally he would have worn a crisp khaki shirt. The overalls were what saved his life.

The engine was not running well; it coughed and then whined up to three or four thousand rpms as though the timing chain were loose, and my father bent over it to listen closely. He had brought a screwdriver with him, and he leaned closer, placing the point of the screwdriver against the bell housing and the handle to his ear, an old mechanic's trick. The engine sang of its ills, and he leaned a little closer to listen. The spinning drive shaft snatched him by the bib of his overalls. He went two revolutions around the shaft, striking his head each time under on the corner of a railroad tie. On the upward thrust of the third revolution, the fabric gave way, then the entire front panel of the garment came unpeeled from him, wrapping itself around the free-spinning shaft in a wad no larger than a baseball bat. He landed unconscious on his face and lay for an hour bleeding, the back half of his overalls still clinging to him. When my mother found him, she ran to telephone Mr. Frank Arneau, who came with a truck and bandages.

As we sat in the living room drinking iced tea, she told me that she had heard the shaft grab him, had heard a deep, vicious growl from the engine, an alien change, and had looked up from the TV with a frown on her face and then at the clock on the wall. Figuring from the beginning of "Gunsmoke," he had been gone only twenty minutes. It was not unusual for him to check the pump, fiddle with the mixture a bit, then take the long way back past the hog pens and the farrowing house just to see that all was well.

When "Gunsmoke" ended and he had been gone an hour, she took a light and went to look for him. She rode in the truck bed with him in her arms to the county veterinary clinic, where they waited an hour for the resident who served the county. Dr. Billy Hardget, the local vet, stood over him, holding compresses to the severed artery in his head, and talking in his low, calming voice to his two neighbors, telling them not to worry, while he glanced too often at his watch. Assisted by Dr. Hardget, the resident closed the artery, then sent my father by ambulance to the hospital in Live Oak for the bone work.

"He's lucky, the old fool," my mother said. "How many times did he tell *you* to stay away from that shaft?" She looked at me, wanting the answer, as though it would explain something.

"A hundred. At least." I sipped tea and looked at the door of their bedroom. It was the room in which my sister and I had been made. My father would sleep and recover and my mother would lie with him again, with luck, many times. I thought how nearly it had become the room she would not go into, could not enter without unbearable pain. I turned back to her and said, "It only takes once. That's what he always used to tell me. 'You just have to forget once, Toad, and you don't get another chance.' "

She listened carefully as though I could explain. Finally she shook her head. "He's just too old. He forgets now. He's strong here," — she took herself by the upper arm — "but here" — she touched her temple — "he wanders now. He's just spent too much time going up and down those rows swallowing dust and hearing all that noise and getting his inside rattled. He starts dreaming now. Last month he turned a corner wide and tore out fifty feet of wire with the harrow. Didn't even know he was dragging it down the highway until some Yankee tourist honked him over to the side of the road."

After a while, she told me what she had said as he lay bleeding in her lap in the truck bed: "I told him, 'You better wait for me. You just better wait.' "

I shook my head. It was all reproach, all of it. "What do I need to do, Mommer?" I put down my glass of tea.

"You bring any clothes?" She meant work clothes.

"Sure." I lifted my old boots from the carpet. She glanced down at them. They were still smeared with the hardened Black Jack roofing cement we had used that January on the new farrowing house. "Go on over to Mr. Frank's and see if he's caught up with Sir Alfred yet. Somebody's got to get the plastic off that tobacco bed." She tossed me the keys. "Here, take your daddy's truck."

I was farming again.

Early morning, and a crew of us were going to pull plastic. We were Mr. Frank Arneau, who should have been in his own field but would help until I was on my feet, and his son, C. Randle, and we were expecting Sir Alfred, who was the unofficial labor broker for the local black community. It was no community really, just a collection of families united by membership in the Greater Liberty Hill and Zion Primitive Baptist Church. No one, including Sir Alfred himself, knew how old Sir Alfred was, but somewhere back in the first fifth of the present century, as he often told us, his hopeful and progressive parents had named him Sir Alfred Lancelot Pinkney so that he could get respect every day of his life. "All's you did is call my name, and you done gizz me respeck." In the county, his unwieldy moniker had been reduced by way of *Sir Al* to *Srall*, or occasionally, *Sraffid*. He had been getting respect for as long as any of us could remember. When times got hard and the local farmers needed labor, you could hear the emphasis on the "Sir" come rising up. This was one of those Sir mornings. C. Randle and Mr. Frank and Sir Alfred and I were going to strip a hundred yards of clear plastic sheeting from our tobacco bed. It was hard, delicate work.

While Mr. Frank went inside to say hello to Daddy, I stepped out to give C. Randle my greeting, which was a left hook to the shoulder muscle. It made my wrist ache. "Hi y'all doing?" I asked. C. Randle was man enough to handle one side of the plastic by himself. His upper body would have put Tory Hubbel's to shame. I had seen him hoist two hundred-pound sacks of fertilizer to his shoulders and walk plowed ground without breathing hard. When he drew back to give me a punch in return, I danced out of range and he answered, "I be all right if I don't drop through my asshole and strangle myself. How 'bout you?"

"Awright," I said. "I'm awright."

We both blushed and turned to watch Sir Alfred come bouncing across the pasture toward our tobacco bed in his white '58 Cadillac El Dorado. He jumped out, willowy and spry, to greet Mr. Frank with a solemn handshake and then turned to me and went into a Sugar Ray Robinson crouch. "Look out now, it's Toad Turlow." I noted that I was not *Mr.* Toad.

I said "What it is, Sir Alfred?"

He stood up and said, "It's mighty fine, mighty fine. All right. All right."

We all stood around like bowling pins, rocking on our heels with our hands shoved deep in our pockets, kicking clods and spitting and marveling inwardly at how it was all mighty fine and all right. We were trying not to think how godawful hard it would be to pull that long sheet of plastic off those tobacco seedlings without damaging them. We knew that Sir Alfred was not going to be much physical help. In fact, we knew he was with us mostly to consolidate his own position. We were in travail, and when he had seen us in it, there would be no denying later that we needed him.

Finally I said, "C. Randle, whyn't you and Sir Alfred take one side and I'll see if I can't keep up with Mr. Frank over here?" C. Randle lowered his head, which seemed to make one of his massive thighs rise up, and he was off and shuffling with Sir Alfred toward the far side of the bed.

The trick is to get the plastic started and keep it doubling on itself in a curve rather than digging down. For the first few yards, it's easy. It's only moderately difficult for the next fifty. But during the last forty or so, when the accumulated weight of the wet, dirt-encrusted plastic is in your hands and wrists, it's agony.

The whole operation, which has to go fast once it starts, lasts only minutes and is roughly comparable to running a half mile flat out carrying an anvil.

I positioned myself behind Mr. Frank and looked across the eight feet of miniature greenhouse at Sir Alfred, who was just ahead of C. Randle and squatting down. We all dug the edges of the plastic out of the rich earth and took a few deep breaths. I looked for a moment at thousands of dollars worth of seedlings sleeping between us, then at C. Randle, who looked over at his father, Mr. Frank, who said, "Y'all ready?"

We said yes, and I saw Mr. Frank's hard old shanks up and running in a cloud of dirt and a rustle of bending, crackling plastic. To keep up with Mr. Frank and me, C. Randle was soon hard upon the heels of old Sir Alfred, who, with a whoop and a laugh and a "Be god dog!" let go and jumped out of C. Randle's way. After that I saw nothing but Mr. Frank's back through a mist of sweat and various promises to myself not to let go no matter what happened. We got it done.

When we were standing around puffing and drying afterward, I started my negotiations for the tobacco crew. It would be a few local high school kids earning summer money and the six or eight black folk — men, women, and children — that Sir Alfred could supply for the price agreed upon.

"I can get you Ellis Teagarden — he done quit that drinkin' — and might could get ole Doreen Drawdy, if'n she done weaned that young'un of hern, and . . ." I knew some of the names and some of the faces and considered telling him it didn't matter much, that I trusted him. I decided to listen while he displayed his human wares and his knowledge of whereabouts and good habits and the small changes of their lives. Otherwise, who was he and, for that matter, who was I? Mr. Frank stood nearby, half–turned away, staring at a piece of the weather and listening. I knew he would jump in and help me if I needed it. He wasn't going to do anything unless Sir Alfred got greedy.

I stood listening and rocking on the balls of my feet and staring at the same patch of weather that absorbed Mr. Frank and nodding occasionally and occasionally intoning, "Right, right, I see." And after a while, Sir Alfred finished with a promise: "Yes, sir, young Mr. Toad, I bleeve I can gizz you as good a crew's anybody roun' here got. I do."

I said, "Right, sir. You just send over who all you think is best and we'll go with it. We'll do that."

I looked at him, communicating trust and acknowledging the deep responsibility we shared for the maintenance of the minor formulae and the well-being of the good people who would show up, mostly in rattletrap cars and the beds of pickup trucks, a few days hence when I had my equipment serviced and ready for the setting of the tobacco plants in one field and the topping and suckering in another. We shook hands and stared for three or four beats into each other's eyes, and then Sir Alfred sprinted away to the old white Cadillac and bounced across the furrows to the hardroad.

A rooster tail of dust curled up after him on the sandy track that went to parts of the piney woods none of us knew. He was off to collect his labor. I knew he had got the best of me for a few dollars, but not as many as would have made Mr. Frank come into it. And the system we all subscribed to had got the best of him and his all their lives and always would.

Twenty-Five

I FARMED ON through that hot August, remembering old habits and getting myself promoted right and left, while Daddy slowly got better in the bed where I had been made. He and I held long conferences late in the night. He seemed to take as much delight in my decisions, even in our disagreements, as in the assurances I gave that things would get done. I knew I was doing the work only medium well and was shaving his profits to a transparency that would send him to the bank next spring with his hat in his hand. I told him so. He answered that it was a whole lot better than nothing at all, *with* doctor bills, which was what he'd have without me. I told him he'd be better off to hire a practical nurse and send Mama out to the field — she could farm with the best of them — but he only grinned.

The weeks became a month and then another, and through the long hot days, we got the tobacco gathered and cured and auctioned. It was a good auction that year, as good as anyone around could remember, a fair one the local men said. Our tobacco graded out high and sold at a good price.

I picked most of the corn myself because it required no skill, only endurance and a hugh tolerance for boredom. Inside the glass cab of our Alice Chalmers Four-Row Gleaner, I bounced down the rows pouring a golden stream of corn into the hopper behind me. The green mandibles of the machine chewed the crackling corn stalks in front of me, and the country music came tinning at me from the cheap transistor that hung from the rearview mirror. I made up my own songs, combining verses and bits of what was available, and sometimes at night, picking by headlights in a delirium of din and vibration and monotony, I sang, "I got tears in my ears from lying on my back crying my eyes out over you," or "If I had it to do all over again, I'd do it all over you."

Through all of this, I tried to put Bainesborough out of my mind by nurturing the attitude of a soldier on a long and arduous march. A day's work was sufficient to the day. I rose before light each morning, stiff, calloused, rashed, sunburnt, tobacco-stained, leaner, stronger, harder, and more benumbed and did a day's work and half of a night's if the dew fell late, with no thought but to build time.

But sometimes, late at night, just before sleeping, I could not censor that world of Bainesborough. Reeba and Ardis and Lindy Briggs and, most of all, Eldon Odom came crowding into my mind's eye, preemptory and strange-seeming now that I was on home soil. The strangeness was how easily I had absented myself from my dream closet at the call of blood, and how strongly that blood still sang to me now that Daddy was better.

By the third week in September, when the corn had gone to the scales in Live Oak and the peanuts were mature and ready for the gas dryers, Daddy was up and hobbling around and wanting the reins back from me. One afternoon we stopped to watch the sun set and feel the first breath of cool air from the northwest. We were standing by the peanut dryers, big fans that channeled heat from a rushing blue gas flame through the collected tons of our labors. Our backs were warm and our chests were cool. Daddy hung from his crutches. With a thumb and forefinger, he formed a pill of tobacco in a pouch of Red Man. Reflexively, he offered me some. I thanked him, no, and lit a Camel.

A cold western light was dusting the tops of Mr. Frank Arneau's windbreak of pines. Daddy watched the pale fire in the pines, sniffed the air, and said, "It's gone be a hard winter, I can tell it."

I thought: Look back at the summer you survived by the skin of your teeth. But I said, "How d'you know?"

He laid a forefinger to the side of his nose, thick with exploded capillaries. "Nose tells me," he said. I looked at all of him, ace-bandaged and crutch-propped, at the two deep purple scars that crossed his forehead and plunged into the gray hair at his temple. He was still soft at the broken places and would be for some time.

"I allus could smell weather, Toad. It's a Turlow trait. Your mommer's people ain't got the nose to speak of, but a Turlow can tell you weather if he wants to."

He tweezered the pill of tobacco and stuck it under his lip. *If he wants to:* It was his warning never to deprecate the hidden powers. I had discovered some hidden powers in myself those last weeks, and so I decided to venerate the idea of the supernatural nose.

"You gone mend fence and take it easy for a while?" I suggested.

"Usual," he said, watching the fire grow dim in the pines. He meant that he would negotiate the fall season as usual, a work load not quite as heavy as that of August and September, but almost. In anger, I turned away, blowing smoke at the gathering darkness. The terms under which we took each other had changed, but not enough so that I could turn as I wanted to and say, "Old man, if you don't take it easy there won't be stitches and rest enough for your next mistake. And there won't be me either. I have done my bit." After a space, my anger subsided and I was ashamed.

I walked over and put my hand on the warm cowl of the gas burner. "I wish you'd give yourself a season to get stronger. I'll call Sir Alfred and get you some help with the fences and the stock. You can lay up and rest some more and do some bird hunting. You don't have to work so hard."

He looked at me with an expression complicated by the growing darkness and the lump in his cheek. Not knowing exactly what was in his face, I was only sure that, in his way, he had asked me to stay. Maybe he had even threatened me with the consequences of leaving. He would not say more. After spearing me with that look for a count of three, he turned and spit brown juice into the gas flame.

One night in early October, when the peanuts had gone to market and the combine had been serviced and a consignment of new cypress planking had been stacked teepee-style to cure out for fences and pens, I realized that I had seen nothing but work and no one but my parents and few of their connections for more than two months. I decided to borrow a truck and drive it straight to the first place that sold whiskey by the glass.

After supper, I stood up and stretched and announced my intention to go for a drive. My mother was standing at the sink. "Body'd think you had enough driving," she said to the dishwater.

Daddy pushed himself up on one crutch. The mention of whiskey in this house would conjure my sister Patricia, so I was careful. I followed my father into the living room. He kept his right arm cradled against his body as he walked, leaning heavily on his crutch. He handed me the keys to the truck. "I expect you'll want to try that place across the river at Hatch Bend. Closest."

I thanked him and said I expected I would.

Inside the Suwannee Club, it was as dark as the waters at the bottom of Hatch Bend and just as crosscut with eddies and currents. On the dance floor a clutch of lumpy couples was doing the good old boy and girl shuffle to the tune of "Help Me Make It Through the Night," sung by Kris Kristofferson. Leg to leg and crotch to crotch in the lurid light of the jukebox, they were turning and grinding like there was no tomorrow. I didn't see anyone I knew, so I took a corner table and waited for service.

When I had been overcharged for a bourbon and branch to the tune of "It Wasn't God Who Made Honky-Tonk Angels," I sat back to sip and meditate. I had only just entered the realm of long thought when C. Randle Arneau came lurching out of the Gents. He was a massive delta of muscle driven into a thirty-inch waist, swaying metronomically to "Satin Sheets," sung by Miss Jeannie Pruett. Heartbreak eddied and swirled around me, dark and deep and cold as the waters hard by the door.

"C. Randle!" I called across those beautiful words: "Long black Cadillac, tailor-mades on my back, but still I'm not happy, don't you see?"

"Ho?" he shouted, stopping in good-natured confusion in the gale of lust and music and darkness.

"Here!" I hailed.

"Ho!"

I waved at him from my corner redoubt. A few listless heads turned as he came toward me. We shook hands. His was an oddly gentle grip, given with concentration as though he had carefully taught himself not to mangle. C. Randle Arneau lived in that placid world very few ever locate: He was bad enough to be left alone, and too good to bother anyone.

When C. Randle had sat down and the shock wave that attended the event had subsided, we surveyed the human comedy. Ours was an easy silence. We had worked together. I had begun with doubts about my ability to keep up, doubts that had more to do with a species of ingenuity in the face of the ten thousand mechanical and logistical problems that plague a farmer's day than with anything physical. Now I was easy in the aura of all the muscle and the pleasantly masculine odor of whiskey and cheap aftershave and boot leather; also, and not incidentally, I was safe with C. Randle Arneau.

"You come down here to do some titty hawking?" C. Randle queried.

"Naw. My dick done dropped off in the peanut field."

C. Randle laughed a big, full-throated laugh. "You didn't go back and look for it?"

"Not after it got all dirty." I mentioned that this was the unwholesome prospect before us all, and he sipped and stared at the notion until two unattended cowgirls circled past us. One of them spoke to C. Randle, who introduced me. "Oh," the visitor said, "I didn't know Trish Turlow had a brother."

After a night in a place like this, I mused, Trish usually didn't know it either.

Some time and three bourbons later, after C. Randle and I had remembered and congratulated every tobacco leaf and peanut and ear of corn of that summer and had looked forward with philosophic weariness to the castrating and vaccinating and fence-mending of the fall, I excused myself to the call of wild nature. When I returned, C. Randle was on the dance floor enveloped in the limbs of some faded former Alligood County Tobacco or Soybean Queen, drunkenly swaying as Ray Price crooned, "Make believe you love me one more time . . . for the good times." I stepped into the thumping silence of the parking lot.

It was early yet, and I did not want to go home. I headed out 249 west toward the edges of the Savannah. I had no thought except for the feel of the night wind in my face and the raspy sound of a radio that might have been broadcasting from the dance floor at the Suwannee Club. I had been driving for twenty minutes, just spinning down the white corridor of my head-lights, when I saw the sign: Hardentown. I had already lurched into a turn before it came home to me that I was heading back into my other life.

I slowed at the outskirts of the town, a little grit stopover like Isle Hammock or Swinford and dozens more — a water tower, a gas station, a hardware store, a feed and seed store, a post office, and a storefront lawyer selling farms and acreage and divorce. I could feel the attraction of the home place somewhere behind me in that maze of roads, but more strongly the counter-pull of Hardentown, which I knew by name only and as the new residence of Eldon Odom.

It was one of those narrow lots common on Florida lakes. A small waterfront and a long backyard. As I drove the winding dirt lane to the house, a glimmer through the trees, I could hear faintly the sound of a booming base guitar. Ardis's Mercedes was parked in the yard. Its paint was lashed dull by branches; she had been putting in some time on country roads. I parked beside it and stood in the side yard listening to the music and watching the moon on the lake. It was a bright, clear night, chilly enough to show me my breath. Far across the lake, maybe three-quarters of a mile away, I could make out rooftops and the glimmering white stalks of a boathouse.

Odom's "retreat" was of whitewashed frame with long veran- dahs and a sharply pitched roof. It reminded me of the govern- ment buildings below the lighthouses on Amelia Island and Captiva. It must have been forty years old. I could see shadows moving on the old paper shades. The stereo rejected "Sympathy for the Devil," and on came "Bad Moon Rising." In the silent interim, I heard Eldon Odom's loud, raucous laugh, and then the following laughter of the group. Still following, I thought, and so am I.

I walked around to the lakefront. Tall pines stood in the dooryard; further down the sandy slope canoe paddles, weight benches, a barbecue grill, and deck chairs were littered about. A Hobie Cat, trailing its sail in the water, was snubbed to the shore. I climbed the porch and knocked loudly.

The music continued inside but the voices stopped. Then I heard the whispers and the rushing footsteps of people who are hiding something. I felt a brief thrill of power and something else, too. I wanted what was hidden.

"Yeah?" Tory Hubbel threw open the door. His belligerency gave way to wild relief when he saw my face.

"Shit, Toad," he wiped his nose with a thick wrist, "you had us back-peddling there for a minute."

"What you doing, Tory, having a fire drill?" I moved past him into the warm, lighted room. All of them were in postures of recovery and relief — Shine, Sarah, Hubbel. Eldon Odom was sitting in a chair with a book upside down in his hand. He put it aside and said, "First time you been here, Toad." My power was high, but I could think of no way to use it.

I nodded. He looked around at the others, then back to me, his wary eyes commenting upon my long absence.

"My daddy hurt himself," I told them all. "I had to go back and be a noble son of the soil for a while. Got so eat up with nobility I couldn't stand myself." I shrugged and raised my hands in mock appeal. My palms were tobacco-tanned and rough as new corncobs. Sarah said, "When you can't stand yourself, always come and see us." The group laughed, Odom was amused, and so was I, but I felt also the cut of my own disloyalty. I had used it to buy my way back among them.

Eldon Odom rose and stepped toward me. The others, including Ardis, who had come in from the kitchen with Lindy, closed around us. "We're doing some crank." Odom was up in my face. "You want some?"

"Sure," I said, flinching from him.

Shine walked over to the coffee table and carefully lifted a newspaper, exposing a woman's hand mirror with a pool of white powder on it and a razor blade. Shine placed the powder, like a votive offering, on the dining room table. The group gathered around.

The house was a hunting camp. Moldering trophies were mounted on the walls — the head of a little key deer, hardly larger than a spaniel's; a whole bobcat, running; a molting red-tailed hawk. There was a display case of pickled snakes — a coral, a good-sized diamondback, and a moccasin with an aged, yellow mouth. Currier and Ives prints hung on the walls — horses with all four feet off the ground, frilled and high-hatted passengers riding in carriages, and the steamboat Robert E. Lee. The furniture was thick and functional and greasy from too many pairs of dirty pants. It must have been some country bachelor's last stand, this place on the lake. A string of real mahogany decoys lay in the corner by the Franklin stove, and there was a standing cabinet full of the lethal gleam of gunmetal.

I wondered if this old hunter and taxidermist was Odom's culture vulture.

The house bore the marks of his and Lindy's more recent passage. A typewriter flanked by stacks of new manuscript rested on a card table on the screened porch facing the lake. A newly-opened carton gleamed with the bright dust jackets of Odom's recent triumph, *Sojourners Under the Mountain*. Apparently the two of them did not bother much with house-keeping. Peering down the dim hallway to the bathroom, I could see a riot of Lindy's pastel dainties and Odom's running togs. Lindy was no wife. She may have been Odom's muse, perhaps his goad, perhaps even the living curse to the *poete maudit,* but she was no housekeeping amanuensis like Reeba.

I noticed with a relief that annoyed me that MacEvoy was not among us. I could not grow used to him, the hawk face and droll, leering eye, the casual possessiveness of Ardis. When I was around them, I had to keep reminding myself that my rights to the usual feelings were cancelled. As I stood watching the white powder become smoother and whiter, I reflected that none of us had rights, except Reeba who was not one of us.

Silently we filed by Shine's communion table, throwing our heads back and clutching at watering eyes, then passing on into the world of nostalgia. After that, time was synchronized with our fast-paced hearts, and we each began to perform a trivial miracle. Mine was a game of darts with Tory Hubbel. Wordless and furious, it was the best game of darts I had ever played.

And yet, even as I gloried in the heartbeat of the drug, I knew that I was destroying honest time. When the last dart had struck the center of the target, I wandered out under the moon. I found Ardis there, sitting in one of Odom's deck chairs. I watched the long slope to the glassy water. What had earlier been a chaos of litter was now the cleverest of all possible arrangements of objects in space. I marveled at it, deciding to disarrange a chair only so that I could sit by her.

I grinned fiercely at her in the moonlight, but she only stared at the glimmering shapes across the lake. Perhaps the powder seized her differently than it took me. Or perhaps — the thought was trouble — she had not filed past our table to the other side, to the world of nostalgia. I might be with a stranger

"So, how's it going?" I asked carefully.

She turned and stared at me. "He knows."

I couldn't imagine what she meant.

"He knows you've been . . . *seeing* her. She *is* still his wife. If he weren't so goddamned interested in hurting himself, you'd be in very deep shit." Anger was in her voice, and more, a kind of mournful concern not so much for me as for all of us.

"Oh, I don't know," I said. My voice was jaunty, hollow, scared. My heart seemed to crawl toward the fuse of my neck. All I could think was, "How did he find out?"

"Tommy told him. He saw you coming out of there one morning. He . . ."

"I could have been . . . could have been . . ."

"Were you?"

Frantically I tried to rewrite it, to say that I could have been an innocent bystander, a delivery boy, a victim, a telephone man. Why did the truth have to be assumed?

Ardis shifted in her chair and looked straight at me, and I was certain she had not taken our communion. This was not the way it used to be. This was some nightmare of what might be, of what I had no power to prevent.

I held up my hand between us, pushing her eyes away. "Ardis, listen," I began, with no idea where I was going.

"I'm listening," she said, "but I don't hear anything. I don't hear anything from any of these people but bullshit and self-deception and plans that never go and books they never write and a whole lot of talk about drugs, as though drugs were stories or better than stories.''

Something occurred to me, and it came with a blossoming rage. Suddenly I was standing on the other side of nostalgia, the beneath, the dark. "What the hell are *you* doing with that asshole MacEvoy, that pimp, that scumbag, that . . ." It was loud, echoing across the lake and coming back crazy. She was backing away from me, and when I stopped and stood trembling, my hands were extended toward her in hate and supplication. I looked at them. They had torn something that until now had still existed between us. I sat down and listened to the glassy sounds of her bare feet on the sand. Then I watched the moon, knowing I had worked too hard these last months, missed too much sleep, displaced my dream with too many tawdry country and western fantasies. My funny nobility lay all about me on the sand.

I left the deck chair and walked out to the truck just as MacEvoy drove up in a new black Trans Am. It was gleaming and chromed and scooped and radialed, and it spoke with a menacing grumble there beside Ardis's Mercedes.

"Hey, big'un!" he called to me. "You leaving already? Party's just starting." He removed a parcel of something from inside his denim jacket. Then his face in the moonlight became pensive. "Turlow, Turlow? Hey, don't you have a sister name of Alice? Seems like I used to . . .''

I started the engine. All my rage was gone, drained away into the first few moments of the long, jaw-grinding debt I owed the drug. I said, "Must have been two other guys."

"Sure?" he asked me. He was as friendly as he had ever been to me.

"I'm sure," I said, finding the gears.

"Cause I used to know this old girl named . . ."

But I was backing away, and turning, and starting the long ride back under the moon.

Twenty-Six

I SAID GOOD-BYE to my parents, and in my old Toyota drove off in the direction of Bainesborough, but not before promising I would keep in touch. "Write if you get work," my father called after me, an old joke and a gentle reminder that the only real work was done on the land.

My rented room was dust and disorder, and the dream had to be revived. With a stubborn reluctance I faced my small pile of manuscript pages, the novel rising out of the ashes of that honky-tonk where my sister had burnt alive. As I tidied the small room and squared myself to the now unaccustomed task of writing, I remembered the secret talk I'd had with my mother before leaving the farm.

"I wish you'd stay on another two weeks."

We were standing by the farrowing house watching a litter of pigs which had been dropped the night before. They were our excuse to be alone.

"He doesn't want me to, Mommer. You know that." It was my excuse. True enough, but still an excuse.

"He does and he doesn't." She spoke carefully, staring into the squirming, barely individuated mass of newborn hogflesh. "He does want you back *permanent*. He just doesn't want to be reminded. When you're temporary, you remind him that he bent over that drive shaft. That he forgot."

I told her I had made my decision a long time ago. My tone and the way I stared at the litter of pigs told her I had made it painfully.

"It's different now," she whispered, pulling her pride into her words.

"Aw, he'll be all right," I said. That was my lie, a powerful one. I wanted to believe it because it cancelled time. "He'll take it easy now."

My mother only stared. On the way back to the house, she looked off to the north where the pine treetops were dancing in a brisk cool wind. "I think it will be a mild winter," she said. "I just think it will."

To say that Ardis's words, "He knows," haunted me would be overstatement, but the truth is not far from haunting. I was constantly aware of Odom though I avoided him. I was sick of him and sick with him; that is, with him like a fever, some unkillable breath of the Savannah, not likely to kill me but never forgotten, even as I sat at my typewriter. Was MacEvoy telling the truth? If so, what would Odom do? Did Reeba know we were no longer secret? Why had MacEvoy chosen to tell? (God, to have overheard their conversation! Had the information been passed casually, or as another of the momentous events of the life of Odom? Had MacEvoy carried the fact to Odom in the same way he brought the drug — in delicious secrecy and childish delight?) What and what and how and how, I asked myself, and the fever burned on. In my low grade delirium, I was able to write and meet my dreary obligations, but I avoided the group as much as possible and kept away from Odom's face.

One night Reeba came to the convenience store. The kid who worked the day shift sold hard-core porn under the counter, and just at the moment Reeba chose to enter my working life, I was trying to convince an habitué of the demimonde that *I* did not sell it. He would have to come back in the morning.

Reeba came through the door hugging a trenchcoat around herself and, without looking at me, circled past the dog food to beauty aids. Over the shoulder of my persistent client, a wino named Raven David, I watched her consider the purchase of a mudpack facial. We weren't moving a lot of mudpack facials in Squalor Holler that summer. I said to Raven David, "Look, goddamnit, I told you I ain't selling crotch magazines. If you want one, come back in the morning."

"It *is* morning," Raven David quibbled, pointing to the watch on his wrist. The watch had been rusted solid since the night he was arrested for bathing in the courthouse fountain.

I said, "OK, technically it is morning. But look outside. Do you see light? No, you don't. When you see light, come back and Jimmy the Kid will sell you the T and A."

He looked at me. "I want pink! Ain't he got pink?"

I corrected myself. "Come back when it's light and Jimmy'll sell you some pink."

His eyes got a little bigger and I could see the red color start to come to his face, a sure sign he was about to speak in tongues. His fits of glossolalia sometimes lasted hours. I held up my hand in a gesture of peace. "Look, Raven, why don't you just pay me for the Mad Dog and before you know it, you'll be back around this way and the sun'll be up? We're on your daily route. Watayasay? Huh, big guy?"

The red faded from his cheeks and his lips stopped twitching. He reached into his pocket, shoved aside the erection which was the cause of our problem, and began counting out lint, hair, and change to pay for the wine. I spotted him the last dime because Reeba was showing signs of impatience over by home remedies. "Thanks," Raven said. "Mighty white of you."

When the buzzer on the door had rung Raven David into the night, Reeba walked straight to the counter. Her eyes did not accuse me of avoiding her. Her face without makeup was sallow and sunken. She was excited. She pressed herself against the counter. The trenchcoat had loosened and I thought she might be naked underneath. It was something housewives did, running out to get milk in a robe or raincoat. This time of the morning, the convenience store counterman was like a doctor or a priest. Who cared what he saw?

I reached out and tugged at the lapel of the coat to close it. She smiled, and when she spoke her voice was low. "Can you come home with me?" and I thought she was calling me back into the secret we had started.

Blushing and glancing at the doorway, I said, "Now?"

"Something's wrong. I can't go in the house."

"I don't understand," I said.

She put her hand to her breast and tried to slow her own breathing. "I went out to visit Presley, you know, at camp. I took him out to dinner. It's a long drive and we stayed late. I just got home, just a few minutes ago, and when I went to the door, I didn't hear Leviathan. He didn't come to the door. That's how I know. . . ."

"What do you mean he didn't come? Does he always come?" I tried to control my exasperation. I had nearly convinced myself to stay away from her; I had been told Eldon Odom knew about us. I put a calming hand across the counter, but she drew away from it, looking over her shoulder at the night outside.

"Yes," she said, *"he always comes to the door."*

I looked at the clock above the frozen foods. It was five. I took the keys from under the counter and told her to wait by the door. I might be gone no longer than thirty minutes, and in this neighborhood, no one would complain. Except to me. The bums and street people would bitch about my absence, but no one would find his way to a phone and thence to Billy Soomers, my boss. I hoped.

In the small back room there was a toilet, a floor safe, and a fuse box. I switched off the lights and groped my way out to the front of the store, where Reeba stood shivering.

We took her car. I drove, doing what she told me to do.

"Park up here," she said. "Let's don't make any noise."

We walked quietly down into that cavern of trees. The iron gate that protected the front of the house hung open. "Did you open it?" I whispered.

She shook her head, shivering.

It was then that I wanted to call the police. As a last hope I asked her, "Could the dog open it?"

She shook her head. She had no voice.

I was about to tell her that we should get the hell out when Leviathan's foaming, bloody snout shoved through the doorway. He limped toward Reeba, laboring for breath, then fell and began to convulse as though trying to breathe and vomit at once. She knelt by him, smearing her hands with blood. "Sweet Jesus, what is it?" She looked up at me.

"Get the car down here."

She sat down, pulling his rolling head into her lap.

"Go!" I whispered, hard.

She stood on shaky legs and I pushed her toward the car. When I heard it start, I got down on my knees and used all the strength I had to lift the flopping, blood-foaming dog.

A fancy society veterinarian worked on Leviathan for thirty minutes, but not before asking to see Reeba's Master Charge. We paced his cypress-panelled waiting room in a ridiculous parody of relatives waiting for the news of birth or death. All for a dog, I said to myself, for I was from Alligood County where the truth is not the parable of the good shepherd. Nor did I like this particular dog very much. But I could see how it all moved Reeba. I kept my thoughts to myself and beat back my worries about Eldon Odom and about the convenience store, where I had turned the legions of the Big Thirst out into the night.

At about 5:45, the doctor, a corpulent, balding man with a worried red face and the small white hands of a child, came out to us in great agitation. I was pleased at the collapse of his kennelside manner until I heard what he said: "I have phoned the police, Mrs. Odom. They will meet you at home. I removed a human hand from Leviathan's gut."

Sergeant Elwin Holder, immaculate in police blue and worried, drew his service revolver and led us into the house. He muttered that he had seen it before but did not tell us what he had seen. When he could not find the switch, Reeba, trembling like one of my winos, turned on the lights for him, and the room, a shambles of broken glass, smashed furniture, and smeared blood, leapt to our eyes. A trail of bloody footprints and foam and torn cloth led to the heart of the house, to Eldon Odom's study.

A man was crouched in the closet. "Oh, my Jesus Christ," Reeba moaned when she saw him. She backed away and her heels hit the bed, and she fell back with her head in her hands.

The man's trousers were wadded at his knees and he had removed the belt from them to make a tourniquet for his right arm. Leviathan had seized the hand just inside the iron grill — a luckier snatch than he had made at my own hand once long ago. With the dog pulling and then apparently swallowing, and the man dragging and seeking shelter, they had tumbled and crawled and smeared and fought their way through the wrecked living room, down the long hallway, and into this small study, where the man wedged the closet door in the dog's face, completing the amputation. Sick and frenzied and suffocating, the dog had retreated to the living room to wait for Reeba.

The man crouched with his knees up against his chest, the tourniquet forgotten. A long smear of blood began at his midsection where he still held the blunt wrist tightly against his stomach, and pooled across the floor. The man was Frank Lagano. I sat beside Reeba in a room full of cops and paramedics and the two naked ghosts of our secret and took her hand.

When the rescue squad had taken Frank away, a bloodless white face still surprised on the rolling gurney, and the cops had their report and the neighbors had been shooed away and the last of the revolving blue lights had gone dark and the antlered police cruisers had grumbled into the night, I stood by Reeba at the front door where it had all started. Then I remembered the convenience store.

When we got there in the dawn just before the arrival of my replacement, Jimmy the Kid, the place was dark, deserted, innocent. My hope had held. I went in and turned on the lights and then came out to her.

"I can't go back there," she said, waiting for an answer.

I gave her my keys and directions to my little room. The look of gratitude she gave me when I delivered her from that house full of bloody footprints and broken glass and ghosts was more than I deserved. Before she drove away, she asked me, "Who was he?"

"I don't know," I lied.

She knew it was a lie and gave me a look of reproach. "You'll tell me," she said, my key in her hand.

I nodded, then glanced back at the store. "But not tonight."

An hour later, I was plodding up the stairs with Traymore at my back telling me there had been "a lady" in my room. "How do you know she was a lady?" I asked him. In those days, *lady* was an unreconstructed word.

"Well, you know, she was . . . *old.*"

"How old would you say?"

He looked at me, offended. "I don't know. Fifty maybe." Reeba was forty-two.

"I'm glad she didn't hear you say that."

She had left the door unlocked. My key lay beside the hundred-dollar bill on the desk. She had left a note in my typewriter.

> Dear Sweet: I couldn't have gone back there, not
> while it was still dark. This money is for my rent and
> to help you in case you lost your job on account of
> me. You were good to do what you did.

She signed it *Love, Reeba.* And there was a postscript: *Eldon says to tell you thanks.*

The first time I went to see Frank, a uniformed policeman at the door of his hospital room sent me downtown to see a detective. I thought about it for a day. Finally I decided to present myself, and after a short but thorough investigation of my association with Frank Lagano (but thankfully, not with Rebecca Sullivan Odom), I was given a ticket of admission.

Frank was pale, as though the transfusions had not been red enough. He was still in the slow process of building his own blood, and he lay concentrating on the ceiling. For a long time I stood by the bed waiting. "What did they do with my car, Toad? Where's my car?"

His voice was quiet but anxious. I was surprised by the question. "I don't know, Frank." He looked at me for the first time. "Can you find out? I mean, *would* you find out?" He had to stop. The talking made him tired.

"Sure, Frank. Sure I will." I thought about the ride he had given me the night I had smeared my fists with blood, about his obvious pride in his big salesman's car. To me the Buick was smooth and bright and terrifying because, confined in it with the neon world sliding past, Frank was always an outsider.

His breathing evened a little. "What are you doing here?" he asked me.

"I came to see how you were getting along." It was part of the truth. The rest was my knowledge that no one else would come. Who cared about the outsider? A hundred questions teemed in my brain. I had promised myself to ask none of them. I said, "Can I get you anything?"

He gave a dry chuckle. "A new life. You're the fair-haired boy. How about it? Can you get me outta this trick of shit?" He tried to laugh again, but his lips were parched. I picked up the water glass with a telescoping straw in it and held it for him. I stood there in silence while he drank, concentrating on the ceiling. Finally he returned to me, moving his head on the pillow slowly and with great effort, and I could see that he was lying under an enormous burden. He had been waiting years, years of riding in that car and selling substitutes to others who could not unburden themselves, years of pouring his life story into the jaded ear of the group. Now he wanted to tell me. The way he found to do it was his finest and his most frightening evocation of the storyteller's art.

"Ahhhh, but who is this?" he crooned to me from the pillow. His voice was suddenly changed. Even in the cracked throat and the hollow chest whose energies were gone, I recognized it.

"Where is he?" he crooned.

"Jesus, Frank!" I couldn't help myself. I shrank back from him.

"I'm going to need that kid," he crooned, drawing out the last word just as he had drawn it out into my frightened ear that day on the phone. There were tears in his eyes. They pooled, then flowed across his temples to the pillow. I reached out and touched his arm before I realized it was the arm that had no hand. All I could say was, "Why?"

"I had to get closer," he sobbed. "I had to somehow. I couldn't write worth a shit. I couldn't say anything they would listen to. So I . . ."

He was crying uncontrollably, loudly, unable to speak. I was afraid the officer at the door would come in. I dug my fingers into the flesh of his handless arm, wanting to embrace him and to brain him with the water pitcher all at once.

"You know what I finally realized?" he sobbed with his last energy. "It wasn't him. Oh, sometimes he answered the phone. Sometimes I got close to him, but mostly it was her. And when I saw her at that party, I knew she was just like me. Both of us were . . ." He fixed me with his fiercest gaze. "We weren't close at all. So I decided to go over there. I don't know what I was doing. Maybe I was going to tell her I was sorry, that I was just like her. Maybe . . ."

He was exhausted, his breathing was ragged, his face livid despite the lost reserves of blood. He sank into the counterpane, gasping hard, trying to recover.

I stood there for a while longer, my fingers digging into his arm. It was as close to him as I could get. After a while I forgot that I wanted to hurt him. I had only one reason for touching him. He couldn't talk anymore or wouldn't. I left him there staring at the ceiling, pale and vacant, waiting for what came next.

Twenty-Seven

IT WAS ALL in the papers. The police searched Frank's car and found phone bills listing those moments of closeness. He had been a clumsy criminal. They also found the heaped chapters of his life story. It was, the papers told us, a record of the criminal mind in all its deep perversity. They played up the pornography angle, which kept the story on the front page of the city section for some time. But finally, as Frank's color improved and his Rotarian optimism came back and his pink prosthetic hand began to seem plausible to him, the story faded from the papers and life became pretty much as it had been. Eldon Odom did not press charges. Frank had lost enough. He was abandoned.

The only other person who visited Frank was Sarah Fesco. One day I ran into her in the elevator, and after a short visit with Frank, who was tired that day and not very good company, we left together. Outside on the street, I asked her to have a beer

with me, and after looking up and down the thoroughfare as
though scanning for a better possibility, she said, "All right,
boyo."

So, I thought as we walked down the sunny street toward
Moby's, she's doing Irish today.

Talk about writing got us through the first beer. On the
second, we spoke earnestly about Frank. We agreed that the rest
of them were shits for not visiting the poor bastard, even, Sarah
said, if he was a dirty old man. During the third beer, we gave
ourselves to a pensive silence, and with the fourth we began to
talk about ourselves. Being the more experienced drinker, I was
somewhat at an advantage, and the truth is, I wanted something.
I wanted to know about Sarah. I had seen very little of her since
Odom's new successes. Without the class to rally us, the group
had splintered and only a few had made it to the shores of Lake
Searl in Hardentown.

"Do you miss the class?" I asked her, leaning forward across
the rim of my beer.

Her eyes narrowed, letting me know that we were on new
ground. Not dangerous yet, but new. She nodded. "I do,
indeed," she said, "and so do you. After all, who are we
without it? I'm a waitress and you are . . ." She waited for me to
fill in the blank.

"I purvey truth, beauty, and Mad Dog 20-20 at the Lil
Colonel in Squalor Holler."

"Quite," she said, Britishly. "I serve lunch and dinner at the
Quiche Me Quick, where the fern count is rather too high and
the queer pie is excellent. Come by someday and I'll see they cut
you an extra large slice of the Lorraine." She hoisted her stein to
me.

I had never eaten at the Quiche Me Quick. I couldn't afford it.
"At least you don't get your bottom pinched," I said.

"Oh, don't be too sure. Some of those poofters will run the

odd hand up a girl's knickers just for the reaction. Something to do with mummy. Very deep, psychologically speaking." She smiled, proud of herself. We paused while she ran her fingers back over the notes she had just played to see how they scanned.

"Yes," she said more seriously, sipping, "I miss it, and so do you."

I nodded and said, "But silence has its compensations. I mean, who needs a ritual kick in the ass *every* week?"

"As I recall, yours was not kicked last time out." She was referring to the Old Man's public affirmation of my work. I had been living my dream life on the strength of that moment for some time. In fact, the script of that evening was beginning to curl at the edges from so much rehearsal. I knew the others were jealous, but it was the group's code to be a good loser. Hadn't Tory Hubbel and Mike Shine drawn me closer as a result of that evening? I suppose I expected the same thing from Sarah. I mumbled something about it being her work next time.

"Let's hope so, shall we."

"Yes," I said. "Let's." We drank to it.

"How did you first meet Odom?" I asked her. She sipped and contemplated me. I could see that she was considering the truth. It was winning, but its strong opposition was habit and hurt. I composed a trustworthy face, remembering the night Shine and Hubbel had so casually handled Sarah's private parts. She had been humiliated, angry, but neither strongly enough. What made her accept such things?

"I don't know why I'm telling you this," she said.

"You haven't yet," I said softly.

"No, I haven't, but I'm going to. On the courage of this beer you're paying for, I'm going to tell you something. I'm going to tell you how I first . . . *met* our benefactor and regent, Eldon Odom." She sipped again, and the way she let her mug strike the bar was a little stagey. "I was one of his *undergraduate* students a long time ago. And a *long* time ago it was. In fact, I was once the inhabitant of that hole in his life your wonderful Lindy fills these days."

"She's not *my* Lindy," I said.

"And she isn't mine," Sarah said. "And don't think his stupid charade had me fooled. He once did the same thing with me, pushing me off on another student, a nice boy, so that it would appear I was, shall we say, spoken for. The bastard!"

She had said, "bastar," leaving the "d" somewhere in the beer. I signaled the bartender for two more. When the beers came, Sarah lifted hers up with an air of ownership. She was going to sing for her supper. I moved closer to her and closer to Eldon Odom.

"I was this very young *under*graduate, and Eldon Odom was a much younger, not to say *young,* professor, you see."

I nodded.

"Well, I took his fiction-writing class. Back in those days, when he wasn't such hot shit, you didn't have to have permission to get in or be recommended by someone who was also a benefactor. I think he had only published *Naked in Church* then, and the reviews weren't *that* good, and the university was not convinced that he walked on water. But *we* were. We *knew.* It was just the way he was, that crazy light in his eyes, that swagger, that cock-of-the-walk getalong of his, and even his color. That Indian skin. He was different, he was weird, he was going somewhere. You know what I mean?"

I said I knew.

"I don't know why he picked me. We both know why he picked Lindy, don't we, but with me, it's a little harder to figure. I mean, I'm not exactly your basic boffo chick, am I?" She stared at me fiercely.

I cleared my throat and gave a diagonal slant of the head, an exact cross between a nod and a negative. She closed an eye, which was growing red, and sipped. "Well, anyway. One night I stayed after class to ask him a question about my story. That's another thing that was different then. He would answer questions instead of brushing them off or pointing to groupthink. We were leaning over his desk, and suddenly he was touching me, and then he did the strangest thing."

She stared at me. An old surprise, still barbed, was in her face. She looked down at her beer, and when she raised her head again, the surprise was gone. In its place was the usual pale mask of irony.

"What did he do?" I urged, leaning close.

"He put one of his big hands over mine on my manuscript and he started to tighten. At first it was just a squeeze, and then it started to hurt, and I tried to pull away and he was looking at me, close, like he was trying to study something, and I tried to pull away, and then I . . . didn't. I didn't pull away. I just let him hurt me, and after a while he said, 'You're smiling,' and I said, 'Yes.' He took me to a motel."

Sarah left her beer on the bar and went to the toilet. I waited, staring at my reflection in the mirror, a blurred, clouded face shoved among the bright bottles.

She returned and we drank in silence. Finally, I said, "Isn't there more? I mean, every story has a middle and an end."

"You mean, tell me the delicious details, is what you mean. After all, you're a writer."

I looked at her in the mirror. It was not titillation I was after. My calling was a higher one, though it might take me to some very low places. I wanted to be closer to the source.

In the mirror, she gave me a withering look and said, "I'm a better storyteller than you think. And I am certainly no dry hump, no sir. Just let me . . ." She took a long swallow. "Just let . . ." She drank again and gasped.

"So," she said, squaring herself to face us in the mirror. "We

carried on in the usual manner for quite some time and no one
the wiser. I was . . . *very* young and thought it was wonderful,
and I thought *he* was wonderful, and, if you can believe it, I even
thought *I* was wonderful. And he said my work was very good,
and for a while we were going somewhere, you know, together.
But then it started to change. He kept asking me for more, for
things I couldn't give him." Her voice became small, her face
began to flush. "He wanted me to *do* things." She appealed to
me. "Things I just couldn't . . ."

She turned to me, the real me, not the one in the mirror. "You
know?" I nodded, not exactly sure.

With great effort, she blurted, "Things that *hurt* me. Finally I
realized he was trying to eat me alive, use me up for his work, or
for something inside him that wasn't right, that wasn't love, or
. . ." She paused. " . . . or wonder. That wonder I told you
about. One night a new student came to his class, a girl named
Carlin. To make a long story short, he started up with her, too,
and he kept me, and then he asked us to come with him one night
together, and we did because we were both very *young*, and we
both thought he was wonderful. It was the first time, as far as I
know, as far as I have been able to . . ." Her voice took on the
abstracted tone of the researcher, one of the keepers of the lore.
" . . . to determine, that he ever used that lovely white powder.
He offered it to us like it was something from God in heaven, or
was his god, or was his work, his talent, his gift, like it was
everything, and certainly more than we were. I remember
looking over at Carlin, this sweet young girl, a girl just like me,
and asking her with my eyes, Where *are* we? Who are we?"

"Did you do it?"

"We did it. Of course, we did it."

She took another long pull and said in a small voice, "If I
have one more of these, will you see that I get home OK?" I
realized then that her Bloomsbury airs had been packed away.

She was speaking to me in the colorless, flat-voweled voice of a girl from the suburbs of Topeka. I nodded. "Sure," I said.

We had one more beer.

"Well, that night we had your basic *ménage à trois*. I will never forget the first time I rolled over in that white powder haze in that sleazy motel down by the overpass on 81 and saw this girl's, this Carlin's tits rolling toward me, and his mouth. . . . I hated him and I loved her. It's as simple as that. I loved her because she was me, the new Sarah, my replacement. I hated him for needing her and for never getting enough. He made us do things that night to each other. And we did them, and some of them hurt. He dropped us off together on the same street corner, and told us good-bye collectively because we were one girl, just arms and legs and tits. We stood there on the street corner, and Carlin was having some sort of paranoid reaction to the white powder, or maybe to Eldon Odom, because I know now Eldon Odom *is* the white powder and the powder is Eldon Odom. They're both just power, and it's false. Anyway, I was the more experienced slut, so I took Carlin home with me. We spent the day holding each other."

She gave me a hard look. It was a hardness that never found its way into her writing. I thought: If you could find that voice, the voice you have used here in Moby's. . . .

"He came over a few more times to visit us. He laughed about us being a marriage made in heaven and about his being the matchmaker. A couple of times, he asked us to do things for him and we did. I don't know why, and those are the only things I truly regret. I wasn't young anymore, but I did them because there was still that wonder. I knew I shouldn't, but I did. He would stand by and watch us and not say anything, only smile that snake charmer smile of his and take notes in his head. Finally I told him to go to hell, and it was the best day of my life. It's the day I really became a writer."

She drank the last of her beer and went wobbling on her antique heels to the toilet.

I took her home in a cab. She gave directions lucidly, rising up from the crook of my arm each time she was needed, saying "Left turn" or "Stop at the light, then right" very clearly, very Topeka, then lapsing against my shoulder. I stroked her hair.

When we stopped at a duplex on the fringes of the student ghetto, Carlin opened the door. She sniffed the air among us. "Pissed, are you?"

I had to think a minute to remember that world of BBC programming where "pissed" means drunk.

"Yeah," I grinned, "sort of."

"Well, all right," Carlin said. "Thanks for bringing her home." I handed Sarah over. There was no expression on Carlin's face, nor any intonation in her voice except that single one, of wonder.

Part V

Twenty-Eight

THAT FALL I visited Eldon Odom's Lake Searl retreat, though not as often as Shine and Hubbel and MacEvoy. We drank and drugged, and to make up for it, we ran the country roads and lifted weights under the tall pines. But the accounts can't be balanced by pain indefinitely, and the strain of trying was visible in Eldon Odom's fevered eyes and in his gaunt frame and in his behavior toward his friends. He was impossible to predict. He lashed out at the slightest provocation. He told us wild stories of his journalistic exploits — he had parachuted into Cuba, knew the identity of the second gun — things that could not possibly be true. We told him what he wanted to hear.

The financial strain of maintaining two households and of providing cocaine and crystal methedrine for so large a retinue drove him more and more often to the quick and easy returns of long-distance journalism. He was as likely to be in Key West covering the buskers of Mallory Square as in New York uncovering the whores of Soho — anywhere his redneck insouciance struck sparks from the local *mise en scène*. But the traveling consumed him even as the white powder kept him going, and finally we were certain of something. We had feared it but had put it out of sight, believing him too large a personage to fall by the usual route. But I worked in the Lil Colonel, and Ardis worked in the halfway house, and consequently we were the first two to see it. Eldon Odom was an addict.

It was not all pain and payment on Lake Searl that fall and winter. We went sailing in the Hobie Cat, skimming down the long, windy lake with only the soft groan of the boom and the snap of canvas to violate the autumn quiet and only sundown to bring us ashore. There were many parties and most were quite civilized. After his separation from Reeba and the public trouble with Frank, Eldon Odom tried to normalize relations with his university colleagues and city friends. He was a good politician and a better luminary. He knew that a star must not orbit too far from the eyes that glut on its light. His colleagues thought him a romantic, a disdainer of suburban entrapment. They thought him lucky and resented him in equal measure for doing what they had no courage to do. He had gone farther out. And if Odom was a little weathered, a little diminished, even a little mad those days, it was the strain of the divorce, the demands of fame and work, and of course, the rigors of country life. Back in their university offices, they filed him under *Byronic*.

On civilized occasions, I hung on the fringe with Shine and Hubbel and Sarah and, sometimes, MacEvoy and Ardis, and we behaved ourselves. If we were quizzed by these professors — "Tell us about him" — we gave press releases, then laughed at ourselves. "He speaks perfect Gaelic," Sarah said one day, and I added, "He bench-presses six hundred pounds." The scholars believed us. We drank, but only moderately, and the white powder stayed in the metal fishing tackle box out in MacEvoy's black Trans Am.

It was a vagary of Odom's affliction, a game he played, that he would not keep his own supply of drugs. He bought small consignments from MacEvoy, who was growing wealthier by the day. If the powder was brought to him in this fashion, then each time it was a surprise, and Odom could believe he had no habit. On those few occasions when the supply dwindled or the connection could not be made, Odom became agitated, a trip wire, a hair trigger.

During those days, I watched Odom closely, observing what I was already calling his decline. I had seen him write at night, often all night long, out on the little porch facing the lake. I knew that he wrote by the drug. It had become his sustenance, his muse. If the curve of his fame was still rising, that of his physical vitality had long ago bisected it on the downward slant. I watched the others — Shine, Hubbel, Sarah, Lindy. They hung in suspension, waiting to see how Odom would raise the ante or change the rules.

I watched Ardis, too. Several times I had come upon her and Tommy MacEvoy in some quiet place, a hammock under the pines, a nest of tall grasses by the lakeside, and always she seemed to be doing good. And her earnestness impressed me, for it was unchanging. She really was trying to save MacEvoy from himself or some other demon. I began to be proud of her. She had planted herself in our midst and was nourished by detritus and waste.

One afternoon I arrived at Lake Searl carrying my jogging gear. It was our practice to run the country roads, Eldon Odom and I, the two gimps, as he called us. We ran in order to improve our injured limbs, sometimes with Lindy along to show us how

it was done. I entered by the kitchen as usual and found Lindy
alone. She was dressed for running in a pair of brief nylon shorts
and a mesh T-shirt. She wore no socks, just an expensive pair of
the imported running shoes that were becoming popular in those
days, and the hard, supple swell of her calf above the amorphous
bulge of that shoe was a thing to see. I told her so. She looked
down at herself, flexed her calf this way and that, and said, "I
miss dancing."

"Where's himself?" I asked her.

"He went looking for Tommy. He's *out.*"

She meant out of the powder. "Don't want to run out," I said.

"He won't," she grimaced. "He'll drive fifty miles so he
doesn't have to spend a day without it."

We wandered out to the screened porch and looked at the
lake. It was a bright, cool autumn day, one of those rare ones
when the air is dry and you believe Florida might actually
conceive a new season.

There were two typewriters on the porch. I walked over to the
new one. "What's this?" I asked. "You writing, too?"

"I am," she said in a determined tone.

"Lady Narcissus," I laughed.

She looked a little defensive, then laughed with me. It was
awkward, all of us writing, dividing up the experience we
shared, telling each other "You can't have that, damn it!" each
time a good line was loosed among us. Lindy the dancer had
been the refreshing difference.

"You gonna let me read it?" I didn't know what *it* was but
thought I'd better ask.

She looked at me with a strange intensity. We had been
trying, both of us to keep it light, and now came this straight-
ahead look.

"Sure," she said. "You're the one who really wants to
know."

"Know what?" I asked her.

"Him."

We were running well ahead of Eldon Odom, Lindy and I. It was embarrassing in a certain way. We had no need to outdistance him, but a mile back he had insisted. It was the way of the group. You didn't stop for stragglers. "Get your workout, get your workout!" he had shouted in this testy, not-to-be-disputed voice when we had begun to slow down for him. He looked as though he were dying. His red chest was inflating and emptying like a punctured bellows, and his head was thrown back and pitching side to side. His long legs wobbled and stumbled. We did what he told us to do, the alternative being a confrontation with his pride.

We were striding easily at about an eight-minute pace, grooving after the shakedown of the first two miles, on a five-mile loop that included the curve of the lakeshore and an old sawmill road that let down to the rim of the Savannah. My knee was unusually fluid, and I was nearing that moment runners woo when breath and sweat and pace become an ecstasy and running is almost effortless. You are drugged by your own blood and believe you will never stop. I could feel Lindy beside me entering the same door. We ran along that way for most of the fourth mile, and it was only in the last three quarters that we began to compete.

We matched strides, accelerating, passing into the realm of pain, then into agony. We were sprinting like dash-men when we reached the front door of the lake house. Lindy nipped me in the last twenty yards, but what surprised me was lasting as long as I had. We were still making aimless circles, gasping, our heads thrown back watching each other through a bleary happiness, when Eldon Odom came struggling into the yard.

"Feels good when it stops hurting," Lindy said.

I took a last long gasp of that blood-drugged euphoria and began to come to earth. Lindy and I sat on the back porch waiting for Odom to join the living world. He made the same distressed circles we had made, gasping "Ah, ah, ah," his flesh steaming in the cool fall air. I watched him closely, and I could feel Lindy beside me doing the same thing. Now it seemed there was always a vigil. Now Odom was a miracle of diminishment, of survival. Drugs and work had carved so much flesh from his bones there was an illusory youthfulness about him. His running shorts hung loose on him, but his skin, which was yellowing and liverish, told the truth.

He was leaning with his hands on his bent knees, his back arching with each labored breath. Without opening his eyes, he reached for Lindy. She supported him as they walked past me into the house. It was an alienating gesture, Odom's reaching for her. When Lindy went under his arm, I was excluded. The house was the place where a hundred such intimacies had come up between them, more all the time now that Odom was a sick man. I was ready to leave, but Lindy looked anxiously back at me from the porch, calling me across their barrier of privacy into the house.

Odom was splayed on a spindly kitchen chair. Lindy had placed a glass of cold water in front of him, but he only stared at it, swallowing air, his eyes red and bulging. Unsteadily, Odom heaved himself up and Lindy reached for him. Suddenly, viciously, he shoved her away with a fist to the throat that left a white mark, a star, in the rosy flush of her neck. She gave a sharp cry of pain and outrage. Then I thought she would strike back. Her fists balled white, as the white star at her throat became a welt, turning livid, then an ugly blue. But she didn't strike. She let her fist go soft and stepped toward him again, and this time he took her with both big hands by the throat and held her in a strangler's embrace, not hurting her, not yet, while I watched uncertain of everything.

He held her at arm's length, his face miserable as though pushing the world away from him, saying to her and to me, Get away, all of you get away, you are strangling me.

Lindy raised her soft hands to his forearms and let them rest. I doubt she could have pushed a word through the compressed fuse of her neck. She only smiled at him, and after a space he let go, shoving her again, and me too as he parted us and stumbled to the little screened porch overlooking the lake where the typewriters, his and hers, were standing.

Dripping with sweat, he flung himself into a chair. We could hear his fingers jamming the keys, and him grunting, then moaning as he extricated them, then trying to unstick the clotted letters inside the typewriter. I imagined mad words appearing on the page. They would be his best — they were from pain, his muse. Then I remembered it was only journalism.

Lindy stood by me massaging her neck. "He's got a deadline," she whispered. "Some shit for *Esquire* about fashion models. A shitload he knows about fashion models." As she watched him and I watched her, a new expression came into her eyes, the same bereft longing I had seen in Reeba's. Abandonment. She gave a nod that said I should go.

I left by the kitchen door but not before taking a step or two toward Odom. The page was soggy, smeared with sweat and ink, and the words were solid chaos. He clawed the keys and moaned, and I heard him say "Where *is* it?" as I was going out.

I was opening the door of my old Toyota when I heard a rumbling noise, like thunder, then understood it was something heavy striking the old boards of that house. A picture formed of Lindy falling, and those chemicals which had gone to rest in the long swoon after our run came clamoring back to my blood. I was turning to run when I saw her at the door and heard her calling me, "Come back. He's . . ."

Eldon Odom lay belly down on the floor by the typewriter. His lips were blue, his jaw was clamped and leaking, his eyes were open, enlarged. He was convulsing. Lindy knelt beside him. "Help me turn him over," she hissed at me. I dropped beside her and wedged my arms under his torso and tried a shove, but he was too large, too inert. "You get on the other side," I said, and Lindy jumped across our burden and began straining at his shoulder while I lifted. In my hands, his hot chest was thumping madly, without rhythm, and I was glad to feel this heat and the movement of his heart. When we had him over, his face going from blue to white, unclamped but awful in its loose expressionlessness, neither of us knew what to do. All that came to me were old movies in which you loosened the victim's collar and slapped his face. I strained to remember Boy Scout manuals and cardiopulmonary pamphlets and decided to do whatever I could vaguely recall. I straightened his head, arched his neck and plumbed his loose and furry mouth with my index finger. His tongue was a stubborn slippery clot in the back of his throat. I was about to press my lips to his in that desperate kiss I knew might help when Lindy touched my arm.

"He's better," she said, with such authority that I withdrew from the prospect of that kiss. We watched. He seemed to be breathing a little easier. The twitching had stopped. Lindy lifted his T-shirt, soaked with sweat from our long run, and we looked at his chest. His ribs were stretched wide and under them something was skittering about like an animal in a cage. "Jesus," she said as we watched this misfiring flurry of impulses. Lindy pressed her ear to his chest and I waited, hoping for news.

"What did you get?" I asked when she raised up.

"I don't know. You try."

I listened but heard only my own blood beating in my ears. In scared impotence, we stared at each other over the mass of Odom. Finally I remembered that afternoon by the prairie when Reeba had come with the box of things for Odom's new life. "What about those pills?" I asked. "Didn't she give you some pills for him that one time?"

She ran to get them, and while she was gone, I thought about how we might get an unconscious man to swallow a pill. When Lindy knelt again across from me, I read the label: PHE-NOBARBITAL, 60 Mg., *two tablets daily, or as needed*. The doctor's name was Reynolds. Odom was quieter and, despite our incompetence, seemed to be improving. Some of the red color had returned to his skin and some of the shape to his face. There was still the strange fluttering under his ribs, but now and again, he heaved a sigh. He seemed to be settling into natural sleep. Lindy pushed back onto her haunches and looked across at me, and all at once I became aware of sounds from the lake, of bird song and wind and the persistent drone of an engine in a nearby field.

"Did he ever do that before, hit you like that?" We were still on the floor, divided by Odom who was fitfully sleeping.

"A time or two," she admitted. She was still too scared to withdraw into pride. "He only does it when he needs help. When he knows he has to have it."

"What's it like," I asked her, meaning, I suppose, all of it, life with the great man in his decline.

In a tired voice she said, "He drinks all the time and eats that speed, and works for six and ten hours at a stretch and takes those pills sometimes. He sleeps when it all catches up with him, and once in a while, like today, we have some healthy exercise. It's a great life here in the country."

Odom's breathing was evening out, and he raised his arm to

cover his eyes. I went to the sofa for a cushion to place under his head. His eyes rolled open and he smiled an embarrassed, friendly smile. Before I could smile back or speak, the smile faded and the eyes rolled off to sleep.

"What do you think we ought to do?" Lindy asked me.

"Did he ever fall out like this before?"

She looked away at the afternoon, pressing blue and shiny at the window. Then she went to the card table where her new typewriter stood and picked up a sheaf of paper. "There's some things I haven't told you about," she said. I looked at her, knowing I could not refuse knowledge of Odom but fearing it for the first time.

She handed me the pages and walked out of the room. I got up from where I was kneeling and walked to the greasy old sofa and sat down to read. But being in the room with Odom, his heat, his battering heart, began to bother me. After a while I could hear Lindy rummaging around. When she reappeared carrying a small suitcase, she said, "Tell him I've gone to visit my grandma. He'll know what that means."

I went out to sit in a deck chair by the lake. It was a fine fall day, crisp and clear with a high blue sky and only those birds and that distant thumping John Deere tractor for company. I picked up the first page and read.

Her title was *Sojourn Under.* It was a good title with three strong suggestions: of subservience, darkness, and temporality. I admired it. She had begun *in medias res,* and the beginning was that day in the little cracker house on the edge of the Savannah when Reeba had come unannounced with Presley and the box of underwear, and bringing that odd calm, that ministering gentleness which we had not expected. But the astonishing thing was the aftermath of the scene, the thing that happened after we were gone on our long grinding glide to earth. It was then that Lindy discovered Eldon Odom's epilepsy.

I'm not certain why this one fact, common enough in itself, so moved and astonished me. There were darker revelations in Lindy's pages. There was the stuff of tabloids and sleazy novels, stories even Frank would not have written.

Alone in the house with Odom, seconds after we had all gone, Lindy was in the eye of one of his fits. Odom seized up still as a tree in winter, blue as ice, drooling, trembling, clutching the walls, falling rigid as a stave bolt while shock after shock of brain-burning current coursed through him. It lasted three minutes and yet was the longest light-year of her life. What *was* this? What could she do?

As he seemed to get worse, then seemed to get better, all she could think was to hold him and be splattered with spittle, then wet with warm urine as he lost control of himself; so she lay with him, speaking mindless fragments into his stopped ears. When it was finally over, he slept the sleep of the dead for twelve hours while she lay on the floor beside him like a dog, unable to move, unable to leave except when her burning bladder finally made her. She watched him, felt him, touched the places on his neck and wrist which gave the medical knowledge she could understand. Yes, his heart still hammered, his blood still flowed, his breath came and went.

This coming and going finally put her to sleep, but in her sleep there was an awful unfolding, a nightmare. In it, Reeba came again with Presley and the box of linens, and she took the box and gave it to her lover, but under the first layer of white cloth slept a black snake, and the snake struck and this twisting, burning, clutching fit was the result. Reeba stood by and the boy with her, howling the laughter of the damned, and this noise from hell woke her and she found herself draped across the chest of the awakening Odom, whose weeping she had heard, mistaking it for that howling in the warp and woof of her dream.

There were darker revelations, and Lindy did not spare them. Her account of the night we two had climbed the trellis to look in at Odom's dog's moan, that noise of animal success, was accurate and moving, and she followed it with a long, weary description of their sexual life together. Odom's resorts to her usually came when he was drunk or drugged, and they were all prolonged reenactments of that night at the Thrash Palace with the little flower girl. They had struggled in Lindy's room, and on the floor of his office, and later in the house by the Savannah, and more recently in this lake retreat, fiercely and sorrowfully. Odom was always the rapist, but Lindy refused the victim's role. When not fighting him off, she was trying to woo him with gentleness.

His night terrors, his insomnia, even moments of extraordinary physical cowardice; all were recorded in Lindy's pages with a remorseless, unornamented clarity. This reading brought sweat to my palms and the stink of fear to my armpits as I sat in the deck chair by the lake.

The writing itself was unadorned, often clumsy, but always pushed toward new revelation. Odom's scars, his mythic wounds, were mostly self-inflicted, the tracks of his epilepsy. Since boyhood, he had built stories on these scars to cover their origin. As I read, I learned the history and physiology of the disease and learned of Odom's secret, costly search for a cure. Many of the flights we had believed carried him to New York for editorial conferences and literary fêtes had been trips to clinics and hospitals where the newest procedures were being tried. Odom kept a secret library, calling it the Grand Mal Collection. In it were clinical volumes on the disease and the stories of the great sufferers — St. Paul, Caesar, Dostoevski, Dante — medical journals and scholarly quarterlies, anything he could read about the affliction and the possibility of a cure. In moments of despair, Odom had frequented spiritualists, conjurors, natural healers, herbalists, and once even an American Indian shaman. He had twice offered himself as an experimental subject for the microsurgery performed by doctors in Minneapolis and had twice been refused because the doctors would not be responsible for opening the brain of Eldon Odom, Southern Writer, national treasure. His very fame condemned him to suffer, while accountants and plumbers might be cured.

Occasionally the memoirist Lindy paused to reflect. Her questions were much more advanced than my own. Why had Odom kept this thing secret? If pain was his subject, why not reveal himself as the monumental sufferer? Why did he seek a cure with one hand and mix his drugs and drink with the other? Knowing that his medicine could control the seizures, why did he go for weeks without taking it, wooing the fits? Lindy had seen only a few such episodes but had heard Odom's agonized tales of thousands more he had endured in his forty-three years. Blankness, he had told her, was what tortured him most — to lie in loss of memory for hours after one of the fits knowing that his mind had been emptied while he writhed and shook and pissed himself. It was fundamental disgrace, for the writer *was* his memory.

And there were pages, long and compassionate flights, about Reeba. This thing had drawn the two women together in a way neither wanted and neither could resist. What Reeba had seen when Odom came running naked from the bedroom of the house by the Savannah was the early warning she knew by heart. By handing over the pills she was chaining Lindy to the demon.

As afternoon became evening and the shadows separated from the trunks of the pines and leaned toward me, I felt a growing discomfort which at first I could not identify. Or would not. Finally I admitted to myself it was jealousy. Unvarnished, unsubtle, Lindy's words had the power of felt experience. They were true. It was a truth my work had not reached. The sun was in its six o'clock configuration when I finished reading, knowing more about Eldon Odom than I, even I, could ever have wanted to know.

It was dark and quiet inside, and I could find no one. The cushion I had put under Eldon Odom's sleeping crown was back in its place on the sofa. There was a note in Lindy's hand on the kitchen counter. *Dear Eldon: I'm going to my grandma in Orlando for a while. You know why. I love you. Lindy.* I walked to the little table on the porch and squared Lindy's pages beside her shiny new Olivetti and stared out at the lengthening shadows, the mushroom tops of the pines just now touching the water's edge. I had made no sound but nevertheless felt I was watched, that nothing and no one could escape the merciless eye loosed by Lindy's writing. I stood that way, immobile, weary, knowing that I was at the end of a search, staring at Lindy's pages, at her title with its heavy suggestion of the temporary. A sojourn was a mere visitation. She had known this from the beginning of her climb and descent. Why hadn't I?

From the bedroom came the heavy padding of bare feet. I turned and watched the mouth of the hallway and soon he was there, propped, big and narrow, red and scratching himself, wearing only underwear and a loose, crooked grin. He launched himself from the doorway and came on unsteadily, making for the table where Lindy's pages were now back in place.

Standing over the table, he said, "You read it, did you?"

I nodded. "She said to tell you she'd gone to her grandma. That you'd understand."

He tapped Lindy's writing with his forefinger. "I understand she ain't got no grandmaw. That's what I understand."

Twenty-Nine

"LET ME GET YOU a drink," Odom said, rambling toward the little kitchen.

"Sure," I muttered, unsure. I had just raised my head from Lindy's book of revelations, and everything was dangerous to me. The world was subtext and murky depths. I remembered the first time we had drunk innocent bourbon on his deck above Hart's Flow. Now whiskey, like everything else, was altered, an instrument of high priests.

We stood in the kitchen holding our glasses, and I knew he was poised, in this aftermath of the fit, at the divide between a morning's recovery and an afternoon's start. He was as sober as I would ever find him, as careful, as balanced. He turned to me with a brimming glass and said, "Did I piss all over myself, Toad?"

The look on his face was earnest, supplicant. I had to think a moment in order to separate what I had read in Lindy's pages —

all the times she had cleaned him up — from what had just happened. Finally I said, "Not this time."

He shook his head and looked at me as though to say, "You see?"

Did I see what he endured? I remembered myself an hour earlier, leaning over him contemplating the cardiopulmonary kiss. The kiss was absolute zero, and yet now we were closer. He brushed past me and walked to his typewriter, his mad writing. He stood looking down at the page, calligraphed with the early warning of his seizure. He shook his head. "Look at this, Toad."

Dutifully, I did what he said.

"You know that old thing about apes and typewriters?"

"Sure," I said.

He shook his head again, then tore the page out of his machine and ripped it across, then longways, and let the four leaves whisper down.

I remembered those pages of mine he had let go without comment. I said, "I guess we're all apes when you get down to it."

He gave me a sharp look, and behind those dark, bewildered eyes, I could see his wits collecting to throw back up the barriers. There wasn't much time.

"Some more than others," he said, the protection gathering.

"Especially me," I said. I remembered that day when he had told me what he liked about me: "Toad, you don't want anything from me." What an insult it had been. How had I contrived to give such an impression of myself, I who wanted everything from him?

We were still standing over Lindy's manuscript, and so I rested my hands on it and said, "Sometimes it seems like . . ." I stared out over the water, waiting for him to supply a word. On the lake, in the gathering darkness, I projected those early images of myself and Eldon Odom — the two of us in his summery office toasting my future, the laying on of hands, the proclaiming. I was still waiting for the word.

"Quit if you can, Toad," Odom said. He spoke the word *quit* with a brutal finality. "That's all I know to tell you. Quit if you can. I used to stand up in front of students and quote it all, shit like 'forge in the smithy of the soul,' and 'purify the language of the tribe,' and on and on, all that milky shit. You can ask the others, the ones been with me longest. Ask Sarah and Tory, they'll tell you what a goddamned quoter I was. I never said anything original because even then I knew there was nothing to say, nothing new. Nothing prettier than the things I learned from the Old Man, God rest him." He raised his fingers to his lips and kissed them and then, oddly, made the sign of the cross and then repeated, "God rest his gorgeous old bones."

In this pause, I remembered my last glimpse of the Old Man in winter clothes, boarding the shuttle, hoping they had whiskey.

"He used to tell me," Odom said, "all the beautiful things, and I knew it was my place to pass them on and, if I could, make a new one or two. And I did, and I tried, but I gave it up finally. It came to me in a dream, one of these goddamned hellhole dreams I have when I have recently befouled myself."

"It?" I asked him.

"What I told you," he said with some impatience. "Quit if you can. It's the only true thing I know about the word trade. The only one I know." Then he grinned, watching for my reaction.

"What does it mean?" I asked him.

"It means just what it says, goddamn it. Nobody should do this. It's too hard. Quit if you can, and if you can't, don't, for Christ's sake, bitch about what happens to you."

He said it straight to my face, underlining every word, and by the time he had finished, I had backed a few steps, knowing that the interview was over. The rest was cancelled by what Odom had learned, at great expense, about "it." I took a step back from him and sipped my bourbon thinking, What a long way we have come.

He turned from me and watched the night come to the lake. I was ready to go. I had learned all there was to know. And if it was not what I had wanted, then so be it. Or so I told myself, standing back from him.

I said, "Well, if you don't need me I guess I'll just be . . ."

"Need you?" he whirled, an angry look on his face. As surely as we stood there, I knew the words that were clarifying in his mind: *I don't need anybody.* I watched anger fulminate, then diminish in that amazing face. He relented a little. "Thanks for . . . helping her out." "Her" was Lindy. She was gone somewhere but would be back to give him whatever was not help, whatever he could accept. I had finally dragged him into manners, things that had to be said. It was true that I had helped her out. It was also true that he did not know what I had done; how could he? That he could thank me only for what I could not prove had happened was somehow an essential truth about him.

I raised my glass in salute and farewell and thanks, a gesture that said, Yes, you are welcome, said all those things with a diffidence that was irony. For I had learned my lesson in irony.

I put my glass on the counter-top in the kitchen and was moving to the door when he said, "You *are* good." He spoke with a wincing resignation, as though it hurt him physically.

He said just that — "You *are* good" — and it was enormous in its ambiguity. Was I Reeba's *good boy* to him now? Was that it? I could see the two of them deciding what a good boy was, the sort of boy who should leave early, whose innocence should be preserved, not because it is good but because it could not tolerate irony. I kept on walking.

"Your work . . ." He spoke again emphatically, in a rhetorical, from-the-lectern voice, as though the night were pulling from him those long-ago tones the Old Man had taught. I stopped at the door. He stood beside his writing table, staring at the black darkness at the edge of the lake, and he let his hand fall to Lindy's pages. ". . . is very good. Better than mine was when I was your age. It has . . ." I stood at the door while he searched his orator's throat for words that should not sound like a blurbist's effusions. ". . . a voice." That was all he said. He tried for more. Then I saw him smile and edit himself back to that one word. *Voice.* The smile told me the word was perfect.

He didn't turn and I didn't speak. I left him standing there looking out at the night, his hand on Lindy's book, which was their collected life.

Thirty

THAT FIRST STEP back, the one I took when Eldon Odom turned to me and said "Quit if you can," was followed by another and another. I didn't quit, but I didn't go on in quite the same way, either. Each time I sat down to write a word, one of Lindy's invited comparison. The only truth, I began to believe, was biography. Odom had been wrong that day at the birding place. Fiction could not be life. Only biography, the empirical observation and record of life, could be valid. Or so it seemed to me then. For I knew that Lindy had no artifice. By the accident of experience and by her own persistence and the power of love, she had the closeness I had sought. She lived with Odom. She recorded him and he was worth it.

The distance I now stood from Odom took me away from my own work, though I continued to labor out of habit and the fear that if I stopped I would become no one. I began to fear my winos. They came too close for comfort. I lived in a small rented room, owned nothing, drank more than was good for me, worked at a menial job, and could not justify my existence except as the man who fed their habits. I began to hate and fear them and to take better care of them, as though to care for them were to care for some possibility that was myself.

I saw Lindy but not often. She was shut in with Odom on the lake, or she had left him for some mythical grandma who gave her space to breathe. When we did meet, it was usually for a meal at the Gutbomb, or sometimes she came to my room.

I did not tell her what I thought of her book. I only spoke my manners — wonderful, moving, full of narrative power. If she was pleased, she did not say so, and I respected her silence. She was the dancer who lived with Odom in his decline. To her, the book was survival, not ego, not "work." She wrote for sanity. Our conversations were quiet recitations of the events of our lives. She told me what Odom was doing — the depressing cycle of drink; drugs; sleep; the farce of exercise; the mad, drug-compelled writing; and the rape charade which was their loving. I told her about my winos, the writing I still did in my half-life fashion, and about the letters I received from home, the story of my father's slow recovery.

Sometimes we sat in my room, the two of us occupying bed and chair as we had done that day Lindy had come baring herself to me; I remembered her beauty, those lovely breasts and that scarlet neck. I remembered that forward thrusting stance which offered me flesh as spite to Eldon Odom. Now that we two were closest to him, I knew that impulse. My thoughts took me to spite more and more often, in a way that I could only dimly understand. I dreamt of hurting Eldon Odom and awoke thinking of it.

The group was failing, shriveling, giving up its energies to neglect. Odom often could not meet his classes. There were minor accidents on the forty miles of country road he drove to our Tuesday night class. There were telephone calls at the last minute cancelling us for a week. Several times Traymore came to my door summoning me to hear Odom's furry, fuddled voice on the windy county telephone lines, telling me that I must teach the class for him, saying Lindy would bring the manuscripts, would meet me at the Gutbomb and brief me for the night's work. These were grim, comic occasions. Odom's voice, the long pauses, the bent logic, the moaning exclamations of confusion, all to give me the confidence I would need to cover for him. "You a good reader, Toad, better than you know. You can do it."

The first of these classes, I stood at the front of the room and told them, Shine and Hubbel and Sarah and all the others, that Odom was "sick," that I had been delegated to teach the class. I would go ahead and do it if they thought they could stand me.

My cues, I knew, would come from Shine and Hubbel; so did everyone else. There was palpable disappointment in the room. One young man, a newcomer, rose and drawled, "Aw, shit! I ain't paying to listen to you." He walked to the front of the room and wrestled his manuscript from the bag I had dropped on Odom's desk. Tory Hubbel scratched himself in the deep hollow between pectoral muscles as big as buttocks and said, "Sure, Toad. You go ahead and just *do* it."

Shine, beside him, grimaced at the small, uncertain sound of his friend's voice. "Yeah, Toad," he said. "We'll help you if you need it. Go for it, big'un."

I selected a manuscript and began to read, trying my best to sound like Odom: The sound of Odom was fair, honest to the words, objective, appreciative in spots, but never actorish, never *selling* the words. I tried.

We had an oddly sober discussion. It started slowly. People

tendered their comments softly, as though any moment someone, Odom himself perhaps, might stop our charade. I was the
moderator, appealing often to Hubbel or Shine, trying to create a
consortium of voices. When it was over, a few of the younger
people came up to congratulate me, but they were sad congrat-
ulations, and the absence we all felt so acutely was a bigger
presence than I was on those nights.

Perhaps the strangest thing of all in these long, slow days of
the fall was the flood of publicity that attended the reception of
Sojourners Under the Mountain. The book was a runaway
success. The demand for Odom reached a crescendo just when
he most needed to hide himself. The outcome was as predictable
as it was awful. The university awoke finally to the value of its
homegrown notable and decided to exploit Odom for all he was
worth. The boy who had walked out of class with his manuscript
had complained, along with others, I suppose, but Odom's
public worth made him invincible. It mattered little to deans and
department heads that Odom was casual about meeting his
classes. They had larger plans for him.

The flagship of all their schemes was to be the first annual
Bainesborough Writers' Conference, a gala and symposium that
would surpass in magnitude and pomp even the Old Man's
yearly visit. Odom was invited to draw up the guest list of
writers, agents, editors, and scholars. The fête would be dedicated to the Old Man, whose portrait, stylized and archetyped,
would appear on all the programs and posters for the three days
of celebration.

Odom was to give the opening night reading and the closing
address and to serve as guide and master of ceremonies for the
pride of lions who would attend. Our group was given schol-
arships en masse. These made us insiders, closer than the
paying entrants. The public would be invited to the evening
readings, but only conference members, those who had some

pretensions to the life of words, would attend the more intimate daytime sessions. For a fee, each entrant could have a personal manuscript consultation with one of the luminaries. The list of featured performers was a who's who of the contemporary literary hustings. The poets Jonas Baldi, Elizabeth Bower, and Louis Epcott would be coming, and Odom's brother in Southern fiction, Theron Talmadge, was to be invited. Merit Norman would handle discussions of the New York publishing scene and, rumor had it, would take back a manuscript with him as a way of proving that such gatherings could elevate one among us to that plain where the lions fed. The prospect of the coming conference buoyed us, and Odom seemed to have cleaned up in anticipation. Lindy told me that he was on the wagon; "At least more on than off," she said. There was hope in her voice that reminded me of times I had thought lost.

One day not long after the announcement of the coming event, Odom called me into his university office and asked me to serve as his administrative assistant during the conference. Thinking of Hubbel and Shine and even Sarah, all of whom had been with him longer, I asked, "Why me?"

He seemed annoyed by the question. Through a wrinkled frown, he said, "You the one has what I want. You're dependable, smart, well-spoken, and won't fuck up. That cover it?"

"Sure," I allowed. But I was thinking of the resentment such a promotion could bring to me.

Odom told me there would be a small salary for me and said he hoped I would make some connections. I'd need them, he said.

I thanked him and accepted the first job he wanted done.

Leviathan still had a dirty swath of bandage around his middle and a serious limp. As I stood at the iron gate, waiting for an answer to the bell, he watched me with unabated malevolence. Those yellow eyes said, Don't underestimate me. I heard the footsteps inside that surely would be Reeba's, and with each one I counted a day I had not called her. In my wallet I still carried the note she had written along with the hundred-dollar bill. The note bore her love and the money was her gratitude. I had kept both but somehow had not been able to call her. I was scared.

The door opened only a slit and the pale face in it was surprised, then bemused, then, I thought, helpless with anger. She stared at me for a long time before stepping out. She took Leviathan by the collar and said, "It's all right." He looked at her, then at me and whined. "No," she said, "not this one. He's all right." Then what she had said made her smile. "But just barely," she muttered, and Leviathan watched me, reconsidering.

"Tell him not to eat me," I said, grinning then wincing at the memory of Frank Lagano.

Pulling Leviathan by the collar, Reeba turned and walked through the iron gate. I followed her into the dark, formal living room. As we went, I glanced toward the part of the house where she lived.

She took me out to the deck, leaving Leviathan behind the glass door. He smeared it with his nose for a space, then sat down, licking the edges of his bandage and watching us.

She had been sitting at the little table where we had eaten our breakfast the morning of Frank's phone call. There was a sticky coffee cup and the remains of breakfast, and a chair surrounded by magazines. She sat down again. "You want some coffee?"

"No, thanks," I said. "I'm wired enough as it is."

"I hear you've got a job."

"Listen," I said, "Reeba . . ."

"Don't call me that anymore."

I knew what she meant. I sat down and watched her, remembering what we had done together. I could find nothing wrong in the memory. Neither of us had owned anyone that day, and what we had made was love. So we stared at each other until finally she lowered her head and the dark hair fell around her face like a curtain, closing me out, and I saw again that moment when she had taken me into her mouth as I reached down to guide her with my hands. From under the curtain of black hair came the sound of quickened breathing. I got up and went around and held her in my arms, forgetting my errand. I held her, saying her name, Reeba, saying she couldn't take it away. She clung to me, wet and disheveled while Leviathan whined at the glass door. When we stood apart, I went to the rail and looked out over the lake. It was as quiet as the heart I wanted, and as unclaimed.

She said, "I'm sorry . . . Jedeco." I winced at that implausible name. It was exactly the right thing for her to say.

She said, "What did you come here for? No, let me tell you. He wants me to have the big party. Right? On the last night?"

"Right," I said, not surprised at what she knew. A man and a woman don't break twenty years as easily as they might think they can.

"Tell him I'll be happy to."

We watched the lake and the silence came in again, and with it the awkwardness. Finally she said, "It was nice having your arms around me again."

I nodded.

"But we won't do it again."

I could not say yes and told her so. I don't know what was working in me then — the last of pride or possessiveness or her best interests or my own worst ones. More likely it was all of these and more.

"You know he knows about us," she said.

"Why doesn't he do something?"

"Why should he? He owes me one now, and you're not

the first."

It took me some time to understand her words, and more to place the proud tone of her voice. Why had I assumed it was otherwise? She was my only older woman, therefore I must be her only younger man? In the few seconds she gave me to think, I realized that her revelation did not hurt. She was experience. Those had been the terms.

She took my hand and gave it a squeeze that I can only call motherly. She said, "If he can have me over again, why can't I have my young Eldon? It flatters him. Don't you see that?"

"Me?" I asked, incredulous.

"You," she said, smiling as though it were really a compliment. And maybe it was.

"Remember, I said he'd come back. He always does."

I nodded. There was a pardonable pride in her voice.

"Well, he will. Wait and see."

"If he's being powerfucked," I asked her, "what happened to me?"

"You can figure that one out."

"Give me a hint."

She smiled at me. I will always remember her smile. If there is anything fixed in the relations of men and women, and if that thing is a difference between them, hers was the face of that difference.

"Well," she said, "it has something to do with inspiration, doesn't it?"

Thirty-One

I WAS BUSY with preparations for the writers' conference, doing all that Eldon Odom did not want to do. As he explained it, these things were not so much beneath him as just above me. The best way for me to learn them, and they were necessary to learn, was by acting. And so I acted his agent, his factotum, and sometimes, squirmingly, his boy.

I oversaw the invitations of dignitaries, assuming the title of Executive Director of the conference, and corresponding with the great and the near-great as though I knew what I was doing. After a while, I did know. On the telephone, I talked to the leonine Jonas Baldi, who for thirty years on the American scene had been the bardic voice of the Italian immigrant. I corresponded with poets Elizabeth Bower and Louis Epcott, noting their business styles: the first seeming too unpoetically concerned with earnings (she would be paid three thousand dollars for a three-day stint) and the second unpoetically concerned with how much the first was being paid. Theron Talmadge, who was writer-in-residence of Alabama State University, posed a difficult problem for me. The celebrated author of *Salvation*, also a celebrated drinker and skirt-chaser, declared in a letter to me that he would not come unless asked to give the final address. There were hints in his letter that he knew Eldon Odom was already slated to give it. I wrote to him, all unbeknownst to Eldon Odom, asking him to give the address. In the return post I promptly received a gracious letter of refusal and the assurances that he would arrive on time, prepared to labor in the vineyard.

There were minor lights — a journalist, Tom Stalke, one of Odom's more recent connections from *Esquire* magazine, and a children's author, Millicent Forbush — to round out the field. I carefully scheduled their sessions so as not to compete with anything truly momentous. As the day of the conference neared, I enjoyed my role as man-behind-the-scenes. Enough so that I could occasionally forget that Eldon Odom was sinking again, leaving things to me more often because he could not collect himself than because of trust reposed in me.

The astonishing thing about the conference, the thing that always comes to me first when I think back on it, is that even amidst all those personalities, in that rarefied egosphere where the complexities of literary stress and strife were byzantine, Eldon Odom shone forth, a bold stab of brilliance. Watching him do the introductions, stoop to carry suitcases, shift accommodations, handle petty squabbles, and give his opening address — a magnificent piece of self-analysis entitled "Why We Write" — I was struck by the intensity of his burning. He was the filament of some holy appliance — inflamed, incandescent, febrile, never extinguished. Even his fellow egos, men who had known him for twenty years, who had performed with him, some of them, many times before in such settings, were surprised by his passion and energy. As literary performers, as teachers, they knew how to make fraudulent passion for the crowds and keep the real thing for their work. They were shocked to see Odom so fiery in public. Through it all, I stood as close to him as anyone. The heat was glorious, intense.

Between the acts, Lindy was always near, though often not as close as I. And as much as it offended my sense of protocol there on the literary height, the indispensible MacEvoy was with us, carrying supplies and bringing Ardis. Hubbel and Shine were not with us. Standing in the wings, ready to prompt, I could see their two faces, content in the third row of the house. After all, these were only three days, and they were close, indeed, very close.

On the second day, during one of the intimate sessions conducted by Jonas Baldi on the "Prosody of the Shorter Lyric," I watched Odom suddenly leave the room. We had been standing together along the back wall, our arms folded similarly; the administrative guard. He seemed to wilt, then to catch himself up. He hurried out, straight past me. I waited a few minutes, then followed. On the way up to Odom's suite of rooms in the college Union Building, I wondered what Jonas Baldi would think of our defection.

It was Ardis who opened the door to me, but not before I had knocked several times, my anger rising (for I was the Executive Director), and not before I had been asked to identify myself speak-easy–fashion through the door. Inside, there were only Ardis and I and quiet voices from the bathroom and the heavy muffled sound of large men moving in a small space.

"What are they doing in there?" I whispered.

Ardis stood at the window, her back to me. When she turned, her face was white and sick and she shrugged. "You know," she said.

Oddly, I had the impulse to go and comfort her. And yet she was comfort, was help, was succor to me, or had been. She had always played the part, at the halfway house and with MacEvoy, who had brought that world of the halfway house with him into the group. I remembered I had comforted Ardis, too, that she had shown me the side of her that needed comfort. I went to her and touched her lightly on the side of her head just at the temple where her hair was upswept into a Gibson Girl bun. She smiled at me, but the smile was sick.

I turned and walked to the bathroom. I suppose I was thinking of myself as the Executive Director, of keeping things going, of interfering if need be with what was going on inside.

The door was not locked. When I opened it, I saw Odom, his back to the sink, tears streaming down his face, in an awkward embrace with MacEvoy, who was pressing both hands to Odom's open mouth. A stong rivulet of blood broke from Odom's mouth and across his chin, spilling down the front of his white shirt. MacEvoy jumped back then and said, "Shit!" and then "Toad, hand me that goddamn towel." I did as I was told.

Odom had turned to the mirror, his mouth still open. The look in his eyes was bliss and shock. He was falling into himself, unaware of us. He still held his mouth open, and as I came closer with the towel, I saw that the large blue artery under his tongue was the object of his gaze.

"Jesus Christ," I said.

MacEvoy laughed quietly, wiping the blood from Odom's shirt front. On the back of the toilet lay a collection of things I had seen only in movies. I knew instantly that they were called "works." They were a steel tablespoon, a glass syringe, a disposable butane cigarette lighter, a plastic baggie, and a piece of surgical tubing.

Odom still confronted himself while MacEvoy daubed at him. Finally MacEvoy turned to me. "He got a clean shirt up here?"

"I don't know," I said. I was falling into the mirror, too. A new runner of blood had escaped from Odom's mouth. Strangely, implausibly, I thought of his performance the day before, of the words he had spoken so brilliantly, of the voice I had heard calling those years ago when I had sat one long, hot afternoon in the Alligood County Comprehensive Junior-Senior High School Library, reading *Naked in Church*. That sacred, inviolable voice, now bloodied.

MacEvoy beside me watched Odom with a proprietary interest, the red and white towel in his hand. Finally he began to collect Odom's works. He turned to me and said, "Don't worry, he'll be all right." He must have seen something in my face that demanded more. "You got to do it somewhere it don't show," he said. "That vein under the tongue is a sweetheart."

With one of my post hole–digger's hands, I clutched him by the throat. Whatever madness was running in Odom's veins was twice as strong in mine. I was trying to put MacEvoy in the toilet where he belonged, and the red bloom of his face looking up at me was turning blue in surprise and anguish. "You dirty hunk of grunt," I said. He tried to hand me the tackle box.

Ardis pushed through the door, shoving me into Odom, collapsing us all in a heap that loosed my grip. MacEvoy punched me as hard as he could at that awkward angle, and the blow took me just below the right cheekbone on the raised cartilaginous lump where Lindy had booted me. I don't know what I was thinking. I was about to hit back when Ardis reached down and took me by the wrist. The three of us were all tangled up for some seconds. Eldon Odom pushed past and ran out the door.

As Ardis and I rode the elevator down, I sensed below a turmoil, a psychic disturbance, a whirling tangle of mixed emotions and public outrage, even before the elevator doors opened. Then I could hear it.

When I turned the corner to the conference room, there was no sign of Odom. Jonas Baldi, the immigrant lion from Boston was lying spread-eagled on the polished terrazzo floor, a bright blue lump glowing on his forehead. He looked up at me in numb outrage, then shrugged, and a boy I did not know, a recent member of the Tuesday night class, shrugged in imitation and said, "He punched him. Just walked up and give him a good hard shot to the head."

The boy and Jonas Baldi looked at the corridor, the exit to the parking lot. Walking a few steps in that direction, I found three drops of bright red blood on the white terrazzo. The questions in all of the faces surrounding Baldi were aimed at me, the Executive Director. I knew where my duty lay. I was suppose to stay and get things moving again. I turned with Ardis and followed the trail of blood out the door.

In the parking lot, I did not know what I would do. There was no sign of Odom. Ardis passed me walking resolutely. "Come on, I've got my car."

We drove toward our first decision, the intersection of University Boulevard and 18th Street. Which way had Odom gone? My feeling — but more than a feeling, strange and peremptory, a magnetic sense of closeness — was toward the country, Lake Searl, the Hardentown retreat. I said as much to Ardis, but she said no. We looked at each other. I tried to recapture that sense I'd had standing in the elevator, of something happening in special knowledge without being seen. It was fading, along with the adrenal rush of my encounter with MacEvoy. In the very last of it, I knew she was right. "OK," I said, and she turned left into the heart of the city, but not before reaching over and touching me on the bruise MacEvoy had built atop my old one. Her touch was cool and tender. Where had it been?

We drove in heavy traffic toward University and 18th, and I tried to keep my mind blank, prepared for the next guess. I didn't have to guess. We heard the wail of police sirens and saw the snarl of a traffic jam. When we had gone as far as we could, I jumped out and ran ahead. Eldon Odom stood at the center of the intersection directing traffic. He stood absurdly erect, about a hundred yards from me, raising one hand imperially to stop a flight of oncoming cars, then gesturing toward another, hopelessly stalled, to come toward him. In his red-Indian face, I saw the petulant impatience of authority disobeyed. Why didn't the cars follow his baton? Then together we heard the moan of approaching police cars, and Odom sprinted away, weaving among the tangled cars and red faces and waving arms and shouts of "Asshole!" I watched him out of sight, running toward the parking lot of a nearby pizza parlor. I ran back to Ardis's blue Mercedes.

We had to guess again. The police were on one side of him and the traffic jam cut him off from the western side of the city. If he had parked at the pizza parlor before going out to conduct traffic, then he could only head toward one quadrant of the compass. "The Savannah," I told Ardis. "Maybe the Thrash Palace."

She grimaced at my words, for the Thrash Palace was the beginning of the nothing we had made, but she ground her jaw in resolution and shoved the Mercedes into gear. We pulled into a side street, skirting the snarl of traffic, passing three rushing police cruisers with an air of nonchalance that made us laugh even as Ardis accelerated toward the rim of the city.

When we pulled up to that junkyard and carnival which was Shine and Hubbel's dooryard, we saw that we had chosen wrong. Odom's car was not there. "Damn it," I said, and Ardis put a gentling hand on my shoulder.

"Let's go in and wait a while," she said. "He might show up

here anyhow." It was a possibility but not a very likely one. I could think of nothing better, and so I agreed.

We hid the Mercedes a hundred yards or so down one of the dirt tracks that meandered off into the scrub. I began to have second thoughts. What were we going to do with him once we found him? I remembered his size, his strength. He had become that manic, imaginary policeman in an instant, stopping traffic on the authority of the drug.

We went in and walked around the place, hearing our own footsteps too loudly, looking in all the hiding places we could find, not finding anything. The place was strange, full of the voices of all those wild nights. We walked through the rooms, skirting the piles of weights and speaking in low tones about new holes in the plaster and scars on the floors and ceilings. We ended up on the screened porch where we had seen Tory Hubbel under a giggling pile of jailbait. Ardis sat down on the lumpy sofa, raising up a puff of dust and an effluvium of sweat and musk. She spread her skirts in prim fashion and then patted the cushion next to her. I sat as directed. We stared out at the quiet afternoon, watching the birds circle over the Savannah. A flight of egrets rose from a raft of hyacinths, circled, and returned to alight again. Above them three turkey buzzards ploughed their serrated wings into the rising thermals. Further out and high above, a lone hawk, dun-colored and thick as a bullet, swerved in the hot air. We watched, and I remembered something Eldon Odom had said to me about the birdlife on the Savannah. "You can see, just by watching for five minutes which are the kings and queens and which are the minions." The hawk, I knew, held the highest circle. There was something about this memory of Odom, his love of birds that called me, but Ardis's fingers were lightly drumming on my thigh and I let go of memory.

Still watching the highest circle, that swerving bullet bird, I let my own fingers cover Ardis's, cool and therapeutic on my leg. A shyness descended on us that made my ears ring and my face hot. It seemed to carry me years back, all the way to the country and times before I had followed the voice to Bainesborough. We didn't move or speak. I counted the circles. Finally Ardis said in a quiet, interested tone, "What's she like?"

I thought of asking, "What's he like?" but knew that I could not abide any number of answers and couldn't trust even Ardis, even now, to answer well enough. I said, "She . . . knows things. *Not* . . . what you think."

"I don't think anything," she said, still in that quiet, interested tone that did not judge.

"You do," I said. "You have to. Anybody would."

"No," she said. "No, I don't. I'm not anybody. I've learned that much from all of this." There was something a little cold in her voice. I turned and moved closer to her and placed my hand in her lap. She drew in her breath sharp but kept looking out at the afternoon and, almost imperceptibly, opened her legs for me.

After we had sat for some time watching the hawk make his circles, holding hands and not speaking, we knew that Eldon Odom was not coming. And if we were not exactly wasting time, we were losing the edge we had on the others who were after him. My last glimpse of the hawk, just as he plummeted after something that would be instantly dead, gave me the guess I needed. Eldon Odom would have gone, if he went anywhere on this part of the compass, to his favorite place. His birding spot. I grabbed Ardis up, and we were running for her car.

The birding spot was only a few miles from the Thrash Palace, if we could make the right guesses on that skein of dirt tracks that networked the rim of the Savannah. With Ardis driving and me pointing and urging, we traveled fast, and as we went I had ever more the sense that I was right, that we were homing, that sense of a thing in special knowledge. When we pulled up in the little clearing Eldon Odom had brought me to only once, his sanctum, the place he had not even shown Lindy because, he said, it was male ground, a place where the predator could commune with his kind, we saw his car ahead. I put my hand on Ardis's arm, "Slow down. Go slow." My voice was urgent and she responded, "Yes." We were together.

We parked beside his car and saw him plainly, sitting under an oak, his head to the bark, drinking from a pint bottle.

Ardis and I got out on either side of the car and walked slowly up to him. As we approached, I had the hunter's feeling from Alligood County, the tense, expectant feeling as you walk past the quivering flanks of a liver-and-white dog to flush the covey. Anything could happen. I tried to put down those thoughts, to keep myself as calm as I sensed Ardis to be. We stopped about ten feet from him, looking across his right shoulder, and when he turned, slowly, lowering the near-empty bottle, the grin on his face was maniacally wide, so splitting, that it froze us where we stood. "You ort'nt have brought her here, Toad," he said. And he grinned.

I said what came to me. "She is help, coach. She's always help."

"I *know* that," he said. "But not *here*. You *shouldn't* have." He drank and looked out across rippling grasses.

Then he was up, flinging the empty bottle and running, plunging as fast as he could straight into the Savannah. I caught a glimpse of him among the green and splashing, a flash of the red blood on his white shirt front. Then I saw him again, farther out, covered with blood in the knifing saw grass. I stood for a moment, undecided. Ardis seized me, but I tore her hands away and ran. He had broken trail for me, but the slash and cut of the grass, the hot witching suction of the water and mud, the rising insects around me, the fever of my pain and the brilliant wake of Odom's madness, his pain, all took me to a frenzy, and I was running, heedless of the flaying, cutting grass. I saw him quartering to my left and followed and knew we were making a circle. Then suddenly he leapt up in front of me, a monster rising, throwing water and weeds and laughter all around him and holding in one hand an uprooted saw grass sword. "Stop, Toad!" he called.

I was afraid to stop, afraid my courage or my madness would fail me and I would be trapped, unable to go forward or back, stuck in that blinding sawing pain forever. I came on, and he called out again, angry, "Don't . . . come . . . any . . . closer! See this?" he called, brandishing the firm stalk of saw grass. Then he plunged on. I heard him, echoing to the hot heavens, turning, circling, plunging in the stinging grass.

I could not make myself move again, not forward at least. I stood for some time, stuck, bleeding, paralyzed. I don't know how long. Through the grass, I saw him one last time. He stopped, saw me, made a formal bow, and made with his sword a gladiator's salute. Then he opened his mouth wide and with both fists plunged the tip of the saw grass blade straight down his throat, turned, and ran on. After that, I lost him.

I made my way back, utterly defeated, along the trail twice broken. It took me a long time. I tried to put my feet exactly where I or my prey had already been, picking my way through the razor edges that had closed in around me, thanking the hot blue above, those circling birds, for the easy places. I was astonished at how far I had come, at how long it took to return sane the way I had gone so quickly by madness. I was near the edge of the Savannah when I heard Ardis calling out to me. "Toad, are you in there? Tell me if you are in there!"

"I'm close," I called to her. "I'm right here."

She was sitting under Odom's oak, her wide, white cotton

skirt spread under her, and Odom's unconscious head was in her lap. He still held the sword in one hand. His face, peaceful now under Ardis's stroking fingers, was awash with blood. It ran steadily from the wound in his mouth. "I couldn't move him. He just came and said to me, 'You're help.' I didn't know what to do, so I was just going to wait. I was hoping you'd come out." She was crying and the hand that stroked Odom's brow and the one that held his head in a red grip began to tremble and tremble wildly.

In the university hospital, floating on Thorazine, Odom slept for three days. When I was bandaged and in a few places stitched, I went back to try to stitch the conference together. I was surprised to find that it had a new and close cohesion. Odom's brothers in art, even the pummeled Baldi, had rallied round him. They had gone on performing according to agreement, and this, along with the many nightlong orgies of gossip and rehearsals of the lore, had made the conference a famous success. Watching it all come to its glorious end, with Theron Talmadge at the lectern giving the closing address, I was pleased. Not at their success, which was to me the success of vultures, not of hawks, but at how little was really needed. The Executive Director was as dispensable as was Odom, the brightest sun. Literature, gossip, and lore would flow on, great current and undertow, without any single one of us, large or small.

After the three days of his long sleep, Odom awoke refreshed, seeming quite sane, though terribly bruised and cut and mortally embarrassed. There seemed no end to his penitential impulse. It was pleasant to see him in a forgiving and forgetting mood. I needed his forgiveness for more than he knew. I needed it for chasing him, for failing to honor his last crazy wish, which was to be alone there on the wild grasslands with his torment and his cure, and with that kingdom of birdlife circling above him. And for much else, too. I remembered when I had at last seized MacEvoy by the neck and wondered why I had not done it much sooner or why someone had not, and I silently apologized to the silent Odom for that, too.

When I went to see him, we did not speak of these things. He thanked me formally and, I knew, sincerely for bringing him back. His voice, the gorgeous voice I had loved, was a strangled croak in his throat. The doctors were divided as to whether it would always be so. I imagined him at the lectern, speaking in that croaking animal fashion to audiences who knew by heart the story of his hurts. They would love him better than ever.

"I appreciate what you did for me, Toad. It's not everybody would haul ass out into all that . . . terrain after a crazy goddamn fiction writer." I nodded, and didn't say that I had needed to chase just as surely as he had needed to bolt. Nor did I say that there would be no reprise of that day on the Savannah. He knew it. We chatted on into the afternoon, easier than we had ever been together. As I was leaving, Lindy came in. He said to me, "Toad, I meant it. What I said about your work. You are good. I gave a copy of your book to Merit Norman. I was going to tell you. I was waiting to see what he said about it first, so you wouldn't be too . . . cut up, if he didn't think . . ."

I watched him; so did Lindy.

". . . but who gives a shit what those New York blood-suckers think. I'm telling you right here and now, it's good. Do you hear me?"

I heard him and I told him so, but it was a strangely uneasy moment. As I was going out, he grinned, "Course, you ain't as good as Lindy, here. Not by a damn long way," and my last glimpse of him was of a man reaching up for a woman and of her going gladly into his arms.

Thirty-Two

A WEEK LATER the news came that my father had suffered a stroke. He had been found wandering along the highway. It was a week in which I had done nothing but work for winos and sit in my room damning myself for the anticipation I felt as I waited for news from Merit Norman. It would be wrong to say I was glad of the news about my father. It was a terrible sorrow, though not an entirely unforeseen one. The gladness was that the stroke was mild, and my father was alive and better already, and that he gave me the deliverence of something to do.

I stayed with my mother, helping take care of my father. He had lost his power of speech and the articulation of his right arm. He lay in the bed looking at us, able only to squeeze my mother's hand — once for yes, twice for no. The doctors told us the sooner we began working at speech therapy, the better his chances were, and so we sat with him by the hour, talking to him, urging him to respond, knowing that he was with us, just at a distance behind the cloudy blue of his eyes, with us and trying. For me, it was also the crossing of an old boundary toward a closeness I had thought I would never achieve with my father.

Sitting with him by the hour, I began to tell him stories. At first they were our reminiscences. Do you remember the time, this time or that, do you? And I could see in the heightened color of his face and the milky blue of his eyes that he did remember. I passed beyond reminiscences to stories of my own, things I made up right then and there, compulsively going on and on until I realized that I had longed to display this skill before my father. I was writing to him. Writing the voice I had kept disguised from him since leaving to follow the call of *Naked in Church*. And what a joy it was to unmask myself there in that quiet room before the man who listened so carefully.

There were two weeks of this. I talked myself blue in the face, and my father listened, and my mother sometimes came to the door of the room where I gabbled on, looked in on us, shook her head, smiled, and walked away. After two weeks of being submerged in my own voice and the listening, discerning eyes of my father, I heard the unmistakeable rattle of that Mercedes diesel under the tall pines and left my father to greet Ardis.

We embraced under the pines, and as we walked to the house, I saw my mother watching at the kitchen window. There was no mistaking the look on her face. Inside, she and Ardis remembered each other politely and remembered that lovely day, as they both called it, when Ardis had come for her visit. My mother asked Ardis what had brought her our way again, and Ardis said, "I came out to help. I hope that's all right." Of the six or so "right" things to say to my mother, this was the ace. The two of them left me standing in the kitchen and went directly to my father's room and stayed for at least an hour.

Merit Norman returned my novel. When I went into Bainesborough to my rented room to collect my things, Traymore came to my door and handed it to me. "What's this?" I asked him, just to see what he knew.

"I don't know," he said, mildly offended. "It came for you. I signed for it. Is that all right?"

"Sure," I said. I put the manuscript in its neat, padded mailer inside the bag I was packing.

"You leaving?"

"Yeah."

"Coming back?"

"Don't know. Maybe."

I finished shoving things into my canvas duffle and turned to him. He stood in the doorway watching, uneasy. I went over and put my hand on his shoulder. "Don't worry," I said. "You can stay. And you can forget that twenty you owe me." I smiled at him.

"Naw," he said. "I'll send it to you. It's better that way."

We were not specific about how he would send it. Still, I nodded assent.

When I was putting my things in the front seat of my father's International truck, Traymore stood by me. "I started a new canvas," he said.

"I'll come back in and see it . . . soon."

"It's good," he said. "It's the big one. You know?"

"Sure," I said.

We shook hands. After a while I heard him on the stairs, then looked up as he lowered the shades. In my mind's eye, I saw the shadows in his room and, for a moment, those perishable expectations that lived in the shadows. I took an envelope from the glove compartment of my father's truck, scrawled his name on it, put a twenty-dollar bill in it, and stuck it in his mailbox.

Lindy's apartment was locked and silent, so I drove to the dance studio. When she saw me peeking into that dim room full of sweat and perfume and music, she left the line of gliding women and walked straight to me, scared. She was ready to help. I said, "It's OK. Nothing new. I just came in to get some stuff."

"How much stuff?" She touched the sweat in her eyes and went into one of those absent, erotic slumps of hers, legs parted, arms akimbo.

"Most of it."

"Just most?" She squinted at me, and something happened to her eyes, something I had not seen before. I could not tell the sweat from the tears.

"Yes," I said, and she was up against my chest, wetting me, and my nostrils were full of her. I pressed her to me just as the music stopped and all the exhausted dancers pushed past us. "Just most," I whispered to her.

She pushed me away roughly. "As long as you promise."

"I do." Then I held her close again for a little while, knowing we wouldn't think of more to say, and that of all our promises, it was the one I would break.

Merit Norman's letter was businesslike but encouraging. He said that he had read my manuscript at first only as a favor to Eldon Odom, then later with real interest. His beginning was a disarming bit of honesty. It drew me into the editorial conspiracy. Next he told me that he shared Odom's high opinion of my potential as a writer. I paused to reflect that Odom had not spoken of potential; he had said my work was good. Norman's next words were about the marketplace and what it would support. I cannot very well remember that part of the letter.

There was some discussion of fashion and the winds of change and what was going to sell that year. The small town book, the family chronicle, Norman gave me to understand, was not going to be big for a while. He thanked me cordially and suggested that I keep him in mind when next I finished a novel.

Ardis and my mother went to work on my father. Ardis moved into the guest room, displacing me to one of the empty tobacco barns. I didn't mind camping out. I enjoyed the smell of the old smoke and cured broad leaf, and when it got too quiet, sometimes I would sneak into Ardis's room. My mother would have switched us both to the bone had she caught us. Since the two women had taken over the medical chores, there was nothing much left for me to do (I was talked out) but take up farm work. It was the slack season. I worked along at fences and vaccinations and castrations, moving at something less than a killing pace. One day while I was hauling cypress for pens, my father said his first word — to Ardis. It was "heart" or "art," we aren't certain.

About a week later, one evening after supper when my mother had retired early and things were quiet, Ardis and I had the serious talk I had seen coming for a long time.

There was one thing left for me to ask her, and there were a few things I suppose she had left to say to me. We strolled out to the hog pens first, but the wind was from the east and it was not a very good place to contemplate the ultimate. I suggested a turn past last summer's tobacco beds and then a promenade along the banks of the little pond in the south eighty. Ardis, who didn't know south from down, agreed.

My question was a simple one, albeit an important one, and she let me ask it first.

"What kept you coming back . . . to the group, I mean? I mean, if it wasn't really him?"

"You."

We walked on about fifty yards, fifty paces by my count.

"Blackford, stop that."

"Stop what?"

"That counting."

We stopped at the edge of the tobacco beds where the most recent of my episodes as re-emerging son of the soil had begun, and I picked up a few hard clods and scaled them toward the pond. They landed with a plunk and gurgle in the darkness.

"It was you, Toad. I kept waiting for you to give up being sorry and come back to me." Ardis was using "sorry" in the country way. It meant worthless, half-assed, no-account, feckless, bothersome, careless, and, above all, cruel. It meant all those and more. It's about the sorriest thing you can be and not be hopeless.

I scaled another largish piece of the home dirt and listened for it to fall. Then Ardis said the thing that sealed it.

"You were so goddamn busy following Eldon Odom and disgracing yourself and being sorry, you couldn't turn around and see me following *you.*"

"But *you* weren't getting sorry," I said, grinning in the dark.

"I wish I could believe it," Ardis said, and there was a genuine sadness in her voice. She pulled me by the shoulder, around to face her. She pressed herself warm and urgent against my chest. "You mean, you didn't know it all the time?"

I told her I didn't.

"It's sad," she said, burying her face in my neck. "It means you didn't know you were worth it."

She was right about that.

There isn't much more to say. Hubbel and Shine, who have three strong hands and an enormous gift for dedication, are running a chiropractic clinic. When I think of them as two bone-crackers, I remember that night under Odom's deck — Hubbel's strength as he held Sarah aloft, and Shine's fine, one-handed delicacy with the drawstrings of her unmentionables. By all accounts, they are quite successful, and I hear that they have almost achieved respectability. Almost. The Thrash Palace, those years of bachelor disgrace on the rim of the Savannah, aren't easily outrun. Still, each year that passes pushes them forward along a highway made of money.

Sarah still waits on tables, and Lindy owns the dance studio. She is as graceful, lean, and strong as ever, and she still comes to Eldon Odom by night and by the back door.

Eldon Odom seems to his friends and admirers, of whom there are still a great many, to be eternal. He cannot hurt himself badly enough to stop what is beyond his control — fame. He is the celebrated literary man, generous and spiteful, grandiose and humble, a mean drunk, and as utterly enslaved as he has always been. He has gone back, of course, to Missy Sully, to sojourn in the house under the hill. It will be impossible now for him to escape. His reputation grows, though his powers diminish. He still speaks in public, on all manner of subjects, his voice a self-inflicted croak, beautiful still — a bright, terrible calling.

My father is up and walking and doing a little light, one-handed work. Nothing like the old caught-up days. He is doing some talking too, and his favorite words are the ones Ardis taught him. The two of us work the place and take what it gives us, and take care of our two women when they are not taking care of us. I am a country man. I live the bad and the good life on the land.

Ardis runs the County Medical Health Clinic, caring for the walk-in traffic. You will believe me when I say that what walks in drunk and bent and sometimes bleeding from these towns and hamlets and the fast country roads and the sun-beat farms is sorely in need of her. She is help. Though an outsider, she has earned her way here as well as I have earned my way back.

We go for long walks in the evenings, holding hands. We speak less and less it seems. Ardis uses her voice all day long in exhausting work and it is depleted in the evening. She tells me that she only wants my hand in hers and the country quiet.

For me, it's a little different. I have gone so many miles now in the bouncing saddle of a John Deere tractor that my head is alight with the poetry of engines and of disks that slice and curl the earth and of streams of corn in the hoppers, of prices and weather reports and auctioneering yodels and at dawn the rushing South wind and at dusk the mourning dove. So full of these that in my evenings with Ardis, I am pleased to stand in the last light under the tall pines and listen to the silence.